GIDEON'S VOTE

'So it's a general election on November 6th.' Suddenly, Gideon realised why the date had registered in the way it had. 'Great Scott – why didn't they make it the Wednesday?'

'Eh?'

'Wednesday, November 5th.'

'Good Lord!' gasped Rogerson.

They sat there, these old friends who knew more about the crime of London than any other two men in the country, who knew the potentialities of criminals and the opportunities for crime. They sat within a stone's throw of the Mother of Parliaments, where on the fifth of November a man had tried to blow up the House of Commons. Over the centuries there had been many who hated politicians, but never had there been such an organisation as that of the group of high-minded idealists in the Fight for Peace campaign.

'You know, George, it's the kind of bloody-minded thing some of the hot-heads might think up.'

'A bomb under the House you mean?'

'Something like that.'

Gideon's Vote

John Creasey
writing as J. J. Marric

CORONET BOOKS
Hodder and Stoughton

First published in Great Britain 1964 by
Hodder and Stoughton Limited

Coronet Edition 1966
Third impression 1977

Printed in Great Britain for
Hodder & Stoughton Paperbacks, a
division of Hodder & Stoughton Ltd.,
Mill Road, Dunton Green, Sevenoaks,
Kent by Richard Clay (The Chaucer Press) Ltd,
Bungay, Suffolk

ISBN 0 340 00883 0

CONTENTS

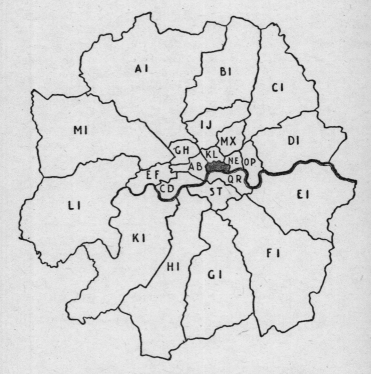

SKETCH MAP OF GIDEON'S TERRITORY

The map conforms only approximately to the boundaries of the
Metropolitan and City Police Forces, and the divisional reference
letters do not coincide with the real London divisional letters or
boundaries.

1

DISSOLUTION

THEORETICALLY a policeman, like a priest, should be above politics, or at least untouched by party politics, yet it is the policeman who is responsible for enforcing the laws made by the politicians. Gideon, politically a middle-of-the-road man who did not always agree with middle-of-the-road politicians, felt that the law which made civil servants political neuters was good in principle but as it affected the individual, quite intolerable. In the course of most years, he could have made half a dozen vigorously uncomplimentary speeches saying what he thought of members of Parliament and members of the Government; when he did make them, however, it was within the privacy of his home. His colleagues at New Scotland Yard might guess what he felt and how he would vote, but none of them could be sure.

The Headquarters of the Metropolitan Police was, among other things, a spawning ground for rumours. When Gideon reached his office just after nine o'clock on a clear, crisp October morning, the gleam in the bright eyes of Superintendent Lemaitre, his chief assistant and good friend, told of rumour or sensation.

"Morning, Lem." Gideon hung his grey trilby on a peg of the hatstand, eased his collar, and stepped across to the window. A sight of the Thames in sunshine always did him good, and this morning the stream of cars and people going over Westminster Bridge looked bright and eager and shiny in the sun. "Nice one, too."

"If this is how you like 'em," said Lemaitre. He was a tall, angular man, almost scraggy about the neck, with thin dark hair brushed carefully to hide as much pate as possible, a bony nose and chin, a taste for bright ties and colour in clothes. This morning his greeny-brown jacket hung on a hanger on the hatstand, his silk bow tie was made of green-and-white spots, and his white shirt could have been used as an example of perfection by any detergent manufacturer.

7

Gideon turned to study him.

"What's up, Lem?"

"Haven't you heard?"

"Somebody planning to blow up the Houses of Parliament?"

Lemaitre's voice dropped in disappointment. "So you *have* heard."

"Haven't heard a thing this morning," Gideon assured him. Then he frowned. "The Fight for Peace crowd haven't been making any trouble across there, have they?"

By craning his neck he could see the terrace of the Houses of Parliament, and the reflection of Gothic grandeur in the calm surface of the river. He stared towards it, then looked back again, and repeated: "Have they?"

"If you ask me, it wouldn't be a bad idea to put a bomb under that place when they're voting for an increase in their own salaries," Lemaitre said. "Get the lot of them at one go then. The Prime Minister's handing in his chips today."

Gideon moved from the window to his desk and sat down. The big, leather-topped desk was set cornerwise across the room, so that all the light from the window fell on it. Trays marked *In*, *Out*, *Pending*, *Urgent* were secured to the far side of the desk, and in front of him was a thick folder, filled with reports which had come in during the night. Somewhere in this rabbit warren of a building a dozen senior detectives were waiting to see him, each of them in charge of one of the cases covered by these reports. He alone had to know the details of each major case at the Yard, had to be able to discuss it with the man in charge, to put his finger on errors, to make suggestions, above all to think. All of the men were sound, some were brilliant, but over the years they had come to regard him as a kind of father figure; now and again, silently, he looked upon himself in the same way and wondered if it was a good thing. Certainly there were times when it made him feel as Atlas must have felt.

Lemaitre was watching him intently but less eagerly, obviously he was disappointed by his reaction.

"Got a private line to Number 10?" Gideon asked at last.

"Good as," asserted Lemaitre.

"Sure about this?"

"Paterson said he heard the P.M. saying that he was going to have an audience this morning, and a dissolution's been in the air for months. Waited too long, if you ask me. Mark my word, they're going to spring it on the electors. Won't give 'em any time to think about it. Snap election, that's what it's going to be."

"Can't be much of a snap if it's been in the air for months," Gideon pointed out.

"It's the date they choose, voting day itself," declared Lemaitre, warming up. He pushed his chair back and began to waggle his forefinger. "It's October 10th now. If the Queen does dissolve Parliament today, they'll fix the earliest date they can. Lemme see, when——"

"Lem," interrupted Gideon, "how's crime?"

"Eh?"

"What's on our plate this morning?"

"Oh." Lemaitre looked a little abashed, he had been so carried away. "Not interested in the next government of the country, eh? Philistine. There isn't much that's new. Curson's coming in, he's got stuck on that skeleton in the well down in Cornwall. Only reason they sent for us, they knew it was going to be next door to impossible. Riddell's got those two swine who did in the bank messenger last week—arrested them in the night, and says it's as good as over. They still haven't got the mother of that kid found gassed in Hendon, but she'll turn up. They had a bank job out at Acton, two or three men burrowed under the road—right under the road from the opposite side, mind you—and broke through the wall of the strong room. Took about fifty thousand quid."

Lemaitre broke off, leaned back in his chair, linked his fingers, and thrust his chest out.

"Oh, I forgot. The Quack's at it again. Over at Peckham. Same drill as before. Answers an advert for a locum, gets the job thanks to faked certificates, takes over the doctor's job for a few days, until some of the women tumble to the fact that he's no more a doctor than I am. A woman in her forties didn't like the way he listened to her heartbeats." Lemaitre gave an expansive grin. "Takes all kinds to make a world. You've got to hand it to the Quack in a way—he gets away with it time and time again."

9

It would not have taken much then to make Gideon angry, but he passed this story over, opened the file, and said shortly:

"All right. I'll look through these before seeing anyone."

"Okeydoke," said Lemaitre.

Gideon thumbed through the reports, including that on the Quack. There were now known to be seven instances of his special trick, and there might be more which no one knew about. It was not until a woman patient's suspicions had been aroused by a locum, four weeks ago, that the British Medical Council had realized that the same man was involved in a number of cases. The B.M.C. had gone carefully into it before presenting the problem to the Yard. So far there had been no publicity, and no general warning had gone out to doctors; unless they caught the Quack soon, a warning would have to be sent to all general practitioners.

There was a question at the end of the report from the division: "Please advise whether we question all the women patients the man examined so that they're bound to realize he was a phony or let it ride?"

Gideon thought: No point in stirring up a lot of embarrassment yet. Then he wondered if he was right.

Lemaitre, unaware of Gideon's mood, looked up suddenly.

"Old Charlie Kimble fell off a roof, chasing a couple of cat burglars who got away. Broke his leg. Nothing much really," finished Lemaitre. He was an ebullient character, seldom subdued for long. "It's all there. Who are you going to start with?"

"I'll see in a minute," Gideon said.

Lemaitre had listed a few of the crimes on London's calendar, sweeping through and glossing over them with the casualness of long experience with crime. 'Nothing much' included a murdered child, a big bank robbery, an attack on a bank messenger, and a hundred other crimes, most of which had been committed in the London metropolitan area. The whole of the Criminal Investigation Department's force was heavily involved in the inquiries, every one of the divisions had plenty of work on hand, most of them were understaffed. All over London new crimes were being plotted, some by old criminals, some by people who had never committed a crime in their lives. Crimes of violence were being planned, some perhaps taking place, children were being starved and ill-treated, in a hundred offices and a hundred shops little men, clerks and assistants were slipping a few shillings or a few pounds into their pockets out of the till or the cashbox. Every one of London's police courts had at least a dozen cases up for hearing this very morning, from prostitution to indecent assault, from murder to being drunk and disorderly. The rash of crime, like acne upon the face of London, was neither better nor worse.

"Nothing much really," Lemaitre had insisted.

Lemaitre's preoccupation with the likely dissolution of Parliament and the coming general election confirmed what Gideon had suspected for a long time: Lemaitre was doing his job almost by habit, skimming the surface of each case instead of probing. That was worrisome. In this office of the Commander of the C.I.D., the chief executive's office, there was no room for superficial reactions, for a shallow, cynical assessment of such crimes as the Quack's. Lemaitre was stale, of course, he had been at this particular job too long, and he was a man who should be out and about, carrying the war energetically into the criminal's camp. He probably did not realize that, but he was bored and something like the Quack brightened life for him.

He was Gideon's oldest and closest friend at the Yard— and he was not doing his job.

This thought passed in and out of Gideon's mind during the morning. He tried to be fair and dispassionate. By some standards, there was nothing much today, certainly no great spate of crime. The newspapers headlined the bank robbery, of course, and spared paragraphs for the others, but any experienced Fleet Street man would have agreed that it was a dull day. Was it really surprising that Lemaitre, immersed in such comparative dullness, should look elsewhere for his excitements?

It was one of the not uncommon periods at the Yard when everyone was stale, up to a point. There had been no great stimulus, no great incentive to all-out effort. Taken by and large, it had been a quiet summer in England, even in the provinces and the big coastal resorts. It was almost as if the continual and continuing efforts to raise the level of the national conscience and the social good were paying off. At heart Gideon did not believe this; they were in the middle of a kind of lull. Lulls had come often enough before, and the danger was that when this one broke the Yard would be caught napping.

He did not go out to lunch, but had a plate of cold meat and some salad brought into the office; salad was not his idea of the right provender for human beings, but he was putting on weight and wanted to check it. He was drinking a cup of lukewarm coffee when a telephone bell rang. Lemaitre was still over at the pub in Cannon Row where the Yard men usually gathered, as a kind of club. Gideon lifted the receiver.

"Gideon."

"Can you spare me a minute, George?" That was Rogerson, the Assistant Commissioner for Crime.

"Now?"

"Yes."

"I'll be right with you," Gideon said. As he put down the receiver he pressed a bell-push for a sergeant, who came in as he was smoothing down his thick, iron-grey hair. The sergeant was a lean, brown whippet of a man; Gideon's massive body made two of his.

"I'll be with the Assistant Commissioner," Gideon said. "Stay here until Mr. Lemaitre gets back."

"Right, sir!"

The passages of the Yard had an almost bleak look; plain light-coloured walls and plain dark-coloured doors with name plates so small one could hardly read them. Gideon walked with his head thrust forward, thick shoulders slightly rounded. As he turned a corner he heard a man say behind him.

"Always looks as if he owns the place."

In a way, Gideon knew, this was true; sometimes he *felt* as if he owned it. Though he knew, too, nothing could be further from the truth and nothing could be more nonsensical.

He tapped perfunctorily at Rogerson's door and then went in. Rogerson's secretary, a youngish blonde, looked up from her tidy desk.

"Good morning, Mr. Gideon."

"Morning."

"Mr. Rogerson's expecting you."

Think I didn't know? Gideon thought. He nodded and stepped into the larger office. This one also overlooked the Thames and was bright with sunlight. Rogerson was sitting at his big pedestal desk. He was an ill-looking man, slightly purplish about the cheeks and lips at times, with eyes which always seemed tired. There had been talk of his retirement, years ago, but he stayed on; Gideon thought secretly that this was an instance where retirement would probably lead straight to the grave. Here was another man who sometimes felt that he carried the cares of the Yard on his shoulders.

"Hallo, George."

"Hallo, Hugh."

"You heard?" Rogerson was looking up, and motioning to a chair.

"Heard what?"

"A general election's coming up."

"Official?" asked Gideon. Lemaitre would be cock-a-hoop.

"The Prime Minister announced it in the House five minutes ago. I've just had a flash."

"Couldn't have been delayed much longer," Gideon observed. "This government's been in over four years. It will keep Uniform busy for a bit."

"Not only Uniform," Rogerson declared. He leaned back in his chair, and Gideon had a feeling that he was worried, as if there was something on his mind that he didn't relish talking about. "The Home Secretary thinks that we might have a lot of bother with the Fight for Peace people, and the Q Men. We've had an official directive—check both of them even more closely than we have already, so that we know just what they're up to."

Gideon wrinkled his nose.

"What's the matter?" demanded Rogerson.

"Don't like it much," Gideon remarked. "If we start probing into political or neopolitical groups at this stage, a lot of people will start talking about unconstitutional methods, and we might find ourselves running into trouble." When Rogerson just sat staring at him, he went on almost irritably: "What's the real size of it?"

"There's a rumour—it could be stronger—that a lot more money has been going to both campaigns lately, and that the

Fight for Peace people as well as the Q Men have had their ranks thickened by a lot of toughs who will stir up as much trouble as they can at the election." Rogerson was emphatic. "All we need to do is make sure that there are no foreign influences at work, no funds from overseas. Fair enough?"

"Fair enough," Gideon conceded. "I'll get on to it." He felt a deeper sense of irritation, partly because he hadn't given this possibility much thought. He regarded both of the extremist political factions as fanatics, each having some members on the lunatic fringe, but knew enough about both groups to be sure that most of the members were wholly sincere. The trouble with sincerity when it became passionate enough to grow into fanaticism was that it could persuade one to tolerate what was bad, or at least to excuse it. Then, almost disgustedly, he thought, *Moralizing ass*. He sat down at last. "That the lot?"

"Er—not quite," Rogerson said.

Now there was no doubt that he had something serious on his mind. It was seldom that he felt any kind of embarrassment or awkwardness with Gideon, yet obviously he did now. He was going to ask him to do something he didn't want to do, Gideon thought, and even speculated that he *might* be saying that he was going off for a few weeks and would he, Gideon, stand in for him again? Rogerson was almost too conscientious, and had been away on sick leave a great deal recently. He was immaculately dressed, still the Guards officer, and oddly enough his crimpy hair retained its natural brown colour, but in the past year something had seeped out of him.

"Let's have it," Gideon said, almost impatiently.

"Straight from the shoulder, eh?" Rogerson said unexpectedly, and gave a wry smile. "All right, George. How long is it since you had a holiday?"

Gideon was so surprised that he only stared.

"A year?" asked Rogerson. "Or even more?"

"Er—eighteen months or so, I suppose," Gideon answered at last. "That's if you mean two or three weeks in a row. I take the odd weekend off, and Kate and I slipped over to Ostend for a week last summer." He finished almost aggressively. "Think I need a holiday?"

As Rogerson stared at him, Gideon was acutely conscious

14

of the contrast between them. He, Gideon, was in the middle
fifties, as fit physically as he could be—except for that ten
pounds or so overweight—and he had not had a day's illness
in the past ten years. He had never felt more completely in
control of himself, and the only thing that made him lose
patience was the attitude of some of the staff, for instance
Lemaitre, who seemed to have lost their energy and their sense
of dedication.

"As a matter of fact, George, yes. I think you need a good
one," Rogerson declared. "I know just what it's like, remember—it's a long time since I had any zip to lose. But, then,
I'm just an old crock. You———" Rogerson broke off, spread
his hands and went on: "You'll go on until you live to be a
hundred if you look after yourself. Working too long at a
stretch is asking for trouble, and you know it. You tell other
people about it often enough, and send them packing. Is there
anything to stop you taking a couple of weeks off before the
general election? The date's fixed for Thursday, November
6th."

2

OWN PETARD

GIDEON'S first reaction was one of resentment, almost of
anger. He sat staring at his Chief, having a fair idea what was
going through Rogerson's mind. He, Gideon, had often wondered how some of the senior C.I.D. men would take his blunt
declaration that they were losing their zeal because of overwork. Now he didn't have to wonder. *Overwork?* This had
been the slackest period he could remember for a long time.
Rogerson didn't look away from him, and the only sign of
tension was the way he pushed his tongue against his lips,
giving them a swollen look. An echo sounded in Gideon's
mind: *The date's fixed for Thursday November 6th.* The echo died
away. Another replaced it. *Nothing much*, Lemaitre had insisted, and had remembered and related with such gusto the
story of the Quack. Lemaitre was bored, remember, and
getting slack—my God!

A quick, spontaneous grin curved Gideon's lips.

Rogerson spoke almost too quickly.

"Glad you see the funny side of it. I thought you'd want to throw me out the window."

"I shall when I've digested this fairy story." Gideon half wished he had controlled that grin, but it would be better to appear to take this well, no matter what he really felt. "Coming along here I was telling myself that Lemaitre's getting slack. That's what's funny. Hoist with my own petard." He didn't now think it funny at all, but kept smiling and hoped that the stiffness of the smile didn't show. "Anyone else put you up to this? I mean, the Old Man?"

"No one at all," said Rogerson. "All my own work. You look as if you would like to tear some of the chaps apart—you've been a bit lacking in that patience you're famous for." He was still talking too quickly, perhaps now with relief. "You need a rest, and I need you here when the general election's closer at hand. I can sit in for you meanwhile."

Gideon said, "You've got enough on your plate." He was still put out, but his mind was working more normally, ideas flashing through it. "Like to give Lemaitre the break he's been waiting for?"

"I don't get you."

"Let him stand in for me for a couple of weeks, and if he comes through all right, make him deputy commander. It would be just the incentive he needs. He's a bit browned off always playing second fiddle."

Rogerson pursed his lips.

"I don't know that Lemaitre's my idea of the right man for the job, but I suppose he knows the drill pretty well."

"Inside out."

"If only he wouldn't jump to conclusions," complained Rogerson. Then he spread his hands. "All right, but tell him if he's in doubt about anything at all, he's to come to me." Rogerson grinned suddenly, broadly. "Like *you* always do! George, you're quite a guy. Two minutes after being kicked in the teeth you start thinking about how to help someone else."

"Got to be sure the job's handled while I'm away, and I wouldn't like you to try it on your own," Gideon retorted. He made himself thrust the unpalatable aspect out of his mind.

"So it's a general election on November 6th." Suddenly, he realized why the date had registered in the way it had. "Great Scott—why didn't they make it the Wednesday?"

"Eh?"

"Wednesday, November 5th."

"Good Lord!" gasped Rogerson.

They sat there, these old friends who knew more about the crime of London than any other two men in the country, who knew the potentialities of criminals and the opportunities for crime, and the whole range of crimes from petty larceny to murder. They sat within a stone's throw of the Mother of Parliaments, where on the fifth of November over three hundred and fifty years ago, a man had tried to blow up the House of Commons because he had hated what its members were doing. Over the centuries there had been many who hated politicians, many fanatics and much resentment, but never in Britain's history had there been such an organization as that of the group of high-minded idealists in the Fight for Peace campaign, who were fighting their strange cold war for unilateral nuclear disarmament.

"You know, George——"

"If you ask me——"

"Go on."

"No, you."

"It's the kind of bloody-minded thing some of the hotheads might think up."

"A bomb under the House you mean?"

"Something like that."

"Yes," Gideon said. He looked like a graven image for a few seconds, then shook his head. "No, it's unthinkable. They're capable of a lot of things, and when we have to shift 'em from sit-down strikes and marches a few of them get violent, but a bomb——"

"George," interrupted Rogerson, "you know what I mean as well, as I know myself. No one connected with the Fight for Peace Committee would do it, but the very nature of the group means that there are a lot of lunatic fringes. After all, they're a splinter group from the old Ban the Bomb campaigners who were too mild for the F.F.P.'s liking. You might find one or two among them who would think it worth trying

17

to blow up the House, and the date makes it almost irresistible. Eve of Poll rallies will be all over the country on November 5th—what the devil was the government thinking of?"

Gideon said heavily. "The Prime Minister's a crafty old bird. He might have had his reasons."

"No one could be so inept as to choose that date accidentally." Rogerson asserted, but was probably a long way from convinced. "Will you brief Lemaitre and everyone concerned so that all the reports and preliminary information will be available as soon as you get back?"

Gideon stood up.

"I will. I'll come in tomorrow and Saturday, then take a couple of weeks off." He nodded, opened the door, and strode straight into the passage, bypassing the secretary's little office. The door closed with a snap. He was in no mood to say anything else to Rogerson, and now that he was alone he stood quite still, bracing himself to face the situation. He did not feel like telling Lemaitre or anyone else about it yet; he wanted to cool off, to make sure he had himself under full control.

That general election date, even with Guy Fawkes Night the Eve of the Poll, had receded again.

He passed the door of his own office, hearing Lemaitre on the telephone, his voice raised. Gideon went up one flight of stairs, nodding to the people he passed, speaking to no one. A long corridor with open doors on either side led to the offices occupied by the chief inspectors and the detective sergeants. Through the open doors he saw men sitting, talking, lounging, smoking, speaking into telephones, poring over reports. Every now and again someone moved away from a window or a desk quickly, as if caught out in some guilty act; and those who lounged looked aghast when they saw him. Usually the fact that Gideon was on the prowl reached the offices well ahead of him, but today he had caught them by surprise. He knew what was happening in those offices, the kind of thing that was being said:

"My God, Gee-Gee's around."

"Why the hell didn't someone tell us?"

Looking as if he were unaware of this, Gideon turned into the last office on the right. Here, where there were six desks, two people were working, one of them staring at a lot of drawings on his desk, a bald-headed man, grey moustached, on the plump side, and with very big hands. A pencil in his right hand looked like a matchstick. This was Piper, one of the older chief inspectors. The other man, twenty years younger, was Cummings, a man recently promoted from sergeant's rank, and a member of the Fraud Squad. Both men were immersed in what they were doing, and looked up vaguely. Cummings almost dropped his pen as he jumped to his feet.

"Good afternoon, sir."

Gideon nodded. Piper pushed his chair back.

"After me, sir?" Had Cummings not been there he would have said 'George,' for they had known each other for nearly thirty years.

"Yes. All right, Cummings," Gideon said. Did the idiot think he would eat him? "Give me a chair, will you?" Cummings snatched a chair, lifted it, banged a leg on a corner of a desk, muttered "Sorry," and put the chair too close to Piper's desk. "Thanks," said Gideon, and shifted it and sat down. "So you haven't got the Quack yet?" Gideon said to Piper.

"I've got some pretty pictures of what he might be like, and some *Identikit* make-ups," Piper said. "I've been studying them for the past hour—since I got back from Sydenham, where he did his latest stint." Piper was mildly amused, and yet took this quite seriously. He was the Yard man in charge of the inquiries into the pseudo-medical man, and liaison with all the divisions where the 'doctor' had practised. He had interviewed the first woman who had been suspicious of the locum with roving hands. She had told the locum she was going to the police, and had got out quickly.

Piper had also been in touch with all divisions concerned and with the British Medical Council.

"I can't say I'm much further on though," he continued. "I've talked to four of the women this chap examined in Sydenham. The trouble is, most of them get so damned embarrassed. Faked, I sometimes think. The one thing in common is that all four say he's about thirty and has dark hair. In all, that gives us five different hair colours!"

Piper was pushing papers across to Gideon, who had put everything else out of his mind so that he could concentrate on this; concentration on a problem was what he needed more than anything else.

"*Five colours?*"

"Very fair, yellow, grey, black and auburn-ginger," explained Piper. "Which makes him good at dyeing his hair."

"If he's really the same man."

"Don't think there's much doubt about that," said Piper. "I've talked to the Sydenham doctor, who came rushing back when he heard what had happened—he looked as if he could have jumped off a roof, he was so upset because he'd let some of his women patients in for this. This chap's the same build, and has rather moist hands. That's been mentioned eight times."

"Fingerprints?"

"All wiped away. He hasn't once slipped up over that," Piper went on. "He's no fool, he knows what we'll do the moment he's been around. He always judges the reaction of the patients well, and gets out the moment he thinks anyone might complain about him. Did you hear from Sydenham?"

"Yes."

"Dowsett would like to interrogate every one of the women the man examined—wants me to do the rounds with him." Dowsett was a chief inspector at the division. "Symes isn't so keen." Symes was the divisional superintendent. "He thinks it's going to cause the women a lot of unnecessary embarrassment, especially the married ones. And he doesn't think it will help much—we know what the chap looks like, we've got plenty of descriptions including the doctor's. The doctor dislikes the idea of tackling each of the women—for obvious reasons."

"What do you think?" inquired Gideon. For the first time since leaving Rogerson he thought, *November 5th*, but the date faded quickly from his mind.

"Can't see it would help much, unless——"

"Go on."

"The more women who know what happened to them the more will be keeping a sharp lookout for him, and we might strike lucky one day," said Piper. "Can't afford to be too pernickety. If a woman patient doesn't want to tell her husband what happened she can say she only talked to him."

"Except that she's already told her husband what a thorough examination she had," said Gideon dryly. "I'm sure you're right, and so is Dowsett. I'll have a word with Symes, and fix it."

"Thanks," Piper's rather tired smile suggested that that was exactly what he had hoped for.

"What else have you got on?" asked Gideon.

"Nothing that can't wait. I've been checking chemists' shops for drugs which might have been bought on the cheap—we've had three vanloads of pharmaceutical stuff stolen in the past five weeks. It's routine, mostly, and I've got a couple of sergeants and the divisions on it. Like you said," Piper added hastily.

"We'll put the sergeants on to the pharmaceutical job, so that you can concentrate on the Quack," Gideon decided. "If you need a man, let Mr. Lemaitre know. It's time we got this character, and he warrants a man full time. Handle it as you think best, check with me or Mr. Lemaitre, and I'll let all the divisions know that you're going to get right behind it."

"That's what it needs," Piper said, with satisfaction. "Sometimes the divisions want a bomb under them. The trouble over this job is that too many of them think it's funny. Mind you, there *is* a funny side." Piper gave his rather tired grin again. "When he was over at Streatham, this chap had one of the local prostitutes as a patient. She tumbled to his game pretty quickly, and threatened to sue him for indecent assault!"

Cummings, silent until then, burst into a guffaw. Gideon smiled, chuckled, nodded, and went out. He knew that Piper was delighted that he had been given this job, and no one would put more work into it. In a much more relaxed mood Gideon walked back to his office; no one was lounging in his sight this time. Lemaitre was sitting back at his desk, one telephone at his right ear, another pressed tightly against his chest.

". . . no, he's not. . . . Well, I told you. . . . Yep. Hold on, I've got NE on the other line." He switched telephones. "Hallo, Christie . . . the great man's here, hold on." Without lowering his voice, he called to Gideon: "Christie thinks he knows who did that bank job at Acton, want a word with him?"

Gideon was already lifting a receiver from his own desk. "Hallo."

"Micky Bane was out last night," Christie of NE Division declared. NE, the East End Division, was still the home of a greater proportion of men known to the police than any other London division. "And I've just discovered that his wife rented the shop opposite that Acton Bank under her maiden name—she took in dressmaking and repairs. Ideal place for Bane to drill from and he went very deep so as to dodge all the supply mains. She's given the shop up, of course, but if I bring both her and Bane in for questioning——"

"Do it right away."

"Going to send anyone over?"

"Not yet. Let Lemaitre know what happens. If you think it's safe to make a charge, he'll send someone. Thanks."

Gideon rang off. Lemaitre was putting down the other telephone, and staring across at Gideon frowning, one eyebrow cocked above the other. "What's your game?" he demanded.

"What about?"

"Me," said Lemaitre suspiciously. "What did you tell Christie to contact me for?"

"I've come to the conclusion that you haven't enough to do," said Gideon. "So I'm going to put a lot more work on to you."

Lemaitre almost screeched. "You're going to do what?"

"Find out how broad your shoulders are," said Gideon. He sat at his desk and pulled the accumulation of papers towards him. "Get me Symes of C.I. will you?"

Lemaitre put in the call, still eyeing Gideon suspiciously. The call came through at once.

"Hallo, Sy," said Gideon. "Oh, I'm fine. Overworking, of course, but fine. . . . Yes, that's it. Sy, I think Dowsett ought to talk to all the women, he'll do it discreetly, I'm sure. . . . Good. I'm putting Piper on the Quack full time, he can go round with Dowsett. Thanks. . . . Yes, Kate's fine." Gideon rang off, put his right hand to his pocket and fiddled with the bowl of a big pipe, then said to Lemaitre, "Piper will contact you if he gets into any difficulties. Now I want to run through all the outstanding cases and find out if you really know what's going on around here."

Lemaitre looked baffled.

"You retiring or something? You—" His eyes rounded, and he caught his breath. "Hey! You've just been to the A.C., haven't you? He's been looking like death warmed up lately. He's retiring? That it? He's retiring, so that you can get pushed upstairs, and I——" He broke off, eyes glistening.

"Lem, I'm going to have a couple of weeks off, that's all there is to it," Gideon said. "Rogerson's not fit enough to take on extra work, so you'll take over from me, with someone to stand in for you. That's if you think you can manage it."

"Do it on my head," declared Lemaitre, and then realized what he had said, and went on hastily, "I didn't mean any offence, George. There isn't a man at the Yard who could do it half as well as you can, but I do know the ropes and I know how your mind works—well, some of the time!"

"Let's go over every case," Gideon said.

There was Lemaitre's great failing: jumping to conclusions. If he was ever to be cured, it would have to be soon. But for the failing, he would be a certainty for the deputy job, with it, Gideon had his doubts. Could one cure a man of a life-long trait? Lemaitre sat at Gideon's side, going through every job that was being handled, shrewd, knowledgeable, practical, full of ideas, bursting with energy and satisfaction. This wasn't the time to try to warn him.

They did not finish until six o'clock.

"Now how about a beer over at the pub?" suggested Lemaitre. "My mouth's like sandpaper."

"Good idea," Gideon said. Soon they walked across the courtyard, watched by Flying Squad men and others in the vicinity, pointed out by several men. When they were in the coziness of the pub, with a dozen other Yard men, mostly big and making it look as if it were peopled by giants, Lemaitre said:

"I was right about the election, George, but not about them springing it on us. Got nearly five weeks. Plenty of time. Think we'll have any trouble with the Fight for Peace mob? I've got a feeling they might try to pull off a stunt."

3

THE F.F.P.

GIDEON and Lemaitre were not the only people who were thinking about the activities of the Fight for Peace group on that Thursday afternoon. Within an hour of the date of the general election being known, a meeting of the Battle Committee was called to discuss action. The discussion, as always, was level-headed and quite dispassionate; only now and again did a glint of extreme emotion show in the eyes of the people gathered in the room.

"We are agreed on one thing," the chairman said. "This gives us our greatest opportunity for making our views heard by the general public. And we should also be able to make our views *felt*."

A small, young, very smooth-looking man sitting in a corner of the room shifted his position.

"Not before it's time," he said.

"I think we all agree with you too, Daniel," said the chairman. He smiled; he had a great natural charm as well as exceptional gifts in dialectics. "We have a skeleton plan of campaign in existence, of course, but I wonder whether we have fully realized the significance of the situation."

"It's the chance we've been waiting for," said a plump, rosy-cheeked young woman in her twenties. She had fluffy hair, a tweed suit and a scrubbed look.

"Yes, indeed, Jane," said the chairman. "But we have to remember that a general election is the supreme example of democracy in practice, and above everything else we have to preserve democracy. We must—I am quite emphatic in my views about this—we must make sure that we use the weapons of democracy, not autocracy. We have to make quite sure that all the local groups are alerted and know exactly what to do, but that we must *not* use the actual polling day as one for physical demonstrations. We must restrain our over eager members. Or our ebullience will look as if we were deliberately impeding the progress of democracy. That in turn will antagonize a great number of the electors who might other-

24

wise be sympathetic towards us. We *know* we are right in our aims; we have to use extreme care in our methods."

The young, smooth-skinned man leaned sideways to a very thin, bony-faced girl. She had jet-black hair which fell to her shoulders, wore a black sweater and a black skirt. She had no figure to speak of; the lines of the sweater curved only slightly at the breast. She was not bad-looking in a severe way. Her skin was pale, almost olive in colour, but without blemish. She did not wear lipstick or rouge. The neckline of her sweater was very high, and the sleeves were pulled low. She wore black stockings and black sandals.

"He's going to let this chance slip out of his fingers," the smooth-looking man whispered.

Out of the corner of her mouth, the girl replied. "Well, we're not."

"We certainly are not"

The chairman glanced their way, paused and made several others look round towards the whispering couple. No one spoke.

"What your Battle Committee suggests is that we prepare a form of questionnaire, all to do with our subject, and that this questionnaire be sent to every newspaper, to ensure publicity, and to every candidate. Then we must arrange to have members attend every meeting—*every* meeting, I'm sure we all agree—of *every* candidate. The same questions must be asked at each meeting. We have to phrase these questions in such a way that everyone who hears them knows that we have the purest humanitarian motives and also knows the unbelievable danger to humanity which the existence of nuclear weapons creates. We have to use the general election as a platform, always—I repeat in a strictly democratic way— from which to tell the people of this country the suicidal folly of the present policy."

When the chairman paused there was a chorus of "*Hear, hear.*"

"Now, as for the questions themselves . . ." the chairman began. Two members of the committee began to hand out mimeographed lists of recommended questions, and the meeting got down to detail.

The young-looking Daniel and the black-clad pencil-slim

25

girl took what appeared to be a polite interest, until the girl said in a clear, penetrating voice:

"Don't you think the first question asked of a candidate should be: *Do you want to live?*"

After a pause someone round the table said in a muted voice, "Oh, shut up, Amanda."

The girl in black took no notice.

"I see exactly what you mean," the chairman said. "You want to make a dramatic start to the questions. The trouble is, Amanda, that if you find anyone in an audience of an—ah—a ribald nature, and election meetings seem to breed hecklers with a peculiar sense of humour, they might answer for the candidate somewhat curtly. That could easily—ah—spoil the effect of the question."

"We need a more detailed first question," said a well-dressed young cleric with gingery hair and many freckles. "We need to ask: *Do you believe in the destruction of humanity by nuclear explosion?* If the candidate says no, then one of us wants to jump up and start a barrage of supplementary questions. Certainly he won't say *yes*."

"Some of these extremists will say anything," a middle-aged man put in cynically.

"We'll have to have questioners sprinkled about the halls to keep the pot boiling," said a sweet-faced little woman with silvery-white hair. "I always feel that if an audience believes that a great *many* people among them have the same sentiments as the questioner, there is a deeper sympathy, less tendency to scoff."

"What we have to make sure is that the campaign is run as the chairman says—on strictly democratic lines and in complete conformity with the law." The speaker was a tall, dark-haired, earnest-looking man, faintly like the woman in black. He wore thick-rimmed, thick-lensed glasses and kept pushing back his untidy hair. "The British people are very jealous of their democratic rights, and we shall get results only if we respect their views."

"How can we if we're dead?" inquired the girl Amanda.

"Amanda, you can be sure that the Battle Committee will do everything in its power to make sure that the questions asked of the candidates are effective, succinct and pungent. In fact we shall need a Question Drafting Subcommittee. Will you serve on it?"

Most members of the committee were staring at Amanda, and the youngish-looking man by her side whispered:

"Say yes."

"If you wish, yes," answered Amanda.

The chairman looked relieved, as if feeling that by putting Amanda on the subcommittee he had drawn her claws. The sweet-faced woman said, "I'll second that, if you need a seconder." The man with thick rims and lenses to his glasses was frowning at the ceiling, as if he was a long way from satisfied. From that moment on, however, the meeting made good progress. There was tremendous enthusiasm and great vitality in everyone present. Whenever a member showed a tendency to make a speech, the chairman gently headed him off. The silver-haired woman appeared to be very happy.

After the meeting Amanda Tenby and Daniel Ronn went off together. They walked without speaking for five minutes, to a black and white MG sports car which had a much-repaired look about it. The leather of the seats was patched and the wire wheels were rusty. Daniel Ronn opened the door for Amanda, who slid her long, very thin legs in, and sat down, then shook her head and slid her hands beneath her hair and lifted it clear for a moment, so that the wind blew about it. Ronn took the wheel and started off. The engine roared, going much too fast to the corner. Ronn braked sharply, and went round the corner cautiously, as if he were aware of the big man at the far end of the street who was staring after him.

Once they were clear of other members of the committee. Amanda said in her clear, precise voice:

"They're going to throw the opportunity away."

"Don't I know it."

"We've got to think of something—drastic."

"Sensational."

"Drastic. We've got to make sure that members of Parliament *and* the people know we're serious."

"Any ideas?" Ronn asked.

"I'm working on it," said Amanda. "I'm working on it."

Ronn glanced at her. Her high-bridged nose gave her appearance a touch of arrogance, and she wore false eyelashes to

27

heighten the grey brilliance of her eyes. She was staring straight ahead, but he did not think she was studying the traffic in the gathering dusk.

"It's got to be drastic," she said again. "We've got to make them realize what they're doing."

Ronn said, "We will."

Detective Constable Ashenden of the division made a note in his report that night, reading:

Amanda Tenby and Daniel Ronn left the F.F.P. C'ee meeting looking as if they hated everyone they'd been talking with.

There were reports about other members of the committee who were known to be firebrands, for Gideon's request for detailed information was already in the hands of the division. No report was made on the chairman, however, nor on the silver-haired woman with the sweet face and dulcet tones. She was Lady Lucy Wallis, a lady with decided views of her own and a passionate hatred of everything to do with nuclear arms.

The news of the coming general election created a great stir throughout the nation, and of course in every one of London's constituencies. Meetings of constituency associations of the three main parties, Conservative, Labour and Liberal, were hurriedly convened, so that the associations could be wound up for the period of the election, when everyone who worked for a candidate could tell the world what his politics were and how he was going to vote but must not be a member of any party or political association. Men and women who had been members of Parliament until that day faced five weeks of intensive campaigning, and many of them feared that they would not get back into the House, no matter how confident they might seem with their friends. Candidates who had been nursing constituencies for years began to hope, especially those who had been defeated by only a narrow margin at the last general election. Candidates who were on the party lists but had not yet 'found' a constituency also hoped, especially those in the Liberal party who had not been fully blooded in politics but were greatly encouraged by the local and county council election results.

The election agents, eager, patient workers in the constituencies, got busy, checking over their lists of voluntary workers, their committees, their financial supporters. Printers began to gear themselves for the rush of work, the election posters, the election addresses. At least three addresses would go to each elector, one from each candidate. The shrewder agents wrote that very night to the printers they wanted to use, to bill-posting companies, to the owners of those halls which permitted political meetings. At higher pressure still, they telephoned the owners of big auditoriums such as town halls and empty cinemas and dance halls and church halls which were large enough for the Eve of Poll rallies. All over the country, caretakers and clerks began to pencil in provisional bookings for these halls. One in every three or four commented:

"November 5th. How about *that* for a date?"

"Must be daft," some observed.

"There's a reason for it," remarked others sagely.

As candidates, agents, workers, printers, hall secretaries and party machines geared themselves for the struggle, nonpolitical groups made preparations too. The returning officer of each constituency had to arrange for ballot stations so that all the electors in the area under his control were within reasonable reach of a ballot box. This meant that he would need accommodation at many schools and smaller church halls, and on polling day itself would need a host of supervisors and poll clerks to watch over the ritual, to mark off those voters who had cast their votes, and to make sure that no one, out of malice or high spirits, tried to vote twice or more than twice.

Even the criminals would have a vote.

At every polling station, every hall, every meeting, everywhere up and down the country the police would be present, quietly watchful, making sure that the laws were observed. Arrangements would be made for the votes to be counted immediately following the ballot, usually at town halls. There would be the scrutineers and clerks and eager workers, the officials, the returning officer—and of course, the police.

The commander of the Uniform Branch of the Metropolitan Police, recently appointed after serving as deputy commander, had already sent round a directive:

Stop all leave for November 5th and 6th.

Similar directives would soon be going out to all policemen in the land.

Gideon walked from Cannon Row, after his drink with Lemaitre, into Parliament Street and then across to Parliament Square, watching the big face of Big Ben. It was ten minutes to seven. Kate, his wife, would begin to wonder where he was, as he hadn't telephoned to say that he would be late. The stark beauty of the skyline made by the Houses of Parliament and Westminster Abbey always affected Gideon, and he stood with a crowd of people being held back by a policeman on traffic duty, staring up. Someone pushed him. A man said:

"Get a move on."

The policeman was letting them cross the road.

Gideon walked more attentively past the gates which lead to the House of Commons. Four policemen were on duty, and he caught sight of Superintendent Paterson, who looked after security at the Houses of Parliament, disappearing into a doorway. Paterson was going to be the busiest policeman on the force for a while. Gideon walked on, nodding to constables who saluted him. Before he reached the corner leading to the Abbey, a man called:

"*Hey, George!*" He turned round. It was sandy-haired Paterson with his yellowish moustache and his pale eyes and his big knuckly hands and big feet. He had only a suspicion of a Scottish accent. "Getting too proud to know your old friends, are you?"

They shook hands.

"Didn't dare to take up any of your time today," said Gideon.

"Get away with you, you're frightened of your wife, that's why you're in such a hurry. Could you have time for a quick one if I asked you nicely?"

"I've just come from the pub."

"It isn't the only one in the world," said Paterson. "And I'd like a word with you, George."

"That's different," Gideon said.

They walked along Victoria Street and eventually turned into a small public house in Petty France, where there were high-backed oak booths giving a measure of privacy. Paterson went to get the beer, Gideon slipped into a telephone kiosk and dialled his home number. Instead of his wife answering, his son Malcolm did.

"Oh, hallo, dad! Not coming home to supper?"

"Yes, but I'll be a bit late," Gideon said. "Half past eight or so. Where is your mother?"

"She's across at the Marjoribanks'," answered Malcolm. "There's been a bit of an accident—not very serious, I would say. They haven't sent for a doctor, anyhow. Well, I mean they haven't asked me to telephone for one, or go round. How's crime, dad?"

Gideon chuckled.

"Not so good as it ought to be!"

When he joined Paterson at a booth where there was just room for the two big men to sit, Paterson was looking up at him, eyes narrowed in a kind of Lemaitre look.

"What are you grinning about?"

"Young Malcolm," Gideon said. "Wants to know how crime is."

"Don't we all," said Paterson. "Well, here's to the man you're going to vote for." He drank deeply, before adding scornfully, "M.P.s. Sometimes I can sympathize with Khrushchev. What I want to say, George, is that I think you ought to keep a special eye on one or two of the extremist members we've got. There's a peculiar idea that if a man's a member of Parliament he's above suspicion, but I wouldn't like to say that's true where the Q Men and Fight for Peace groups are concerned. I wonder, if I slipped you a few names, on the quiet, would you do a bit of digging? Say nothing to anybody, just dig." Paterson lifted his tankard again, sipped, and lowered it; his pale-blue eyes showed how serious he was. "I'm not saying that there's anything wrong, but the three people I've got in mind have a lot of extremist friends, and there's a lot of feeling being generated at the moment." He grinned suddenly. "As if Gee-Gee doesn't know!"

"I had a directive to take a careful look at both groups," Gideon told him. "This can fit in unobtrusively. I won't be doing it myself for a week or two, I'm having a breather before the election breaks, but I'll get it laid on."

Paterson looked anxious.

"Whoever does this has got to be very discreet, George. If it leaked into the press that you were keeping a special watch on a candidate who was an M.P. there'd be a proper hullabaloo."

"I've got just the man," said Gideon.

"Who?"

"Parsons."

After a reflective pause, Paterson said, "He should be all right, although I can't say I would have thought of him. Parsons," he repeated. "Will you ask him to have a word with me?"

"Yes."

"Here are the three names," Paterson went on, and took a postcard out of his pocket. "I was coming to see you this afternoon but got held up—one of the waitresses in the restaurant helped herself to a couple of wallets. She'll be up in the morning, by the way." He handed the card over. "And you see the names I've pencilled under the members' names? They're the contacts I'm a bit suspicious about. Corby and Hetherington are very extremist anti-nuclear chaps, and they both know a hatchet-faced little weirdie named Tenby, Amanda Tenby."

"Daughter of Sir William Tenby?"

"Daughter disowned," Paterson reminded Gideon.

Gideon nodded. "I remember her. She's been inside three times for causing too much trouble at the rallies and for contempt of court. Do you seriously think she's dangerous?"

"I think she's really dedicated," said Paterson. "She's always pestering members, and I've got a feeling that Corby and Hetherington are very interested in her. I'd have thought she was too skinny for bedlarks. On the other side, the Queen and Country group, the man I'm uneasy about is the leader, Quatrain. He's cold-blooded as a fish, but puts up a big show of emotional flag waving, and he's got a lot of officer-class types about him."

"What do you think he might get up to?"

"I think he hates the F.F.P. people so much he'd like to cut their throats. I see a lot of the lunatic fringers, George, and the groups which come to lobby the members, and the pressure's being stepped up. There's more feeling generated by the present anti-bomb campaign than anything I've ever known. Had a chat with old Charlie Pearce the other day, he's eighty-one and still around Westminster as a watchman and he says that it reminds him of the suffragette days. Says he can't remember anything so likely to get out of hand since then. I don't know how close you've been watching, but take it from me, every member of Parliament is pestered by the F.F.P. people. They've got a genius for making bloody nuisances of themselves. They write to the poor swabs, telephone them and come and push petitions in their faces. It's damned well organized too. And it's been getting fiercer and fiercer. I've got a feeling this election is going to spark something big. They talk mild and they look mild—Moncrieff, the chairman, looks as if he couldn't say boo to a goose, but he gets the craziest ideas. And stubborn mules aren't in it. They're going to use the election as their biggest campaign yet. They'll say how democratic and law-abiding they're going to be and they'll wash their hands of the wild men who go crazy, but the pressure's on all the time. I wish I didn't think so, but I do. The hell of it is, most of those I know not only mean what they say, they feel it. They're fanatics, but they'll make any personal sacrifice for this cause. I've got a feeling that they've been underestimated, George. And I've also got a feeling that the Q Men will start the biggest anti-anti-nuclear campaign they've done yet. I think Quatrain might come out as a new fascist leader. If the two groups do clash at election meetings, it could cause a lot of trouble—the kind of election trouble we've forgotten. I won't be involved until the House assembles again—I'm going to take a week or two off too—but I thought I ought to have a word with you. Don't think I'm a scaremonger, will you?"

"You're a scaremonger all right." Gideon said. "I wish I didn't agree with you so much."

He tucked the postcard into his pocket.

4

THREE WOMEN

WHEN Gideon walked along Harrington Street, Fulham, where he had lived all his married life, over thirty years, he heard two lawn mowers clattering, saw three people clipping their box hedges and two watering their window boxes. Most of these red-brick terrace houses, each of them three storeys high including a kind of attic floor, had been painted recently. His own, Number 43, looked as if it should be painted soon. The last paint job, which he and two of his sons had done between them, hadn't lasted well even for do it yourself. It was probably something to do with the quality of the paint. The little front garden was immaculate, however, with a postage-stamp lawn and some yellow privet clipped recently—probably by Kate, although young Malcolm should have done it. Dark patches on the soil of the only flower bed, filled with chrysanthemums, showed that someone had been busy watering. As he pushed the gate open, Kate came with a full can held with very great care.

"Oh, hallo, dear." Her smile was warm and spontaneous. "I thought I'd get this done before you got here."

She was a tall, handsome woman, with grey hair, a good complexion, clear grey eyes. She carried the watering can with ease, leaning back a little to take the strain and so emphasizing her full bosom.

"Let me take it," said Gideon. He took the can from her, put his cheek to hers in a kind of kiss, began to sprinkle the bed, and went on, "How's the child across the road?"

"Oh, it wasn't much—you know how Lucy Marjoribanks fusses. Alice fell down some stairs and screamed the house down, bumped her nose and bled a little. She's all right now. I'll go and get supper out of the oven." She turned and hurried off, quick-moving and graceful, and Gideon watched her for a moment, then finished the job and went in, swinging the watering can. As he stepped into the dining-room, at the end of the passage by the stairs, Kate was coming out of the kitchen.

"George!" she exclaimed.

"Eh?"

"Look what you're doing with that water?"

"Water?" He glanced down, and saw a trail of spots from the spout of the can, which had dribbled out when he had swung it; he stopped the movement quickly and held the can up in front of his face, in mock defence. "I didn't mean it, honest."

"I don't know what this place would be like if you and the boys had your way," Kate said, obviously vexed. "I only hope those marks will come out."

"They're only water."

"What about the fertilizer mixed with it?"

"Well, if you go mixing fertilizers—— Oh, now don't worry, Kate. It would be so diluted it won't make a stain on the carpet." He sniffed. "That smells good. What is it?"

"You've got about as much sense of smell as you have house sense," said Kate, the moment of vexation not really forgotten. "Sausage toad."

"Be ready in two minutes," said Gideon. He washed at the kitchen sink, and when he came back the toad-in-the-hole was already steaming on his plate, with a huge pile of batter and a lot of sausages. "It's a good job I don't have indigestion," he remarked.

"Well!" exclaimed Kate. "What a thing to say!"

She pushed her chair back from the table and stalked into the kitchen.

Gideon stared after her, open-mouthed, fork poised in one hand and knife in the other. Kate was bending down in front of the oven. She surely couldn't be seriously affronted. He took a mouthful, and the batter was so hot he opened his mouth and drew in cold air; he was looking like that when Kate came back with a vegetable dish in her hands, runner beans on one side, spinach on the other. She was not smiling.

He swallowed, "Kate, what's the matter?"

"If you don't know——"

"Of course I don't know," interrupted Gideon. He began to feel exasperated himself. "If I can't make a perfectly innocent remark without you flaring up, it's a poor show."

35

"An *innocent* remark. You take one look at your plate and talk about indigestion!"

Gideon said, "Oh. Oh, yes, I did. I see what you mean." He watched her spooning the vegetables on to his plate. I've dropped hundreds of heavier clangers than that, he reflected, and she hasn't risen to them. I wonder what's worrying her. They ate in silence for a few minutes, Gideon with increasing gusto. Then suddenly Kate stretched out a hand, pressed his, and said:

"Sorry, dear. I seem to be so touchy these days."

"Touchy," echoed Gideon, and grinned.

Kate stared, not understanding, and he saw from her expression that it wouldn't take much to drive her back to high dudgeon. He waved his fork at her, and noticed the bright sheen that emotion put into her eyes.

"That's exactly what Rogerson said to me this afternoon," he told her. "And what Lemaitre thinks, too. Looks as if it's contagious. I could have punched Rogerson on the nose. Do you know what he said? He said that I had lost the famous Gideon patience and was biting everyone's head off, so it was time I had a long vacation. *Have* I been all that bad?"

"Have *you* been." Kate put down her knife and fork, and laughed in a way that sounded rather forced. There was the eagerness of expectancy in her expression; and hope. "Did he tell you you must take a holiday?"

"Yes."

"Now?"

"Starting Saturday."

"George, it's just what we both want, what we *need!* I'd almost given up hope anyhow, and when I heard about the election I thought we could forget all about getting away this year. You'll go, won't you? You won't let anything stop you?"

"I thought we'd put the car on the train as far as Lyons, and then wander south and finish up at Cannes or Nice," said Gideon. "We can have eight or nine days on the Riviera, and drive back leisurely. We should be about right for the grape harvest. And at this time of year it shouldn't be difficult to get a hotel which doesn't cost the earth. How about Malcolm, though?"

36

"Oh, Malcolm will be all right. If he can't manage to look after himself at fifteen, he never will. Priscilla and Penny will be here at night, and for the weekends too. George, I'm so excited I don't think I want anything to eat."

"What you mean is that you're frightened you'll get indigestion," Gideon said dryly.

Next morning he put an elderly sergeant, Jefferson, on to the job of getting him some literature about the French Riviera, and finding out the times of trains and details of the car ferry and train service to central France. Once the inquiries were in hand, he put the thought of a holiday out of his mind and concentrated on the more urgent jobs. Lemaitre was already a different man, alert, eager, anxious to demonstrate his complete grasp of the situation and each case.

He kept saying, "I've been thinking, George . . ."

Together they briefed several senior officials on cases under review. The last was Fisher, who had been in charge of the investigation about the bank tunnelling job.

"You coming over to West London for the hearing George?" he wanted to know.

"I don't think so. How's it gone?"

"Thanks to Hugh Christie, couldn't have gone better. We talked to Alice Bane first about her tenancy of the shop, and she cracked almost at once. Pretty kid, only about twenty-two, and Bane must be forty if he's a day. He was having a celebration booze-up with some friends in Wapping when we tapped him on the shoulder. Incredible what fools they can be. He had some of the notes he took from the bank in his pocket—some of the new ones. Couldn't resist the feel of them although he knew we'd have the numbers. Beats me," went on Fisher with a shake of his big head. "He can have the intelligence to plan a job, start it months ago, burrow fifty yards underneath a busy street, break through three feet of reinforced concrete—only to slip up like that."

"Has he made any statement?"

"He denies it, but we've got him all right. I thought of asking for the usual eight-day remand, we'll have enough evidence to have him sent for trial after that."

"Then go ahead."

"Er—thanks." Fisher obviously hadn't finished, and as obviously wasn't sure how to go on. "One other thing, George."

"Yes?"

"Bane's wife."

"What about her?"

"We could charge her as being an accessory before and after the fact."

"*Did* she know?"

"Oh, she knew all right."

"Then why the hesitation?"

"I'm not sure that he didn't compel her to help him," explained Fisher. "She's scared of him, no doubt about that. I wondered if it would be a good idea to let her ride, for the time being. We might be able to persuade her to go in the box when the time came. She could be very useful even without giving direct evidence against him. I'm not just being softhearted——"

"You're being mushy," Gideon declared. "I shouldn't charge her, though, just warn her to stay in London in case we want her."

"I'll do that!" Fisher turned and barged out. Lemaitre clapped his hands together, making a surprisingly loud bang.

"*He's* mushy?" Lemaitre stood up, stretched and strolled across to the window. He did not realize it, but some of his actions and his movements were modelled on Gideon, although they often looked out of place because they did not suit his spindly figure as they did Gideon's massive one. Now he stood looking out on to the sunlit Thames, very earnestly. "Well, that's the routine lot, George. What about the election? Can't just sit back and let the water run under the bridge while you're away, can we?"

"What do you suggest?"

"Well, if I was handling it from scratch, I'd make no fuss at all," Lemaitre replied. "There are one or two members of Parliament who could do with watching, they could easily make fools of themselves. Then in each of the local committees of the F.F.P. boys and the Q boys . . ."

Lemaitre was both eager and earnest for over five minutes.

"Who would you put on the job from our end?" inquired Gideon.

"Parsons," Lemaitre answered promptly. "Best chap we've got for it. You agree, George?"

"Let's send for him," said Gideon.

The truth was, he reflected wryly, that it was easy to think one had a kind of divine right to be in charge; that personal belief in one's own indispensability crept up on one, in spite of lip service paid to the creed that no one was indispensable. Lemaitre would do a thoroughly sound job, and the main thing was to make sure that Rogerson realized it.

Parsons arrived at the office almost at once. He listened intently.

"Really think you can handle it?" Gideon asked, when he had finished. "When things hot up it won't be much fun."

"I know what it will be like," said Parsons feelingly. "I think I can handle it, too." The hard note in his voice belied the gentleness of his appearance. "It'll mean contact with each of the divisions and choosing the right man at each. Will you start on that, or shall I?"

"You."

"Thanks," said Parsons. "First thing I'll do is go and see Paterson."

"Yes. And second thing is to ask the Home Secretary to agree to banning all firework displays for the week of the election, Guy Fawkes Night or no Guy Fawkes Night."

"It will be a pleasure," Parsons said. "Am I to drop everything else?"

"Yes. Fix the hand-over with Lem here."

"Won't you be in charge?"

"I'm going away for a couple of weeks."

"Oh," said Parsons. For a moment Gideon thought that his manner would offend Lemaitre, who could be very touchy if his competence was questioned even by inference. Then Parsons gave a broad, canonical smile. "We'll show Gee-Gee how to run this office, Lem, won't we?"

Lemaitre clapped his hands like a pistol shot. Gideon bit back on a sharp comment, realizing that his reaction to the kidding was the clearest possible indication that he badly needed the coming holiday. One of the troubles was that he didn't really trust Lemaitre or Parsons or anyone to handle their jobs without him; he was back in the indispensable mood, although he could not explain why Parsons had affected him like that.

In the next hour Gideon's mind roved over all the cases going through, the big and the small and found himself fidgeting, particularly about the rumours of trouble over the election. Would he be able to pick up the reins where he had dropped them? Would he really be in charge of the situation during the election if he hadn't followed it day by day? It could be more serious than he or anyone else wanted to admit.

Was he right to go away at this juncture?

There was a tap at the door, and grey-haired Jefferson came limping in.

"I've got brochures and timetables and everything you need, sir," he said. "The agency assures me there will be no trouble about booking any class of hotel at this time of year."

"That's fine," said Gideon, with forced heartiness.

So he cleared his desk as best he could, and went away with Kate. For the first two days he was preoccupied with what might be going on back in London, but on the morning of the third day, driving towards Bordeaux, the warmth of the sun and the beauty of the autumn leaves of the vineyards drew worry and anxiety out of him. He slowed down so as to see the great clusters of grapes hanging from the vines, the families gathering them, the children and the women, young and old, carrying the big baskets to the carts, the huge carts with their round containers, bulging with grapes, with men trampling on them, barefooted, to make room for more laden baskets.

"I didn't realize it," he said to Kate on that third night, "but this is going to be a second honeymoon."

"It takes two to make a honeymoon," Kate said.

Later, when she lay sleeping by his side in a huge, feather-filled double bed in a big room with a squeaky, shiny pine floor, he stared at the stars through an open window, and dozed, and dreamed, and did not realize that he was happy.

Until that day Effie Wilcox had been very happy.

She was twenty-three, but young for her age, and she had been married for two years. Her husband lay by her side, sleeping, making a faint noise with every breath; it could hardly be called a snore. He lay on his back, and Effie lay on her side, seeing his profile, his rather big nose, and the small, square window beyond it. They were lucky to have a bed-room as well as a living-room, for flats and apartments were hard to get, and this tiny place was a palace to her. She and Fred had decorated it after they had married, had painted every piece of wood, had put on the wallpaper which they had chosen together—or rather, which she had chosen and Fred had approved.

She worshipped him.

And she was going to have a baby.

Oh, God, why had that other, awful thing had to happen to *her*?

The only man she had 'known' was Fred. He had been the first ever to caress and to fondle her, the first to wake her to an understanding of sexual ecstasy, and from their early meet-ings she had felt no doubts about him, but had submitted with a willingness which would have baffled and frightened her with any other man. In fact she felt sure it could not have happened with anyone else. She had trusted him implicitly from the very beginning.

She knew that he felt about her as she did about him; that there was no other woman, no other girl. She did not know whether there had been in the past, and did not even think about it. They were each other's, and she was young and in-nocent enough to believe that the idyll could last forever. He had a good job as a mechanic at a large garage and was in the running for a foreman's position. She would never cease to be fascinated by the way he handled gadgets; he could 'fix' anything, and often laughed at her ineptness with tools. But as often he watched and admired her taste in décor and in clothes.

There was only one blemish on their happiness, although she felt it wasn't really a blemish, she felt ashamed for thinking of the word. Fred was so jealous it was unbeliev-able. He would go red and then slowly pale, as if to white heat, whenever a man took even the slightest notice of her. When they went dancing she had to be extremely careful to make sure that no partner held her too tightly. She didn't really mind Fred's possessiveness, in fact she was fiercely proud of it, but sometimes it was difficult, such as when after

41

she had seen that doctor Fred had wanted to know everything.

"Did he touch you?"

"Well, *hardly*."

"Come on, I know what doctors do."

"Fred, he only just—well, he just examined me, that's all."

"How old is this doctor?"

"He's about forty, I suppose."

"If he messed you about——"

"Fred darling, I've got to go to a doctor. I'm going to have a baby. Don't—don't spoil it."

"Spoil it!" he had said, and pulled her to him and crushed her lips and pressed his lean hard body against hers. "It's just that I don't want any forty-year-old doctor even looking at you, let alone touching you. So change doctors, see. There's a woman doctor at the clinic over at Darby Street, she's the one for you. If you'd only told me what you thought before you went to see this chap?"

At that time, standing in front of her, half a head taller, dark-haired, strong-looking, very thin, Fred had gripped her so tightly that he had hurt.

"But I wanted to be sure, darling, Don't you see?"

"Of course I see and, okay, I'm a jealous fool—but it's that clinic of women doctors from now on, Right?"

"*Right!*"

And it had been. A middle-aged gynaecologist had confirmed her hopes, and she had been so happy. Fred had too, behaving as if that silly interlude had never happened. She hadn't given it a serious thought—until today.

She had opened the door to a heavy knock and found two big men outside. The flat was on the top floor of a four-storey house in Sydenham, with a front door which opened straight into the living-room. On the right was the bathroom and kitchen, which had just room for a small table, and where they ate except in the evenings, when they sat watching the television after the household chores were done, and ate from an oval coffee table. On the other side of the big room was this little bedroom.

The two huge men had dwarfed Effie Wilcox. She hadn't been scared, but she had been puzzled.

One man was rather like Fred, but taller; the other reminded her of a man she had known at work. He had grey hair, looked rather tired and had very big hands. He had a gentle voice, too.

"Mrs. Wilcox?"

"Yes."

"I am Chief Inspector Piper, of Scotland Yard, and this is Chief Inspector Dowsett," he said.

"*Really?*"

"Will you spare us a few minutes, please."

Then she had thought. *Something's happened to Fred*, and she had felt her knees bending, her legs collapsing. Suddenly her head seemed to burst. The grey-haired man had stopped her from falling, lifted her, carried her into the room, and, a few minutes later, sat on the couch next to her, with a glass of water in his hands.

"Better now?"

"Yes, I—I'm all right. I thought—I thought it must be bad news about my husband."

"It's just a routine call, Mrs. Wilcox."

"I don't really understand."

"I believe you went to see a doctor about two weeks ago. On October 1st, to be precise."

"Well, yes, I did?"

"What was the doctor's name?"

"Warburton, Dr. Warburton. I went——"

"Had you ever seen him before?"

"Well—no. No, I hadn't. I'd expected to see Dr. Nash, you see, but Dr. Nash was away. I saw Dr. Warburton."

"Did he—ah—behave properly, Mrs. Wilcox?"

She had stared, not comprehending. Only as the detective had asked more probing questions had she suspected the truth, and felt the breath of fear. All the time she had sat there, answering the man from Scotland Yard and watched by the dark, saturnine Dowsett, she had been thinking of Fred and what he would say if he ever knew the truth—*that it hadn't been a doctor*. Whenever she thought of it now she went white, both because of what Fred would think, how he would feel; and because a *man* had touched her. A man had laid his hands upon her breasts, a man had mocked the intimacy which was so precious and so right with Fred.

43

She hadn't told Fred. He had noticed that she wasn't quite herself, but she had said she had a headache. He had fussed over her, made her change into her dressing-gown, made the tea they always had as a nightcap. There had been a western followed by a thriller, and he had been absorbed in both. Afterwards there had been a political progamme about the coming election. He was fiercely Labour in his views.

So he hadn't really noticed her nervousness.

She hadn't plucked up courage to tell him about the police as they got ready for bed, and once in bed he turned over and went to sleep.

He had been asleep for hours. That noise was more like a snore now, but she did not worry about it at all, snoring didn't matter, nothing mattered, except that beast of a man who had touched her.

She could almost feel his hands.

That same night Amanda Tenby slept, alone, in a well-furnished room in a well-furnished flat on the Chelsea Embankment, overlooking the Thames. There was no more picturesque position in London. She lived here by herself not because she could not afford servants—she was the wealthy daughter of a wealthy man and money meant very little to her—but because she preferred to do exactly what she liked in her own home, to have whom she liked staying with her whenever she liked, by day or by night. She had one endearing trait, a great love of children, and another which also appealed, she was a good cook, had trained under a *cordon bleu*.

From her infancy she had been used to having her own way. An indulgent mother, a succession of indifferent nurses, a father who was so busy making money to add to money which his father had made before him, had combined with her natural characteristics, a strong will and a determination which nothing could shake. Whatever she wanted she got. If she couldn't get it easily she would fight in every way she knew. If she believed in a thing she would give everything she possessed to bring it about.

It was the genetic aspects of the nuclear horror that had first affected her. The thought that mothers-to-be would be affected by radiation, the thought that a host of babies could

44

be born idiots, imbeciles, beasts or cripples did something to her. At first, when she had realized the significance of it, she had tried to shut it out of her mind, but she had not been able to. She had flown to Japan, ostensibly for a holiday, actually to visit the scene of the World War II nuclear explosions, and she had *seen* some of the 'children' of that awful era, she had visited the clinics and the hospitals and had studied pictures of a horror so hideous, of faces and human forms so grotesque and unbelievably misshapen, that the experience had burrowed deep into her being.

From that moment she had dedicated herself to freeing the world from the nuclear shadow. Being Amanda Tenby, it had never seriously occurred to her that she could fail. She would need a great deal of help, but she could persuade some people and buy others. The committee was a means to an end, but for her it did not work quickly enough and was not drastic enough; it conformed too much.

That night she lay awake staring out the window. The stars were very bright and the night was still. There was no lapping of water against the Embankment, and only now and again did she hear a car. In the distance, across the river, a pale glow shone above the Battersea Power Station, and a faint humming sound came from the station. She often wished that the power station was really a nuclear reactor establishment, which she could destroy. She had studied the theory of nuclear warfare and of atomic reactors, she knew far more about them than most laymen.

She believed that nuclear weapons must be outlawed.

All the arguments against unilateral disarmament left her cold; *her* country need not possess the hideous weapon, it was a moral offence, an offence against humanity, an offence against children and the unborn.

The politicians called it a deterrent, and certainly it was supposed to frighten other nations away from war. But it was above everything else a terror weapon, and such weapons were anathema to her. Yet as she had worked she had realized that the one way to make the campaign effective was to *frighten* the authorities, to plan some move which could embarrass and alarm them. Some of the bolder actions of the Battle Committee had stemmed from her agile mind; but,

45

although she supported the committee with money and ideas, she knew that for really effective actions it had to be by-passed. Luckily there were a few who felt as keenly as she did, who would do anything within reason—or even beyond reason—to make the campaign a success.

There was Daniel Ronn, probably the only man she ever deferred to, a brilliant organizer and a man with contacts in every sphere of public life—with members of Parliament, the friends and relations of public men, with fringe people in the royal household, with the great newspapers and magazines, with the television authorities, the book world, the film world, the theatre world; he was a man with a host of influential acquaintances, and he knew the strength and the weakness of all of them. He could say who could be bought and who could be persuaded, and who could be frightened into helping; and just as important, he knew whom it was a waste of time to approach.

The one thing lacking in Daniel Ronn was ideas; he could work provided someone else did the creative thinking, he created nothing himself. Amanda was the thinker, and had never needed a brilliant idea as much as she did now. It must be something quite devastating, which would bring the nation to its senses, which would frighten the people into action.

The general election offered an unrivalled opportunity, if only she could think *what*.

She felt as if she was in the position of Robert Catesby, and Daniel was Guy Fawkes.

How simple life had been in the days of James I. A few kegs of gunpowder and a taper or two, and they had been able to scare the life out of the King and his courtiers, out of Parliament and its keepers. What would scare them now?

A few kegs of gunpowder . . .

Suddenly an idea came to her. It was like a knife slash in her mind. In the hush of that clear night her thin, boyish body went utterly still and her blood seemed to chill in her veins.

Then she whispered hoarsely to the quiet, "I've got it, I've got it. It's the obvious way, it's the only way, I've got it!"

She was so near ecstasy that tears squeezed themselves out between her eyelids.

46

At half past four that morning Daniel Ronn heard a bell, as if a long way off, then suddenly close by. He started up out of sleep. It was pitch-dark. His flat was in a Mayfair mews, and there was no light by day, no sight of the sky by night. The bell seemed to blast through his head, and he groped for the instrument, struggling to sit up, hating the caller.

He pulled off the receiver and muttered:

"Hallo."

"Daniel!"

"Who the devil is that?"

"Daniel, I've got it!"

"Who——" Ronn began again, and then realized that it was Amanda. Amanda was not a person to shout at, even when she woke him in dead of night. Amanda was a wealthy young woman and he was an eligible young man. "Amanda," he gasped, "what's all this about?"

"I've got it," she said in a breathless-sounding voice.

"You got—my God!" He was awake now, jolted into full wakefulness by understanding. "You mean you've got the big idea?"

"Yes, I know I have. I know it." She caught her breath. "I'm coming round to see you. I've got to talk about it, and we can't talk on the telephone. You'll be up, won't you?"

"Of course I'll be up," said Ronn. "My dear, I can come round to you, if you'd rather."

"No, I'd rather come to you," Amanda insisted. "I want to walk. I've just *got* to walk."

He knew what that meant, that she wanted to commune with herself, to dream her dream, to soliloquize in the tortuous world of her mind.

"I wonder what the hell she's thought up," he said aloud, and then his tone changed. "I've got half an hour, anyhow, if she's going to walk." He picked up the alarm clock, set it for five to five, and turned over and went to sleep again.

At a quarter to five, Amanda left the Chelsea house and began her walk.

A divisional policeman saw her, recognized her, and made a note for his report.

5

PROUD DEPUTY

"It's time you got up, George," Kate said. "Your second honeymoon is over."

It was eight o'clock on the Monday morning after they had reached home. Bright sunlight sparked on frost on grey slates opposite, and on the window ledges. Kate stood with a tea tray in her hand, dressing gown on, hair drawn back from her forehead, straight as it could be. She had refused to pay Riviera prices for a shampoo and set, and had simply brushed and combed it herself after every bathe in a caressing sea. She was beautifully brown; in fact Gideon could not remember having seen her so sunburned. But she had not peeled, whereas his face had been painfully red for the first few days, and there was dead skin on his forehead and ears even now. Yet he had burned almost black, and the colour showed up sharply against the white pillow case.

"So it's over," he said.

"For this year, anyhow."

He said, "Bless you, Kate!" He sat up. "What I need is a couple of days to settle down before going to the office, but I daren't suggest it. At least there wasn't a pile of urgent messages waiting here for me." He took a cup of tea. "If I know Lemaitre, he'll look up at me from my desk and ask me who I am."

Lemaitre sat with his jacket on, a dark-brown tie instead of a bow tie, a subdued dark-brown suit, his hair smarmed down, his hands and face looking very pale. He must have known that Gideon was on his way, for the Yard's grapevine would have started to operate the moment Gideon had appeared at the gate, but he appeared to ignore the opening door. Piles of the familiar manila folders were on Gideon's desk, more were on Lemaitre's, which Gideon had never seen so tidy.

Gideon closed the door quietly.

Lemaitre looked up. "Good morning," he said. "Can I help you?" Almost before the words were out he exploded, "Blimey, you're burned to a cinder!"

48

Gideon grinned; his teeth showed dazzlingly.

"Handsome too," Lemaitre scoffed, and got up and stretched out his hand. "Hallo, George. How'd it go?"

"Couldn't have been better."

"Kate okay?"

"She's as brown as I am."

"Jolly good," said Lemaitre. "And you've lost weight. Oi! How'd you manage to lose weight in France, that's what I want to know?"

"One good meal a day," replied Gideon, slapping his flat, hard stomach. "Nine pounds off, so I can start eating square meals again." He moved towards his desk and Lemaitre moved away from it. "Someone been taking you in hand?"

"Eh?"

"The place looks as if you've had a spring clean."

"Oh, that. Order out of chaos, that's all." Lemaitre now stood by the window, obviously waiting, and Gideon hadn't the heart to hold out any longer.

"How have things been going?" he asked.

"Not bad, not bad at all," said Lemaitre breezily. "In fact I think you'll be damned pleased, George. Not much new stuff in of any importance—one or two wage snatches, a post-office raid, the usual, but nothing to write home about. It's all in the files." He hardly allowed Gideon time to sit down before going on: "First things first. Micky Bane's been sent for trial, but he isn't likely to be up at the Old Bailey until after Christmas. I told Fisher he could prepare the case, and he's been in touch with the Solicitors' Department, don't think there'll be any trouble there. And you remember that skeleton down the old well in Cornwall? They've identified the body, Carson really did it, I think, good bit of sniffing out. It's the body of a young woman who disappeared from Hackney five years ago. The dental work proved it. Carson's still on the job, operating from here. Believe it or not, the Quack's had another go——"

"Speeding up, isn't he?"

"Yes."

"Nothing in about his identity?"

"Nope. It was Chelsea this time. Piper's worried, and Dowsett keeps going off the deep end. Piper's coming in to see you

49

later, he particularly asked for you. Parsons will be in soon too. Parsons—strewth! How that man hates these F.F.P. boys and girls."

Gideon sat down.

"Hates?" he echoed.

"That's the word for it."

"Are you sure?"

"George, he's just as dedicated to stopping them as they are to stopping the bomb, and that's saying something. Funny thing, I didn't think he ever felt deeply about anything, not deep down. But this job—he works day and night."

"Oh," said Gideon.

"Anything wrong?"

"I don't know yet."

"When you see his records and hear what he's got to say you won't think there's anything wrong," Lemaitre assured Gideon. "You know that storeroom they're turning into an office for more inspectors, to give them some elbow room? Well, I've put Parsons into it. He needed room to spread, couldn't have managed it——" Lemaitre was on the defensive now, puzzled by Gideon's manner.

"Good idea," said Gideon. He thought, *hates*. It was not only a surprise, it was something of a shock to discover that he had chosen the man who had become emotionally involved in the issue to take care of it; that had been one of his mistakes. Would he have made it if he hadn't been so flat and tired?

He tried to console himself with the reflection that he wasn't yet sure that it had been a mistake, and shook off the misgivings. Lemaitre was so cock-a-hoop that it was difficult not to be cheered up by his enthusiasm and satisfaction.

"Thought you'd see it that way, George. I don't think there's much else, and with the election only three weeks away maybe that's as well."

Gideon thought, something else is bound to crop up. The run of comparative freedom from major crime had been a long one, and by the law of averages there was sure to be a sharp break soon. The lull might last for the next three weeks or so, though; there was no need to anticipate trouble.

"You going to see the boys for briefing this morning?" asked Lemaitre airily.

"I ought to go along and see the A.C.," said Gideon. "You fix it. I'll be back by half past eleven, for Parsons and Piper."

"Right!" Lemaitre wanted nothing better than to handle the morning's briefing.

Gideon called Rogerson's office, said he would be along, and first went to see Records and Information. A little man wearing pince-nez, Syd Harrison, was in Records and he made the inevitable crack about Gideon's sun tan. Down in Information, where the new room had been in operation for so long that no one thought of it as new any longer, a youngish superintendent named Forbes was on duty. The teleprinters were working, the policemen at the telephones busy, the air of quiet bustle was exactly as when Gideon had last visited it —as it was day in, day out, night in, night out. The room always fascinated him. It was the nearest thing he knew to a true heart of London. Here they were taking the pulse of the nation's crime with the accuracy of a doctor. Yet that wasn't quite true; they were taking the pulse of crime so far as it was discernible; the worst kind of crime, the worrying crime, was that which was taking place unsuspected and unknown, the crime that would never be discovered, committed by criminals who would never be caught. That was always a sobering thought.

He went up to Fingerprints, where King-Hadden, perhaps Gideon's closest friend after Lemaitre, was in his shirt-sleeves examining a broken beer bottle. Gideon studied him as he dusted the neck of the bottle with powder and blew on it gently; they had not yet found an automatic way of looking for fingerprints. Two men wearing khaki coats were also here. The small room was filled with a variety of goods which made it like a secondhand shop and a junk dealer's combined. There was a musty odour, and the windows were tightly closed.

King-Hadden, his smallish eyes half buried as he screwed them up behind a magnifying glass, was as flabby and pale as Gideon was hard and brown. He was big and rather puddeny in build, and wore a shapeless suit of navy blue, the last colour he should have worn on this messy job; there were smears of fuller's earth all over his coat. On the desk by his side was a lipstick and a powder compact.

The thick end of the bottle he was handling was broken

and jagged. One or two of the spiky pieces were bright green, with the translucent beauty of bottle glass, but the others were smeared and brown.

He pursed his lips and blew out a long, slow breath.

"No luck?" asked Gideon.

King-Hadden looked up with a start.

"Oh, it's you, is it? I thought you were still sunning yourself." He put the bottle down on a piece of clean chamois. "You need a holiday, George, can't have you going around looking as pale as that." That was his kind of humour. "Anything I can do for you?"

"What's that?" asked Gideon, pointing.

"A bottle which once contained Guinness."

"Anything on it?"

"Smears, that's all, apart from blood."

"What job is it from?"

"Last night's shindy at Paddington."

"Shindy?" echoed Gideon. Lemaitre had said nothing about a shindy.

"There was a free fight between some of the F.F.P. people and Q Men," explained King-Hadden. "Parsons rushed this over, and asked me for a quickie." So Parsons knew. "Two men got hurt. One of them's in the hospital with wounds in his chest, and a girl got some nasty cuts on her face. We want to stop that kind of lark, George."

Gideon said heavily, "We certainly do." He nodded and went out, knowing that if King-Hadden had anything else of interest to report he would have said so. Outside the door Gideon paused, frowning. He was tempted to talk to Parsons right away, but decided not to jump the gun.

Rogerson was in his office.

"Hallo, George! Glad to see you back." He looked rather better too, as he got up from his desk and rounded it, hand outstretched. He studied Gideon intently, and went on, "Don't need any telling it's done you good. Hating everything this morning?"

"Not yet," said Gideon. "I'm just settling in. Anything in particular worried you while I've been away?"

"Life's one long worry," replied Rogerson, only half flippantly. "As a matter of fact, Lemaitre's done a better job than

I expected. If he can keep it up, you can name him as your deputy. I had a word with the Commissioner, who said he'd like to wait for a few weeks. No urgent need for an official deputy yet, is there?"

"No."

"Seen Parsons?"

"I'm going to, in half an hour."

"He seems to be doing a very sound job," said Rogerson. "He could do with more help, though. My spies tell me that he often works here until the small hours. He's out most of the day at the divisions, and comes back to do the office side of the job. Put a couple of extra men on nights with him if you think it's necessary."

"I will."

"Good thing he's not a married man," remarked Rogerson. "How about lunch today?"

"I'm going to have a sandwich in my office," Gideon said. "Thanks all the same."

It was nearly half past eleven when he returned to his office, to find Piper standing by Lemaitre's desk. Piper's big, knuckly hands were clasped in front of him, but he unclasped them and stood almost to attention when Gideon entered.

"Morning," Gideon said. "Lem tells me that the Quack's been at it again."

"Two days' stint this time, at Chelsea," Piper reported. "Didn't do much harm; in fact, I don't think he did any harm worth speaking of, but he's getting bolder. If it goes on much longer we'll really be in trouble."

"What kind of trouble?"

"The *Daily Globe* is breathing down our backs, and you know what that tabloid's like. One of the victims—that prostitute I told you about—talked to a reporter, and they've haunted Symes and Dowsett ever since. Dowsett thinks that it's time we used the newspapers, anyhow. If the *Daily Globe* and the *News of the World* worked on it together, and published this, we might get places. And if we don't give them the whole story soon, they'll publish what they can get hold of themselves. I believe Dr. Nash had a couple of visitors from the *Globe* yesterday."

Piper handed Gideon a picture made up by the *Identikit*

method, and apparently good. It showed a pleasant-faced, smiling man, a decent-looking type of man, with a square chin and short nose and wide-set eyes. Alongside it were some figures:

Height: About 5' 10"
Hair: Usually dyed: known colours: very fair, yellow, brown, grey, black
Eyes: Greeny-grey
Build: Slender

And there were some notes:

This man, who gives a different name whenever he applies for a post as *locum tenems* at a general practitioner's, has a very pleasant manner and is generally liked by people who meet him.

He is brisk and businesslike with men.

He has every woman 'patient' strip on any excuse, and goes through the motions of a normal medical examination. He appears to have a reasonable knowledge of the normal examination methods.

Gideon studied the picture, as he sat on the corner of his desk.

"We've got to give the whole story to the press, or enough to keep 'em quiet," Piper said.

Gideon shook his head. "There isn't a way of keeping this quiet. If we give 'em a little, they'll start digging deep, and every woman who's been examined by this chap will be rooted out and questioned. I don't know how to handle it for the best. Might give the story to one or two papers." He soon changed his mind. "No, if we give anyone a scoop we'll have the others breathing down our necks." He rounded the desk and tapped the picture with his forefinger. "Any of the patients affected very deeply, do you think?"

"There was one girl whom it seemed to knock badly," Piper told him. "A young woman, really, early twenties and three months gone—married, mind you, nothing wrong about it. When she knew what had happened she fainted right off. I can't say any of the others showed anything more than a bit of embarrassment. One or two seemed almost nostalgic about it."

Gideon didn't smile.

"It's the effect on people like this young woman that we want to watch," he said. "Can never tell how much harm this kind of thing does. Still, we don't have any choice. Have a word with Littleton, and ask him how he would handle it, would you?"

Littleton was the public relations officer at the Yard, a comparatively new man, usually on the ball. Gideon had come to regard him with respect as a journalist who really knew how to get along with Fleet Street, and such liaison officers were rare birds.

"Right," said Piper, and went out.

Effie Wilcox was alone in the little flat, looking through the *Daily Globe* in which there were more pictures than stories. There was one section of four pages devoted, every day, to 'sexy' pictures, and every now and again this section was used for a genuinely sensational story. Whenever a man turned into a woman or a woman turned into a man, for instance— and judging from the *Daily Globe* this biological metamorphosis was by no means uncommon—the whole story was told here with plenty of pictures and hints of intimate details. From time to time, as Effie knew, a different kind of story was told—about women who dressed up as men, and got away with it for years, or men who dressed up as women and lived like women. Only recently there had been a story of a Greek family who had so wanted a boy that when their sixth girl-child was born they pretended that she was a boy. They brought her up as one, and dressed her as one—and got away with it for over twenty years!

Effie sensed that if ever the story of the fake doctor got out, it would be exactly right for this page. The possibility frightened her. The worst of the situation was that every night she knew she should tell Fred what had happened, but every night she put it off for one reason or another. Now she couldn't tell him, because he would wonder why she had kept it to herself for so long. Flashes of jealousy still raised him to white heat, for no reason at all.

If he ever found *this* out . . .

She dropped the paper, leaned back and closed her eyes.

55

By the middle of the afternoon, when she had done the shopping, the housework and the mending, a little of the worry began to recede. The vegetables were ready for the evening meal, a steak already beaten and spread with dripping was out of the refrigerator, because she did not like to put meat under the grill when it was ice-cold. The bell rang. It was a Monday, and Monday was the day when the local savings group collector called, a middle-aged woman from downstairs, Mrs. Mullery. She had a family of seven, she knew everyone in the district, and was a friend in need to every woman who was carrying her first child. Almost eagerly, Effie went to answer the door.

Two men stood there.

She was reminded immediately of the two policemen who had once called, and her first thought was that these were policemen too. They were smaller, but she did not realize that size might be significant. She stood with her hand on the door, the colour draining from her cheeks. One of the men was very young, the other—who carried a big leather box—was elderly and grey-haired.

"Mrs. Wilcox?" the younger man asked pleasantly.

She didn't answer, she couldn't.

"If you can spare us a minute we'd appreciate it," the young man said. He had very fine dark eyes, very fine eyebrows and lashes—they looked as if they had been painted black and had a sheen on them. "We can make it worth your while, too."

"I—I don't know what you mean."

"If you will——"

"I've told you everything I know!" she gasped. "Don't keep coming here, please don't keep coming."

"We haven't been here before," the young man assured her. The older man was taking something out of his box, and was fiddling with it, but Effie did not notice then that it was a camera. "Who has been, Mrs. Wilcox? What newspaper——?"

"Newspaper!" she gasped. "I thought you were the police!"

"Oh, nothing like that," the young man assured her, and then the other man moved, with the camera levelled at her.

56

There was a flash. "We are from the *Daily Globe*. Now if you will be good enough——"

"Look out, she's fainting," the photographer cried in alarm. "Catch her!"

6

THE WORKROOM

GIDEON, unaware of all this, as he was unaware of so much going on which would eventually affect the police, or at least be connected with crime in one way or another, walked along to the office which had been allocated to Parsons for the special general election job. The few hours at the Yard had enabled him to shake off any feeling of lethargy. He felt that he was fairly well acquainted with everything that had happened while he was away, but his absence had made little or no difference to the way things had gone.

He was still uneasy about Parsons and that 'hate' Lemaitre had talked of, but it might just be Lem, exaggerating.

He pushed open the door.

Parsons, in his shirt-sleeves and with the ends of his spotted white-on-blue tie hanging down the front of the white shirt, looked up from a big trestle table. In fact, there were three trestles, close together, and the top was about twelve feet long; it was the width of two average trestle tops too, and filled one side of the room. On the wall behind it were huge maps, brought up from the map room. London's metropolitan area was divided into eight main sections, and these were pasted to the wall so that it made a complete area map.*

On a wall at right angles to this was another map, one of England, showing the county police forces; on a third wall were smaller maps of all the country boroughs which had their own force. Scotland and Wales were shown too, but there was nothing of Northern Ireland.

Parsons sat with his back to the main wall, facing the door; he used the trestle tables as a desk. Two smaller desks, opposite him, were empty; each had two telephones on it, and

* See map opposite page 7.

a green metal filing cabinet behind it; one had a typewriter. To complete the furniture there were two more filing cabinets in a corner, and two rows of bookshelves with a few books on them.

Parsons stood up.

"You look fine," he said. "Glad to see you back."

"I'm all right," said Gideon. "How are you?" He had expected to find signs that Parsons was looking drawn and overworked, but there was nothing to suggest it. His eyes were bright and alert. He had lost a little weight, but that wouldn't do him any harm. It sharpened his features, and gave a new kind of briskness to his manner.

"Couldn't be better," Parsons said. "This job is just my cup of tea."

"You said it would be." Gideon looked round the walls, and began to smile inwardly and appreciatively. There were coloured-headed pins all over the maps, sometimes in clusters, sometimes in ones and two, and he counted the colours. The legend, typewritten on a sheet stuck in one corner, ran:

White: Fight for Peace Committee meeting places
Blue: Q Men ditto
Black: Riot spots
Red: Danger men and women—F.F.P.
Yellow: Ditto Q Men.

"Pretty, isn't it?" said Parsons. "All my own work."

"Don't you ever sleep?"

"As much as I want to," said Parsons. "Nick King-Hadden says you've seen him."

"Yes. What happened at Paddington last night?"

"If you ask me, there was an organized clash and someone was paid to weigh in with this broken bottle to hot things up," Parsons said. "The difficulty is we can't be sure that it wasn't someone who was just out to make a scene. Some of the youngsters these days seem to love the sight of blood. It began as a small demonstration there." He pointed to a black pin. "See how close it is to a Q Men place? Asking for trouble. About two hundred F.F.P. people turned up with banners and placards, and we had men nearby to make sure things didn't get out of hand. A car-load of the Q Men drove up,

58

spilled out, and started to bellow questions and push the crowd around. It didn't take long for the fight to start, and people were hurt. The broken bottle was found at the kerb. If we hadn't had our uniformed chaps on duty, it might have been a lot worse. Nick hoped there might be a print or two on that bottle, but n.b.g." Parsons shrugged. "It's the kind of thing we've got to strangle at birth, George."

Gideon didn't speak.

"Don't you think so?"

Gideon said heavily, "Can we strangle it at birth?" He was frowning. "Why should anyone want to cause that kind of trouble at this stage in the election?"

"That's what I've been talking about all along," said Parsons. "This nuclear age has generated a damned sight more emotional neurosis and nerve sickness than we realize. If it attacks you, it's an acute form of anxiety complex. You're bloody scared, and hit out blindly because you are. Then there's the politically explosive situation of relations with Russia. That's hated by the Q Men. It so happens that most of them are extreme right-wingers who think pacifism is blind cowardice and regard the F.F.P. as the worst kind of pacifism. So what we've got is two lunatic fringes of extremists. They each hit out meaning to hurt, and each sees the other as its natural enemy. That's the chief danger, George. Blind, unthinking, emotional prejudice. And it's fed on both sides by a lot of people who ought to know better."

After a pause, Gideon said:

"I know what you mean. I half agree with you."

"*Half?*"

"That's right, half," repeated Gideon, good-humouredly. "You mustn't overlook the streak of common sense in the average elector. It's there, you know. If we get too much of this kind of behaviour, there will be a revulsion against both groups and neither will be able to stir up serious trouble. Their own supporters will fall away."

"Not the hard core," Parsons objected quickly. "And there's a big hard core in each group."

"Feel strongly about this?" inquired Gideon.

"Couldn't feel stronger."

"Which side are your sympathies on?"

Parsons looked puzzled.

"Sympathies? Who said I had any sympathy one way or the other?"

"Haven't you?"

"No," said Parsons flatly, but he was frowning, and for a moment looked away from Gideon. The window was opposite a blank brick wall, and the dull red of the bricks absorbed most of the daylight. "No," he repeated. "And I don't have any political association either. But I'll tell you what I have got, George. I've got an old-fashioned feeling that this is the best little democracy in the world. When I hear people talk about the Mother of Parliaments, that's what I assume they mean . . the *mother*. I think we've developed the best system of democratic government that there is anywhere in existence, and I don't exclude the Scandinavian countries or the United States. We've got our faults, God knows, but when it comes to the day-by-day practice of political democracy—I mean a democracy which gives everyone a vote—there's no one to touch us. Then these bloody fanatics come along with their half-baked idealism, and they drag along all the lunatic fringe dupes. They pick up the odds and sods, everyone who thinks he or she has had a raw deal, anyone who doesn't fit in, the physical and the mental misfits. If the F.F.P. Battle Committee was dealing with people of its own mental calibre and own intelligence level we wouldn't have anything to worry about, but they're dealing with fanatics, idiots, morons, and dedicated megalomaniacs as well as a lot of poor sods who are plain frightened, and a lot more who are simple-minded idealists who think we can put the world right by waving a wand."

Parsons went on talking in a quiet, low-pitched, even voice. Gideon had no doubt that he felt everything he said with almost passionate sincerity; and Gideon marvelled that he could work with a man for years, give him orders, confer with him, and believe that he knew him—and yet hardly know him beneath the skin.

"These people are more dangerous to humanity than all the nuclear weapons put together," Parsons went on. "They can destroy the mind, they can corrode the heart of democracy, they can destroy everything we've worked for over the cen-

60

turies. *That's* what I hate. That, and the mob at the opposite extreme. Every chance they get the Q Men shout or sing about being for Queen and Country, and maybe most of them are loyalists. Like to be reminded about some other loyalists who've been busy in the last few years? The French OAS, for instance. Remember what they did, George? I was over in Algiers to bring Cotton back on the drug-smuggling job when they blew up a car in a busy street, killed about fifty people and maimed God knows how many more. That's what their kind of loyalty did—turned them into dangerous killers. They stop being nationalists and decent people, they become barbarians who kill, rape, rob, destroy, who will do anything to hurt for the sake of hurting—because they can't get their own way.

"I hate both sorts, George. Any objections?"

Gideon said, very slowly, "I think it's a pity more of us don't feel like you."

Parsons raised one hand. "You mean that?"

"You know I do."

"Oh," said Parsons. He gulped. "Well, I should have realized it. Thanks, George."

"Just one thing."

"Yes?"

"They hate a thing or a system and don't care what they do to hurt it. We hate a thing or a system but we've got to make sure that in beating it we don't do a lot of harm to ourselves."

Parsons was smiling constrainedly.

"Point taken, George."

"Check with me daily, won't you—at home at night if needs be, I'm told you are out most of the day."

"I am, mostly, but I knew you would be in this morning. I've sent the two sergeants out."

"Are they shaping up well?"

"They're pretty good."

"How many more do you need?"

Parsons grinned again. "A dozen!"

"I'll detail six."

"You *mean*—all right, all right! I know you mean it. George; this is the first time I've felt that we're really taking this threat seriously. Thanks." Parsons rubbed his chin, and went on: "And you haven't even asked me how I'm handling it."

"Show me," said Gideon.

"Right!" Parsons turned, picked up a round ebony ruler from his desk, and began to point. As he indicated different places on the map, he talked. There were the known meeting places, the danger spots where the two groups might clash because one or the other held rallies there. There were the key workers in each group, workers who, Parsons believed, might become dangerous because of the passion of their fanaticism. There were the meeting places for the coming election, too, the committee rooms run by the various parties, everything was shown on those maps.

In the cabinets were comprehensive records of the different local committees, and dossiers on individuals, with data as complete as Parsons could make it. Among those he took out was a slim file, marked: AMANDA TENBY.

"Here's one I wouldn't like to trust round the corner," he declared. "She's a weirdie, but she means what she says. She volunteered to fly into the Pacific when the last American tests were being carried out, and she would have gone too. She's worth a couple of hundred thousand pounds, inherited from her grandfather. She's been disowned by her family— her mother's dead, it's just her father, who's a true-blue Tory and still believes in gunboat diplomacy. She's been to Japan and looked at the aftermath of Hiroshima and Nagasaki. She knows as much as anyone on the F.F.P. Battle Committee, and she pays for a lot of the work that the extremists do. She's about as sexless as a carrot, but her money draws the men to her. So do her brain waves, and she has plenty. I rate her the most dangerous of all the F.F.P. people, although we've never caught her out in any serious breach of the peace. She's known to all our chaps and I'm having her specially watched."

He took out two photographs of Amanda Tenby, one so vivid and effective that it was almost as if she was in the room with them.

"See those eyes, George? Fanatic's eyes, that's what they are. Got quite a profile, though." He handed the pictures to Gideon, and went on: "Here are some of the things she's been up to lately: She attends every meeting of the Battle Committee, the real heart of the F.F.P. movement. She's been to seven local committee meetings—and wherever she goes a nasty spot of bother follows."

"Was she out last night?"

"No," answered Parsons. "She doesn't run into that kind of trouble. But last night's fight was at Paddington. She was at the St. John's Wood Local Committee three nights ago. It's a queer thing, but something always blows up after she's been to a place."

"But you said the Q people started last night's shindig."

"I didn't, you know. I said that a couple of people we couldn't place started it, and got away. We don't know whether they were Q Men supporters or F.F.P. supporters. We don't know whether she sponsored them or whether they weighed in just for the hell of it. But here's an interesting graph, George."

Parsons drew out a kind of genealogical tree, drawn up in pencil. At the top was Amanda Tenby. Stemming from her were different local committees, with the names of some of the members. At each there was a red mark. Gideon counted; there were seventeen red marks in all.

"If you study that closely you'll see that she visited each place within seven days of violence taking place there," said Parsons. "Some *might* call it coincidence."

"Was she the only one to visit all the places?"

"Yes."

"Anyone else visit any large proportion of them?"

"Yes—man named Ronn, Daniel Ronn. I can't make Ronn out," Parsons admitted, frowning. "He's got all the qualifications for being one of Quatrain's group. Same kind of background, same kind of social activities, same kind of business and commercial interests as Quatrain, and yet he's a member of the F.F.P. Battle Committee, and seems to be Amanda Tenby's boy friend. I didn't tell you that she left home at a quarter to five the night of October 14th and walked to Ronn's place, getting there at ten past five. Funny kind of thing to do, wasn't it? If she'd spent the night with him and left in the early hours it would be understandable, but this way round looks all wrong."

"Any idea what she wanted?"

"I've got four different reports on her from men who noticed her as she walked, and they all say the same; she looked starry-eyed. And don't tell me that it might have been young love, after all."

"How long was she with Ronn?"

"About three hours."

"Then?"

"She went back to her own flat, and as far as we can judge, behaved normally—if the way she behaves could ever be called normal. I've had as close a watch kept on her and her contacts as I can. Now you're going to give me more men, I can check much closer. I don't like the combination of Amanda T. and Ronn one little bit. Ronn knows everybody."

"What's really worrying you?" asked Gideon.

"I just don't know what they're up to," confessed Parsons. "Now with Quatrain, on the other side of the picture, it's as transparent as glass. Funny thing about Quatrain. I hate everything he stands for, yet everything I find out about the man as a person I like. In his way he's a single-minded idealist who believes in his cause so fiercely that he doesn't care how far he goes to make it succeed. He's stinking rich, remember. He's said to be worth a million, and I know for sure he's worth at least half. He's got a lot of financial support from others." Parsons put away Amanda Tenby's file and took a photograph of a man from another folder. The man was in his forties and strikingly handsome, almost with a film star's looks. In his eyes there was something of the intensity that showed in Amanda Tenby's. A profile photograph was just as striking, and Gideon studied it closely. "My sister always says he's the nearest approach she's ever seen to Ronald Colman," went on Parsons. "And I can have a man full time on him, too. You've done me a world of good, George."

"Pleasure. How about the banning of fireworks? Is that laid on?"

"Yes. Every police force has fixed it, George. Saturday the 8th will be official Guy Fawkes night this time. Fridays and Saturdays are usually the noisiest anyhow, and the election will be almost forgotten by the Saturday."

Gideon thought, a little wryly, that Parsons was almost certainly right about that.

Amanda Tenby walked swiftly along Dean Street, Soho, watched by policemen who were always in the vicinity, and by two C.I.D. men who were making inquiries into the activities of some of the nastier strip shows. Amanda walked with a slight stoop. Her dark hair was blown back from her high forehead by a stiff wind, and fluttered about her shoulders. She wore black stretch slacks, which fitted her lath-like body so tightly that a lot of people turned to look, or stared from across the road. She seemed oblivious to all this, even when she heard a woman ask:

"*Is* that male or female?"

A man said: "Hush! She'll hear you."

"Cut off the hair and she'd be a he!"

Amanda walked on until she reached a small restaurant with faded gold lettering in the window, green-painted woodwork which must have been in the same state throughout the last war, and a very narrow door. This was one of Soho's more famous restaurants. She nodded to the head-waiter, and slipped upstairs, silent as a wraith, noticed by very few. She stopped for a moment at a door marked *1908 Room*, gave a perfunctory tap, and went inside.

Ronn was there, with another young man.

This young man was nearly as thin as Amanda. He wore big glasses with blue-tinted lenses. His mouse-coloured hair was spiky and overlong. His face was bleached of colour like that of a man who worked indoors or in artificial light most of the time. He had a big forehead, a small snub nose, rather a thin mouth, and not very much chin. He sat by himself on one side of a small oak table with a high-backed bench behind it.

Ronn stood up.

"Glad you've arrived, Amanda," he welcomed. "We're starving." He smiled forgiveness. "This is Mr. Travaritch!" His smile widened, and his voice dropped. "Professor Travaritch, I should say."

Amanda did not shake hands at first, but stared at the spindly Travaritch as if she wanted to study every line on his face, and meant to make sure that she never forgot him. It was almost embarrassing. At last she sat down; and, sitting, held out her thin, bony hand.

"Good morning."

"I wish you good morning," Travaritch said. He had a rather hard voice, unexpected from a man with so fragile a figure. "I am very glad to meet you."

"I told Cleo that we would be ready to eat as soon as you came," said Ronn. "If you want to say anything, you'd better get it over. Then we'll have to wait until Cleo's gone."

"I just want to ask one thing," Amanda said. Her eyes seemed huge, it was almost as if she were trying to hypnotize Travaritch. "*Is* what we want possible?"

"Yes, it is possible," Travaritch said.

"If we can come to terms," put in Ronn.

"We will come to terms," Amanda declared softly.

Then there was a tap at the door, and the proprietor, Cleo, came in.

In the late afternoon Parsons studied a written report about all this. Amanda Tenby and Daniel Ronn had been to lunch at Cleo's, in Dean Street, and a waiter had told a policeman that a third person, a man, had also been present. Neither Amanda nor Ronn had used his name in anyone's hearing, and Cleo himself did not know what they had been discussing.

"They were so damned cagey it must have been something nasty," Parsons reflected. "At least we've got a description of the chap they lunched with."

About the same time that Parsons was studying the report Piper tapped at the door of Gideon's office. When he entered he looked annoyed. Gideon was going through some memoranda which had come from the Home Office about the forthcoming election. He was also reflecting that until one was actually imminent, it was easy to forget how a general election affected every aspect of police work. Keeping the public order was as much part of their job as investigating crimes, but it was seldom so obvious. Being preoccupied, he didn't notice Piper's expression.

"What's new?" he asked.

"We're too late, that's what's new," said Piper. Lemaitre looked up sharply, as if there was some implied criticism of him in this. "The *Daily Globe*'s running the story of the Quack tomorrow. Littleton called them this morning, and they were evasive. Now we know why. Dowsett says that they've been to see half a dozen of the women in Sydenham, and three in Chelsea have been interviewed, as well as some of the people in the other districts. They're going to use it in their Sex Special. Littleton wonders if you could persuade them to run the *Indentikit* picture at the same time, and so make the best of it"

After a long pause, Gideon said, "All I can do is try."

7

SEX SPECIAL

AT the top of the two 'special' pages in the *Daily Globe* was a bold declaration of policy. This read:

The *Daily Globe* admits there is such a thing as sex.
It believes that sex motivates human life.
It believes that within the ordinary bounds of human decency and dignity, which amount to the same thing, sex should be fully and frankly featured in a great national newspaper.

When Fred Wilcox went whistling into the garage where he worked he noticed two of the attendants and another mechanic staring at him, and saw one of them fold up a newspaper surreptitiously. He took no notice. He was at peace with the world, with only a faint shadow in his mind—that Effie wasn't quite herself now that she was with child. That was the phrase he used to himself; he had a dislike of the word 'pregnant,' feeling that it was faintly improper. If anyone here wanted to start a fight, they had only to talk in his hearing of Effie's being 'in the family way'. He was a mixture of old-fashioned puritanism and modern tolerance, and at no time did he try to analyse his own emotions: he simply knew how he felt, and acted accordingly.

Effie seemed well enough, he thought, but something seemed to be frightening her. Last night he had told himself that he would have to get his mother to come and stay for a few days and help Effie over this patch. After all, it was her first— but if he knew anything it wouldn't be her last!—and it was only natural she should be worried. He went to his locker, where he kept his overalls and a few odds and ends; beneath the main compartment was a small one, always locked, where he kept his tools, but the upper section was unlocked.

He opened it, and a folded newspaper fell out.

"Funny," he said to himself, and stooped to pick it up. He was half aware of a couple of apprentices hovering near the locker-room door, but didn't give them a thought; they often got into a huddle to tell filthy jokes, knowing that he wasn't interested and would tear a strip off them if they told their stories in his hearing. He put the newspaper, the *Daily Globe*, on a bench as he took off his overcheck sports jacket and slipped into the brown coverall. The apprentices were whispering. He picked up the newspaper, for it was five minutes to eight, and he had a few minutes' grace before work. He always read the *Globe* because Effie liked it, but their copy wasn't delivered until after he had left for work. He skimmed through this one, looking for the political news. There was a double-page spread, headed:

WHO WILL GET *YOUR* VOTE?
NOMINATION DAY—YOUR
FUTURE AT STAKE

He scanned the list of candidates in what the newspaper called the 'decisive constituencies' where the winning margin had been less than 4,000 votes, picked out his own candidate, rubbed his hands, spoke half aloud—as he often did—"I'll have to spend a bit of time on this job. Hope it won't worry Effie if I'm out at nights." He was looking forward to the rough and tumble of meetings and the cut and thrust of question and answer, and his spirits were high when he turned the next page.

On it were four photographs, each of a woman.

One was Effie's.

He stood absolutely still, holding the paper by the sides. It did not even shake. The colour, red in his cheeks when he had first seen the picture, slowly faded, leaving him an unhealthy pallor. Someone whispered, "*Shurrup!*" Someone giggled. He was aware of things but they seemed to have nothing to do with him. All he could see was a misty greyness in front of his eyes. The photographs had vanished, as if cut off by

68

fog. Then, slowly, the newspaper began to shake, as his hands trembled and he could not stop them. Effie looked up at him, in a funny, startled way. He knew that expression very well, it was the one she always had when she was taken by surprise. He had seen it frequently when they had first come to know each other, and he had taken a delight in jumping on her when she was least expecting it.

He began to move his lips together, as if they were dry.

He read:

VICTIMS OF BOGUS DOCTOR

He clenched his teeth until his jaws hurt, and made himself read. It was all there. The places where the bogus doctor had worked, the number of people he was known to have 'examined', the doctors for whom he had acted as *locum tenens*, the names of seventeen women and the photographs of four. *Effie*.

Mrs. Effie Wilcox of Flat 5, Hilton Street, Sydenham. Mrs. Wilcox is soon to have her first child.

Effie!

One of the three young garage hands who knew that the newspaper had been put into the locker and were watching for the reaction, backed away from the door, half shamefaced.

"Let's pack it in," he said.

"It's gone too far," an older one said.

"Look at him," another still gloated, hardly able to choke back his glee. "That'll teach him, the narrow-minded ape. That'll teach——"

He broke off.

"*Look out!*" a third man cried in a high-pitched voice.

Fred Wilcox swung round and stormed towards them, newspaper in one hand, fist clenched. His eyes were glittering, he looked as if he would kill anyone who got in his way. The four men backed off, one of them tripped over an old tyre and staggered against the wall. Wilcox did not seem to see any of them. He pushed past the works manager, who had just come in.

"Wilcox! What's up?"

Wilcox heard him and ignored him. His pale-blue motor

scooter, with the red pillion for Effie, was parked at the side of the garage. He straddled it. He kept the keys in his trousers pocket, and fished them out. The manager came hurrying across.

"Fred, what's *up*?"

He went roaring off. The manager, baffled, turned round and saw the four who had been near the locker room moving towards their benches. No one explained. He went into his office, where a girl of eighteen with lovely legs and an ugly, pimply face said:

"Good morning, Mr. Robson."

"What's happened to Fred Wilcox, do you know?"

"If you ask me, this is what's happened to Mrs. Fred Wilcox," said the girl. She pushed a copy of the *Daily Globe* in front of the manager.

Effie saw Fred arrive, from the front-room window. She was still suffering from shock, and was shivering uncontrollably. She felt terribly cold. She couldn't think. She heard Fred rushing up the stairs, heard his key click against the lock. She was standing in the middle of the room, wearing her fluffy pink dressing-gown, her figure not yet hinting at the child within her, pathetic, pale, with huge eyes and colourless lips.

Fred slammed the door.

"What the hell's been going on?" he demanded in a quivering voice. "Come on, out with it. What's been going on?"

She tried to speak his name, but the sound would not come and her lips hardly moved.

"Listen, I want to know what's been going on." He pulled the newspaper from his pocket, folded to the Sex Special pages, folded over again so that her photograph and that of an older woman showed. "Who took this?"

Now Effie's voice came, croaking:

"A-a-a man——"

"I bet it was a man! Who was he? Come on, tell me his name. I'll break his neck. I'll smash his face in. *Who was it?*"

"F-F-Fred——" she stammered.

He sprang up to her and grabbed her arms. "*Who was the swine?* How come you told him all about the phony doctor and didn't tell *me*? Eh? *How about that?* How long have you

70

known about him? My God, it's bad enough being messed about by a real doctor, but a phony—— Let's have it! What have you been hiding?" He shook her vigorously. "What's been going on?"

"N-n-n-nothing," she managed to mutter. "Fred, listen——"

"Nothing! You can stand there and say 'nothing'—if it was nothing, why didn't you tell me about it? Eh? Answer *that*. This happened three weeks ago, didn't it? Three weeks ago, and you've known all the time and you told this swine of a photographer and lied to me about it."

"I didn't lie!" Her voice was suddenly strong. "Don't say I lied to you."

"You didn't, didn't you? Well, you didn't say anything to me about it, did you? How long *have* you known? Come on, tell me." He was gripping her soft arms very tightly and shaking her with every word.

"Fred——"

"Don't stand there Fred-ing me!"

"Fred, let me go."

"If you don't answer me——"

"Fred, if you don't let me go I shall scream and bring Mrs. Mullery up here," she threatened. "You're hurting me."

He stood still, holding but no longer shaking her, and she returned the furious glare in his eyes with a deliberate gaze which seemed to quiet him. His grip relaxed. Slowly he let her go. He did not look away from her, but the fury had died and a kind of anguish replaced it in his eyes.

"What happened, Eff? You've got to tell me."

"If you'll listen quietly and stop shouting, I'll tell you." She was surprised at her own self-control, by the fact that her voice could be so clear. "I must sit down, even if you don't."

She sat on the couch and put her legs up, while Fred began to walk about the room. She told him exactly what had happened, and tried to tell him why she had not been able to confide in him, but she knew that she wasn't really making him understand.

"If only you'd told me," he kept saying. And then: "If I ever get my hands on him, I'll kill the swine and if I catch up with that photographer I'll break his neck. Why didn't you smash his camera, that's what I want to know?"

"I was too frightened," Effie said simply.

She could not explain, because she was only vaguely aware of the fact that her fear had been of him, Fred. She was beginning to realize that in this crisis she had kept her nerve. There had been a trial of strength and she had won; although she was aware of this, she was also conscious of the fact that Fred might explode again. There was something peculiar about him, both in the expression in his eyes and the twist of his lips.

But when he left an hour later he seemed outwardly calm.

For the first time in their married life he did not kiss her good-bye.

That same morning, all over Great Britain, men and women (in a proportion of about a hundred men to one woman) were going with their chief nominators and seconders, to the mayor's parlours of the land, or to the offices of the chairmen of the urban and of rural district councils. Some of these were as gracious as the drawing-rooms of great palaces, others were as humble as any small parlour. Some were in huge civic buildings erected since the war, square edifices of stone and glass. Others were in converted Georgian or Victorian houses, once private homes, now council offices where the chairmen of the smallest councils presided. The hearts of many candidates were pounding as they waited to accept nomination for candidacy of the constituency. Men and women from all the major parties, seven from the Fight for Peace Committee, five Q Men, one Anti-noise candidate, fourteen Communist candidates, fifty-one Independents and one World Government, seven Welsh Nationalists and four Home Rule for Scotland candidates—all of these met their respective opponents, shook hands, had a drink at the mayor's expense (or that of his corporation, and so the electors) and signified their willingness to stand and to accept the rules of the contest and the laws of the land. It was all very friendly. Only a dozen or so of the candidates refused to shake hands, and stalked out the moment the formalities were over.

At each simple ceremony the press was present.

Outside each room and outside each building, be it local council or city guildhall, policemen waited or plodded or conferred, the outward symbol of a law which gave the people democracy. In certain places where the F.F.P. and the Q candidates were nominated, more police were in evidence, while substantial numbers were held in reserve, discreetly out of sight, in case there was a clash after the nominations between supporters on each side. There were three scuffles, and a few discordant loud-speaker arguments which warned the people of the vicinity what to expect when the election really hotted up.

"But that's all," Parsons reported to Gideon, at half past five. "Nothing to worry about. It went off almost too quietly."

"Good start's half the battle," said Gideon sententiously. He looked down the list which Parsons had brought to his office. Lemaitre had gone home early for some special date with his wife. After a desperately unhappy marriage, Lemaitre had fallen in love and married again and it now looked as if his marital future was set fair. "What about Quatrain?"

"No trouble."

"Hetherington and Corby?"

"I've got a feeling that those two ex-Labour party chaps are going to have their work cut out to hold their seats," said Parsons. "It's one thing to support the F.F.P. movement when you're safely in and you've got official party support, quite another to persuade the electors to put you back as Independents so that you can try to ban the bomb. I gather that Conservatives and Labour are going to send their big guns down to both constituencies."

Gideon nodded.

"Will they also try to unseat Quatrain?"

"According to Littleton, who's got the ear of some of the shrewdest political journalists in Fleet Street, they think they would be wiser to put up weak opponents against him. They feel that he's probably safer in the House than out. But he's got a very lively Independent against him, and he might have his work cut out."

Roland Quatrain did not think, did not dream, he would have any trouble in regaining his seat. He left Williton Town

73

Hall after the nomination that day and saw fifty of his supporters drawn up outside to welcome him. They formed a solid square of men in a kind of uniform, shiny black leather motor-cycle jackets and black knee breeches. On the back of each jacket was a white Q. On the far side of the square near the Town Hall was a larger group of people carrying Fight for Peace banners and posters. These were in no kind of order, but were an untidy, ill-assorted, bedraggled-looking lot of men and women of all shapes and sizes. Quatrain then knew that there was a real risk of a conflict, and that he could cause one with a word. He called Dave Smith, his chief aide, said pleasantly but authoritatively:

"Keep our men away from the F.F.P. crowd, David. We don't want any trouble today."

"I don't know that it will be easy to hold them," Smith objected. He meant he did not want to, for he was not only militant but hot-headed. He had one gift which made him invaluable to Quatrain: he was a brilliant organizer.

"Of course you can hold them," Quatrain said. "If there is any trouble today, we shall be blamed for it. We don't want the electors to think that we're indifferent to democracy, do we?"

"Democracy!"

"This isn't the place or the time for making speeches in favour of a benevolent dictatorship," Quatrain told him. "And you know it as well as I do. Make sure there's no trouble."

Smith's eyes were glistening.

"How about chairing you off?" he suggested. "We could carry you round the square and bring you back to the car. It's sure to hit the headlines, too. And if those weak-kneed baby-sitters over there want to start anything, it would be their fault."

Quatrain, renowned for his split-second decisions, said: "Very well."

Smith hurried away.

When Robert Talmad, the Independent candidate, came down the Town Hall steps with Rowden the Labour man and Saunders the Conservative, he saw the two groups, heard Dave Smith's voice, and hoped that Smith would start something. One fracas now would be worth hundreds if not thousands of votes for him. However, instead of leading a rush at the undisciplined-looking lot of F.F.P. supporters, with their rain-washed and dilapidated banners, the Q Men swooped upon their leader. On the instant, photographers snapped into action, there was a rush of non-partisan sightseers come to see the two groups and now drawn towards Quatrain's Rolls-Royce. With startling precision, Quatrain was hoisted on the shoulders of two enormous men wearing shiny black jackets. Other Q Men fell into line behind them, four abreast, like a storm troop. They began singing their 'battle song':

> *Quat-Quat-Quat-rain*
> *Cast your vote for Quatrain*
> *He will make us great again.*
> *Quat-Quat-Quat-rain.*

The portly, red-faced mayor of Williton, one of the more wealthy London residential boroughs, stood by Talmad's side.

"That didn't do you any good, Bob."

Talmad, tall, in his middle thirties, with a public school and university background and a family almost as good as Quatrain's, smiled, shook his head, and remarked:

"Quatrain's no fool."

"Think you've got a chance?"

"Yes, now that he's Independent and has no Conservative support. If we can lure him into making one major mistake I'll beat him," Talmad said. "But you'd better be careful, you're not supposed to take sides."

"I should think not," chimed in the Conservative.

"Wouldn't like to have to make a complaint against the Returning Officer," joked the Labour man.

Parson's sergeant, on duty at this key spot, heard all of this, reported it faithfully, and also gave as his opinion that the first blood in the Williton campaign had been drawn by Quatrain.

"*Of course,*" the sergeant said, "*it helps that he's got a lot of support from right-wing newspapers.*"

The uniformed men from the local division reported that everything had gone off without incident.

Gideon, knowing all this, felt in a reasonably contented

frame of mind when he reached home. Kate, who had bene-
fited almost as much as he had from the holiday, was in the
garden, sweeping up after Malcolm had cut the lawn. The
scent of the grass was almost ambrosial. The chrysanthemums had been watered, and some small copper-coloured
blooms were beginning to catch the eye.

"Shouldn't have to cut the grass much more this year,"
Gideon said as they went in. "What kind of a day have you
had?"

Kate laughed.

"Interruption after interruption. Canvassers from three
parties have been, and we're getting littered up with circu-
lars." There were several on the small hallstand. "But the
real thrill is——"

"*That you, dad?*" Malcolm came tearing out of the kitchen,
in one hand an apple with a huge piece bitten out of it. His
dark hair was plastered down and for once he seemed to have
washed with enthusiasm. He was the most studious of the
Gideon family, and read a great deal; that might explain the
fact that at fifteen he needed glasses. "What do you think—
I'm the Liberal candidate!"

"You're the *what?*"

"In the school election, I mean. We're all going to have
an election just before the real one comes off. We're going
to do it in style too—everything exactly the same as they do
in the real thing, only the time limit's a bit different as we
weren't prepared for it, you see. There are three candidates
and a freak, and I'm the Liberal."

"Not the freak?"

"No," said Malcolm scornfully. "That's the Fight for Peace
chap. Dad aren't you a Liberal?"

"I am non-political."

"Oh, cut out that official stuff. Aren't you?"

"I like a little of what I see in all of them," said Gideon.
"You won't be able to draw me, so you might as well give up.
How are you going to run your campaign?"

"Well, that's why I hoped you'd be a Liberal. I thought
you could give me some good arguments."

"I can do better," said Gideon. "I can give you two
pamphlets on the party's policy, free, and——"

"Oh, all the parties are supplying us with literature and policy statements, and I believe that there's going to be a big meeting—after school hours of course—when all three candidates are going to be on the same platform."

"Four," corrected Gideon.

"What?"

"Four candidates, you said."

"Oh, yes, I'd forgotten about the F.F.P., but he doesn't count."

"A lot of people might be making the same mistake," said Gideon.

At least Parsons wasn't.

Gideon was sitting back after supper, looking at the news and the flashes of photographs of nomination day, saw the tail end of the Quatrain March, noticed the way Malcolm's eyes kindled at the sight of Quatrain, and knew that he would get much more publicity than anyone else. It might be easy to make the mistake of underrating him, too.

Quatrain, fully satisfied with the way the day had gone and with the space he had obtained in the evening newspapers and on television, spent the evening with David Smith, working out details of his own campaign as well as those of the other four Q Men candidates. He had planned this campaign to be as near a national one as he could, hence the selection of the constituencies—one in Williton, one near Manchester, one near Birmingham, one near Edinburgh, and one in East Anglia. Each constituency had the same strata of electors, including some wealthy ones, and he did not think that any of his men would poll badly.

He wanted a 'sign' from this election—a sign that he was what he had always believed himself to be: destined to lead this nation out of a state of economic and political muddle and confusion into the bright uplands of a benevolent dictatorship.

At half past twelve Smith, a man in his middle twenties, short, stocky, red-haired, with tremendous vigour and vitality, leaned back in his chair, yawned, and said:

"I think I'll have an early night, Q."

Quatrain smiled. "Why don't you? Then you can get off to an early start in the morning."

Good-humouredly Smith agreed. He slipped on his shiny jacket, and Quatrain saw him to the door of the apartment, one of a large block that overlooked Hyde Park. As they went towards the door, Smith was thinking a little uneasily that he might have annoyed Quatrain; he was never really at ease with his leader, although with other people present he always appeared to be. There was an aura almost of mysticism about Quatrain; physically he was nearly perfect and mentally he was far better equipped than most. Certainly he had a kind of personal magnetism which drew men and women to him.

Quatrain opened the door.

"Good night, David."

Smith gave the flick of his hand that was the Q Men's salute and stepped outside.

There was a flash, a sharp explosion, and a blast. Quatrain snatched his hand from the door, and dodged back. Smith went stumbling along the passage, arms waving, making funny little choking noises.

8

PLASTIC BOMB

PARSONS was yawning.

He was in the office with two sergeants, both on night duty, who had been briefed by Gideon earlier in the day. They were youngish men who would probably have to do a lot of legwork in the next three weeks. Tonight they would spend their time studying the maps and going through records, for they knew that when they came on duty tomorrow night, Parsons would put them through their paces.

"I'll call it a day," Parsons announced suddenly.

"Having an early night, sir?" asked the darker of the two sergeants, a man named Petrie.

"You'll know all about early nights before I've finished with you," said Parsons. He yawned again, and peered at himself in an oval mirror over the fireplace. He was looking tired, his eyes were red-rimmed, and for once his mind wasn't working clearly. He took his hat off the peg, and jammed it on. Its round pork-pie shape and rather wide brim made him look more than ever like a priest. "And don't think, because it's been quiet today, it will be like this all the way along."

He went out.

"If you ask me," said the fair-haired sergeant, whose name was Whittle, "he's looking on the gloomy side. When it comes to the point there won't be any trouble. He's got a bee in his bonnet."

As he said 'bonnet' the telephone nearest him began to ring. He got up and lifted it.

"Mr. Parsons's office." He held on. Then suddenly his eyes rounded, he snapped, "Hold it!" and covered the mouth-piece with his hand. "Get Parsons back—Quatrain's been hurt."

Parsons turned into the driveway of Park Towers, one of the tallest and most modern blocks of flats in London. He knew he was ahead of the divisional police, but a man was getting out of a Jaguar, the door of which was being held open by a uni-formed doorman. Parsons climbed out of his car, and the Yard chauffeur with him asked:

"Shall I come with you, sir?"

"No. Wait until the divisional chaps get here and see they come straight up." Parsons hurried after the man from the Jaguar, and the doorman turned to him impatiently.

"Mr. Quatrain's apartment, please," Parsons said.

"Mr. Quatrain can't see——"

"I am Superintendent Parsons of New Scotland Yard."

"*Oh*. Oh, I'm sorry, sir. There are two policemen upstairs now, and this is Dr. Hibberd. It's a terrible thing, isn't it, sir?"

"How is Mr. Quatrain?"

"Oh, *he's* all right. It's his friend, Mr. Smith, who's hurt so badly. You should see his face . . ."

Quatrain came out of a bedroom as Parsons and the doctor, a sharp-featured, dark-haired man, entered the apartment. There was one uniformed policeman in the passage and one inside the flat; this man appeared at the bedroom door, helmet off, coat off. Quatrain was looking completely self-possessed.

"Ah, Howard. Thank you for coming so quickly." So he was on Christian name terms with the doctor. "He's in the bedroom."

"How is he?"

"I don't know. The policeman has been rendering first aid." Quatrain looked at Parsons. "Good evening, Superintendent; I'm sorry you had to be dragged out at this time of night. Thank you for coming so promptly."

"Glad I was still working," said Parsons. "How is he?"

"His face is badly cut about, but the greatest danger appears to be to his eyes."

Parsons said, "Hell of a thing to happen."

"I hope that you find the perpetrator very quickly," said Quatrain. "I shall do everything within my power to help and everything possible to make sure of quick results. Do you wish to see him?"

"For a moment, sir, yes. And then if you will answer some questions . . ."

Smith lay on his back, his face cut and scorched, his eyebrows and front hair burned off. The police constable had washed him and placed pads over his eyes. He was in his underclothes, hands clenching and unclenching, lips working, as if he were trying to keep back moans of pain.

"An ambulance is on the way," the doctor said. He was already pushing the needle of a hypodermic syringe into an ampoule of morphine, and the constable was rolling up the injured man's sleeve. "Here's the spirit, if you'll clean the arm." He lifted the syringe up to the light, the ampoule stuck on the end of it, and the colourless liquid was drawn slowly from one container to the other. "It's all right, David. You'll feel a sharp prick, hardly anything at all, and then you'll go to sleep. From what I can see of you, you'll be all right." He waited until the policeman drew back from the injured man, and then stretched the skin of the arm just above the elbow and pushed the needle in; he seemed to hold it there a long time. "Now just forget all your troubles," he said as he drew the needle out.

Parsons turned away, and Quatrain followed him. Quatrain looked pale, and there was about his lips a tightness which took away something of his looks.

"This is a dastardly political outrage," he declared. "I hope that the full significance of it will not be misunderstood."

"A political outrage, sir?"

"Of course," Quatrain said coldly. "Do you doubt it?"

"I don't take that or anything else for granted," Parsons said. "There could be other motives."

"I find that hard to believe."

"No doubt, sir. Now, if you'll be good enough to tell me exactly what happened?"

While Quatrain talked, the policeman in the passage was reinforced by two plainclothes men from the division. They marked off a large area outside the door, and also indicated a narrow path along which callers could come and go. The policeman put down a sheet covering the doorway, as if to make sure that footprints and other marks could not be damaged or destroyed; there was a quiet and calm efficiency about it which pleased Parsons, for these two uniformed men could not have had any training for C.I.D. work.

A very big, very grey man came walking along the passage; White, of KL Division, which covered London's West End.

"Hallo, Parsons. What's on?"

"These chaps will tell you," Parsons said. "Get your men working and then come and have a word with us, will you?" Parsons could be almost abrupt in his manner. He turned to Quatrain again. "We needn't worry too much about the routine, sir. I would like you to tell me again exactly what happened."

"Didn't you listen to me the first time?" demanded Quatrain.

"Yes, sir," said Parsons, "and I have an almost photographic memory. I want to make sure that you have all the details clear in your mind. After a shock like that the mind plays queer tricks."

"Mine plays no tricks, Superintendent."

"Shall we see, sir?"

Quatrain's expression became haughty, and for a moment

it seemed likely that he would refuse. Then suddenly he relaxed, smiled, turned towards a small book-lined room, and motioned to a chair.

"Yes, we shall indeed find out if my mind plays tricks. Will you have a drink?"

"No, thank you, sir. But don't let me stop you."

"I don't think I will let you stop me from doing anything," said Quatrain. "On the other hand, I am anxious to have this vicious criminal traced as quickly as possible. It was two minutes after twelve-thirty . . ."

It was two minutes to four o'clock when Gideon's telephone bell rang. He stirred in heavy sleep. Kate woke but did not move, although the bell sounded very loud. Gideon grunted. Kate began to struggle up, but suddenly Gideon said, "All right." He hitched himself up, screwed up his eyes and took off the receiver. "Gideon."

"Parsons," said Parsons. "I thought you ought to know that Quatrain . . ."

Gideon listened with growing attentiveness, and when Parsons had finished he said:

"We'll have Quatrain watched wherever he goes, night and day. There mustn't be the slightest suggestion that we aren't bursting at the sides to catch this chap. Do you know what kind of bomb it was?"

Behind him, drowsy, Kate caught her breath.

"A small plastic one—we've collected a lot of the pieces."

"*Bomb*," Kate whispered.

"Where are you speaking from?"

"Quatrain's place," replied Parsons. "Park Towers, in Park Lane."

"I'll come over," said Gideon.

Only now and again was he justified in taking any active part in an investigation, and this was one of his few regrets. There remained a sense of compulsion to be on the spot, a satisfaction in working directly in an investigation which work at the desk never equalled. No matter when he had to go out on a job, it pleased him. Now he was concerned and anxious about what had happened, but that satisfaction remained, and there was no reluctance in his manner as he dressed. Kate was already out of bed. She came in as he was fastening his collar, carrying a tea tray.

"Shouldn't have worried," Gideon said, "but a cup of char will really wake me up. Did I tell you what's happened?"

"You just said bomb, and you mentioned Quatrain."

"That's all you need to know," Gideon said.

"Is he hurt, George?"

"Quatrain?"

"Yes."

"No."

"Who was, then?"

Gideon, sipping tea and breaking a biscuit in his big fingers, said shrewdly:

"Quatrain interest you?"

"Well, yes."

"As a—what?"

"He's so devastatingly good-looking."

"He could be devastating in a lot of other ways if he were given the chance. His first lieutenant has been badly cut about the face, and possibly blinded."

"No!"

"Parsons thinks the bomb was meant for Quatrain. As far as he can judge it was fastened about head height outside the door of the flat, where it was bound to go off in his face."

"How—wicked."

"Wicked's the word," agreed Gideon. "Better the lieutenant than Quatrain, eh?"

Kate said, "It would be dreadful if he was blinded or disfigured, wouldn't it?"

"It would be——" Gideon began, and was about to add "dreadful whoever gets blinded or disfigured," but stopped himself. "You get back to bed, dear. I'll phone sometime during the morning." He finished the tea and knotted his tie.

It was not until he was driving along King's Road towards Westminster that the real significance of this crime began to impress him. Until then he had been thinking only with the surface of his mind, the shallow, automatic kind of mental reaction which came from first waking. He had felt almost smart when questioning Kate about Quatrain and her reaction to him; as if that really mattered. A shadow darkened his mind, and a weight of physical depression settled on his chest. A plastic bomb, used politically, was something revolutionary in England, something almost unbelievable. He remembered how Parsons had talked about the OAS in Algiers and all their savagery, and the weight of depression increased. Had this been political? Was there any reason, any hope at all, for believing that it hadn't? If it had been, what effect would it have on the people, even on the world? England, home of democracy, home of bitter political antagonism in an atmosphere of complete political freedom, freedom from fears and pressures and restraints except those necessary to ensure full rights for the individual—one little plastic bomb, one fascist-type reactionary politician blinded. How far would the effect of such a crime spread?

Was it the first of many? The beginning of a planned campaign?

"Don't be a blurry fool," Gideon rebuked himself.

'Blurry' for 'bloody' was a legacy from the days when his children had been young, and one of them had called a teacher at kindergarten a bloody fool. The only way Gideon had taught himself not to swear in front of the children had been to cut the habit to a minimum everywhere; 'blurry' had been a compromise which had helped him out of many an awkward moment. Now, the explosive use of the word helped him again. He swung past a horse-drawn cart laden with empty boxes for Covent Garden, was passed by a huge lorry overladen with vegetables, bursting their net bags, coming from the market, and then reached Sloane Square. He drove along an almost deserted Sloane Street, past the Carlton Tower Hotel, a block not dissimilar to Park Towers, where Quatrain lived. As he waited on the red light at Knightsbridge, where a surprisingly thick stream of traffic passed, he thought, No need to get into a panic over it.

But he was deeply worried.

The divisional police were coming away when he reached the building, and he recognized the spindly figure of Ben White, the divisional man who had been working with Parsons.

"Hallo, Ben."

"Nasty business. Parsons is still up there with the great Q. Want me for anything?"

84

"Make the report as detailed as possible, and get it over to me fast, will you?"

"Sure."

"Thanks."

Gideon strode into the building, now fully awake and alert, feeling as if he had the situation clear in his mind. His first reaction had been that he must see Quatrain himself; and nothing could have been more right. A uniformed constable at the door recognized him; the doorman took him upstairs. All the evidence of the routine work showed, but the door of the apartment was closed. A policeman outside it rang the bell as soon as Gideon appeared.

"Good morning, sir."

"Good morning."

The door opened, and Quatrain appeared, with Parsons in the hall just behind him. As Gideon stepped inside, he was aware—as he had been often in the past—of the difference between himself and a man like Quatrain. It was the difference between a cart horse and a race horse. This man had a quality which he could never have, and he had a strength and an endurance which this man would probably envy all his life. He had met Quatrain at some official functions, for when a member he had been on two Home Office committees affecting the police, including a committee which had investigated pay and conditions. Quatrain had been progressive and generous in his attitude and had probably helped to sway the committee into recommending improvements which had since come about.

Quatrain held out his hand.

"Commander."

"Mr. Quatrain," Gideon said, "I've come myself so that you will have no doubt that we regard this as the most urgent matter on hand at the Yard."

Quatrain smiled.

"I'm more than satisfied of that, and Superintendent Parsons has already proved by example what you have confirmed. Now I wonder if you will excuse me. I have a very heavy day ahead, even heavier than I had expected without my chief organizer and the party's chief agent. The personal anxiety weighs heavily too. I must at least rest for an hour or two."

"We won't disturb you, sir."

"Thank you," Quatrain said. "Good night."

He entered a dressing-room which, Gideon saw, led in turn to his bedroom and bathroom. The door closed, sealing off that part of the flat completely. Parsons, hand smoothing down his hair, looked at the closed door as if he were puzzled.

"There's something odd about that chap," he said. "Damned odd. I didn't expect to find him human enough to admit that he's tired. Well, George, what did I tell you?"

"I'm more interested in what you've got to tell me," said Gideon.

"I wish it was more." Parsons patted his breast pocket. "I've got it all down here; you'll have a report before I go off duty. It amounts to this: It was a plastic bomb in a red container. It was quite small, and did little damage to the wall or the doors. It was fastened to a light fitting above the door, and there was a kind of trip wire—here are the bits we've found—which make it fall as the door was opened from the inside."

"Inside?"

"Yes. It must have hung about here." Parsons pointed to a spot about six feet from the ground; some blisters on the framework of the door and the door itself, and some stains on the walls, were the only signs of the spot where the explosion had taken place. "As far as I can see—it will have to be checked by the ballistics, of course—as the door was opened the bomb fell to about head height and hung there. As Smith went out he walked straight into it, and it blew up instantaneously. Anyone coming out would be bound to get it full in the face. Quatrain says there was a flash, and the burn marks show that. The actual damage to Smith's face isn't great, though. He will carry scars, but not serious ones, and they might be removed altogether by plastic surgery. The damage to the eyes is a lot more serious. Hibberd, Quatrain's doctor, won't commit himself. Smith's now at the Moorfields Eye Hospital."

Gideon nodded.

"The last person to leave the apartment was Jefferson Miles, second-in-command to David Smith on the organization side of the Q party," went on Parsons. "He lives not far away, in a flat at Park Mews. I called him, and he's been here and gone. He swears there was nothing on the door when he left—he let himself out—and although he could have put the bomb there himself, the record says that he's a fanatical Q man, and I don't rate the possibility high. I've checked with all the people in the nearby flats, and none of them remember anyone coming in here after eleven o'clock. The two doormen on duty swear that they saw no one. I've got the division working on taxi drivers, on our own uniformed men, and on anyone known to have been in the vicinity since ten-thirty. I've been talking to the Yard, and Information has sent out a call to all divisions for information about any explosives expert who might have been here tonight—not that we have many in the country. I've talked to the Sûreté Nationale and made requests to all the other European police headquarters to ask if they know of any bomb expert over here."

Parsons paused.

"Clues?" asked Gideon.

"Nothing on the carpet, wall or doors. No fingerprints we can't identify, nothing but the pieces of the bomb and the damage caused by the explosion. I've had every fire exit and fire escape, every liftman, every door which leads into the building checked—and the result is damn-all." Parsons drew a deep breath. Gideon could not fail to see how tired he looked; his eyes were bloodshot, and he kept rubbing the right one. "All we can do is pray that sooner or later we'll find someone who saw the devil."

Gideon said, "We've got to, and quick." It was a fatuous remark and yet did not sound fatuous to either of them. "I'll get the BBC to put out a request for help from anyone who passed at a quarter to eleven and twelve-thirty to report if they saw anyone coming in. We'll have to get it on television too. The evening papers will play, and . . ."

As he talked he knew that all this had to be done, but for the second time since he had heard of the bombing he felt a heavy weight of depression. In a normal case, even in one of murder, he would have set everything in motion, hoped for quick results, and yet acknowledged philosophically that the odds were against getting them. The investigation would be a matter of patience and perseverance. Whether the pay-off came in a week or two or a month or two did not greatly matter in most cases, for time was not of the essence. Now it was. There was a driving urgency. He hated to think of the effect of a huge publicity build-up in the public mind if the man who had planted the bomb remained at large for even twenty-four hours.

9

REACTION

ROGERSON, his lips and cheeks quite noticeably bluish and his eyes glassy and protruding, opened the door of Gideon's office at a quarter to nine. Lemaitre, called to the Yard early, was rasping into the telephone:

"I don't care who you have to interrupt, get him for me. Bloody secretaries," he muttered, and then caught sight of the Assistant Commissioner. He froze.

"Good morning, Lemaitre. Commander——" this was Rogerson at his most official—"the Commissioner would like to see you in his office at nine o'clock."

"Right," said Gideon.

"Is there any news?" inquired Rogerson.

"David Smith will probably lose the sight of one eye," Gideon replied. "He won't be about again for at least six weeks. So that's put paid to any work he can do for Quatrain in the election. The newspapers are besieging the Back Room. I had five of them on my private line, and had to tear a strip off them before they would stop worrying me."

"I can imagine. But have we any idea who the man was?"

"No," said Gideon.

Ten minutes later, with Rogerson, he entered the office of Lieutenant-Colonel Scott-Marle, the Commissioner of the Metropolitan Police. Scott-Marle was a tall, lean, greying, rather aloof man, always somewhat remote from his men and appearing remote from the job—until a crisis arose, when he proved to be both alert and fully informed. In a way, he reminded Gideon of Quatrain, although he was an older man, an autocrat rather than a potential demagogue.

He shook hands.

"What progress are we making?" he inquired.

"None at all yet," said Gideon flatly.

"I see. So we really haven't any idea who did it?"

"None at all, sir," admitted Gideon.

"Are you making the obvious investigations?"

"Into the F.F.P. people, do you mean?"

"Yes."

"It's being covered," said Gideon, "but we have no reason to think that any of them would do this kind of thing. They've resisted arrest and they've resisted the Q Men from time to time, but in general their methods have been of passive resistance."

"That doesn't mean that one or more of them hasn't lost patience," reasoned Scott-Marle. "Gideon, let me be quite frank. I shall be subjected to a great many pressures. They will come from the Home Office, from Downing Street and from many other sources. I am going to be asked all kinds of questions, both reasonable and unreasonable. I must have an answer for them all. Whatever specific question I am asked about our handling of the case"—a smile teased the corners of his lips—"I want to be able to say that we are investigating that particular angle. I know I don't need to tell you how serious this is. I want to assure you that you have whatever men and whatever authority it is in my power to give, so that you may proceed at all speed with the investigations. If necessary, all but absolutely essential work on other cases must be suspended. The BBC, the ITV and the press will give us all possible help."

Scott-Marle paused. Gideon rubbed his chin. Rogerson shifted his position in an uncomfortable chair.

"Don't you agree?" Scott-Marle asked, almost acidly.

"I agree on the gravity of the situation if it develops," Gideon said. "I also think we could exaggerate it, sir. In fact I'm beginning to think that I overplayed it by calling on the broadcasting and television authorities so quickly." He gave the Commissioner a chance to interrupt, but Scott-Marle simply stared at him, as if in disapproval. Gideon, knowing that look, felt ill at ease; he also felt stubborn. It was as if the bomb, and everything concerning it, was exerting pressures he could hardly withstand. He spoke very deliberately as he went on: "We want the perpetrator, but we don't want anyone to think we're treating it as a disaster."

"It could become one," Rogerson observed.

"Couldn't it?" Scott-Marle asked Gideon.

"If this was an isolated case of a man or woman with a special hatred of Quatrain and what he stands for, it isn't likely. If the worst has happened and it is the first move in a campaign of violence——" Gideon broke off, waving his hands in an uncharacteristic gesture. "But I can't believe it is." He stood there solid, aggressively stubborn. "I'm much more worried about the kind of chain reaction it might set up."

"Chain reaction?" Scott-Marle sounded surprised.

"One effect, and a bad one, could be to start others off," Gideon declared. "Individuals without the moral courage to originate such an outrage might climb on the band wagon. We're always up against reaction crimes, as you know. One bank robbery may set off a chain, as sex murders are inclined to. Any crime which can be committed on impulse is liable to start an impulse in other people. Criminals often imitate one another, and when all's said and done, criminals are only ordinary people with a kink. Some of the F.F.P. people are so involved in their cause that they've got a kink already."

"I think I know what you mean," Scott-Marle conceded. He sat quite erect in his chair, rather like the president of a court-martial. Gideon had never felt more uneasy in his presence. "I think you've overlooked one thing, Gideon."

"Have I, sir?"

"Yes."

"May I ask what?"

"I think you've overlooked the fact that Quatrain's men might already be planning reprisals. Quatrain himself might be able to restrain them for a while, but the only thing that I think will stop them from trying to take revenge is if we find the man who left that bomb there. That's why I think the situation is so serious."

Gideon said, "I see, sir."

Another man than Scott-Marle might have said, "Well, had you forgotten that?" Another man than Gideon might have said, "I've had that well in mind, sir." Neither of them spoke. Rogerson shifted his position again. Gideon wished he would sit still.

Gideon said at last, "There's one thing it would be easy for us all to overlook."

That faint smile played about Scott-Marle's lips again.

"Yes?"

"One man planted this bomb. A few dozen or a few hundred others might lose their heads because of it. We have one dedicated group in Quatrain's supporters and another in the F.F.P.'s Battle Committee's supporters, but put 'em all together and they still represent only a minute fraction of the people—of the electors, sir. We want to show everyone that we're going all out to find the man who planted this bomb, but we should also show them that we don't expect a lot more trouble. We want to make it clear that we rely on the level-headedness and common sense of the man in the street."

Scott-Marle sat like a graven image for some seconds. Then he stood up quickly, surprising Gideon and making Rogerson move again. Gideon thought, Now I've caused it. He himself was caught between the two stools of over-rating and under-rating the danger of the situation.

"You mean, our attitude to the public and press must be that this is one isolated crime, but that internally our whole organization must give it absolute priority."

Thank God for a man with a razor-sharp mind.

"That's right, sir."

Scott-Marle said briskly, "Handle it that way, Gideon. Talk to the press yourself. Make sure that no one else on the force makes any statement at all, we don't want two different stories put out. Report to me twice daily, please, and if necessary more often. I will leave instructions that you are to be put through, whatever I may be doing. Good luck."

"Thank you, sir," said Gideon. He felt a deep relief.

By the time he got back to his desk the newspapers had arrived. Every one of the popular dailies had put out a special late edition, and the two evenings had given the whole of their front pages to the story. Gideon read the headlines and the first few paragraphs of each. There was an interview with Quatrain, quoting:

There was another, more dangerous headline:

Q LEADER ACCUSES NUCLEAR'S

Gideon studied that more closely. The impression given was that Quatrain had accused the nuclear disarmament group, but in fact it was a statement by Jefferson Miles to a news agency. Jefferson Miles had ranted.

There was another:

F.F.P. LEADER DENIES CHARGE

Mr. Cunliffe Moncrieff, Chairman of the Battle Committee of the Fight for Peace Movement, said to a *Globe* reporter: "*It is unthinkable that anyone associated with this organization which seeks only peace could be involved in such a crime. Every one of our Committee—and I am sure every one of our members throughout the country—condemns it utterly.*"

Parsons, who was with Gideon, said gruffly, "I wonder." Then he went on: "Paterson of the House told me to keep an eye on Guy Hetherington and Reginald Corby, left-wing and pro-Ban the Bomb."

"Anything cropped up with them?"

Parsons said, "No, I think they're toeing the party line. All the Communists are too."

"Save us some trouble," said Gideon. "What's the general build-up like?"

"It's off to a slow start," said Parsons. "This will warm it up though."

Amanda Tenby sat in the window seat of her apartment with a morning and two evening papers spread out on the floor about her. She was in her black slacks and black jumper, and the only change in her appearance was that her hair, instead of falling about her shoulders, was held together by a velvet ribbon into a ponytail. Her eyes were aglow. Daniel Ronn sat on an upright chair, back to front, and leaned precariously on it, only two legs on the ground. He watched her as she scanned the headlines.

After she had read one with rapt attention and looked up, Ronn asked:

"Do you?"

"Do I what?"

"Do you condemn our anonymous bomb man?"

She looked at him. "It's a pity Smith didn't die."

"Amanda!" Ronn pretended to be shocked.

"They're not fit to live."

In a more gentle voice, Ronn said, "Amanda darling, we can go too far."

"Not with the Q Men," she said.

He began to frown. "Amanda——"

"Supposing you stop calling me Amanda like that," she said, mimicking him.

He was frowning more deeply and looking at her very oddly. She turned to other papers, leaning forward so that she could read the stories. He stared at the top of her head and the ponytail; he could just see her forehead and the tip of her nose.

"Do you know anything about it?" he demanded.

"What?"

"The bomb."

She didn't look up.

"There's only one bomb I'm interested in."

"Look at me, Amanda."

"I'm busy."

Ronn let the chair settle back on all four legs, stood up, and went towards her. She didn't look up. He trod on one of the newspapers, and the pressure wrinkled the one she was reading. She glanced at the shiny brown toe of his shoe but still did not look up. He put his hand down to her head, and she ducked. He hesitated, then slowly put his fingers round the ponytail and gripped it tightly. He pulled, not hard enough to hurt but enough to make her feel the pressure. She resisted it. He pulled more strongly, and she slapped his leg. He didn't move.

"Do you know anything about it?" he demanded, in a hard voice.

"Let me go."

"Answer me."

"If you don't let me go——"

He jerked the hair so sharply that she cried out. She could no longer stop her head from rising, and for a moment they

93

were face to face. Ronn now had to pull her hair while his hand was round her neck, but he found no difficulty, and kept her neck taut—a beautiful neck pale against the black jumper. She made no attempt now to avoid his gaze.

"I want to know," he insisted.

"I don't want to tell you," said Amanda.

"Do you know what that bomb could do?"

"Wipe out the Q Men."

"Don't you make any mistake," Ronn said softly. "It would wipe us out *and* F.F.P. as a political force. The country wouldn't stand for it. If there was any suspicion that you or anybody connected with the Battle Committee was involved in this, there wouldn't ever be another march, there wouldn't be another effective demonstration. They think we're lunatic fringers as it is, and if they thought we were violent too——" He broke off, thrust his face closer to hers, held her in exactly the same position, and said, "Do you know anything about the bomb attack on Quatrain?"

She smiled into his face. She had beautiful, very white teeth. At close quarters the unblemished smoothness of her skin and the perfection of the bone formation of her too-thin face were more in evidence. She parted her teeth a fraction, as if she were going to laugh at him. He had never seen such an expression in her eyes.

"No," she said.

"If that's a lie——"

"Daniel darling, I said no. Don't tell me you think I'm a liar."

Slowly he let her go. She didn't change her position but sat back with her head arched, looking at him through half-closed eyes, like a Siamese cat.

"You would lie if it suited your purpose," he said, "but I don't think you would to me."

"It wouldn't get me anywhere," Amanda said. "Nor would a lot of little plastic bombs. Nothing would please me more than to think that Quatrain's men were wiped out but that isn't what *we're* planning, is it?"

"No, it isn't," Ronn said.

"Have you heard from Travaritch?"

"Yes."

"Does he still think he can get it?"

"Yes. We'll have to find him help, once he's got it out."

"We can do that."

"And I think he'll want more money."

"We can find that too."

"*We* can't, Amanda," Ronn said very deliberately. He slid his arms round her, but did not go close enough for their bodies to touch. "You can, but I can't. I don't want there to be any misunderstanding."

"There isn't any misunderstanding."

He pulled her a little closer; their bodies touched. She didn't look away from him, and still watched him from narrowed eyes; she gave no sign whether she liked or disliked, approved or resented what he was doing. He confirmed something he had long suspected. She could make his blood run hot. It was the way she smiled. It was the sight of her shiny teeth, parted a fraction, and the glistening red of her tongue showing beyond. It was the crystal beauty of her complexion.

"Daniel," she said.

"Amanda, I want to take you to bed."

"I know you do," she said. "But first things first."

"That *is* first."

"It isn't," she said.

"It needn't interfere with——"

"Darling Daniel," Amanda said sweetly, "we have to concentrate on one thing, just one thing only, and to me that is first and last and every place in between. Afterwards."

"Is that a promise?"

"Afterwards," Amanda said.

Slowly, reluctantly, he let her go. She didn't move from him; he had to move back from her. He felt a strange disquiet and dissatisfaction and desire. She stood up, so slight and boyish, yet his heart pounded in his ears and he had to clench his teeth to stop himself from pleading with her; only one positive fact stopped him: Amanda Tenby would not be influenced by pleading.

"Are you sure about Travaritch?" she asked.

"I think so."

"Can't you be absolutely sure?"

95

"How can I?"

"That is what I mean about first things first," said Amanda. "You have to think more, darling." At last she moved, slinking back to the window seat and sitting cross-legged. "I don't believe that Travaritch has led a blameless life, do you? There must be some skeleton in his cupboard, something we could find out that he wouldn't want the world to know about."

Ronn watched her closely, a smile touching his lips but not his eyes.

"I shouldn't think he has any guilty secrets," he said.

"How innocent can you be?"

"You forget one thing."

"Do I, Daniel?"

"You forget that everyone who works in nuclear research for the Government is very closely screened before he is allowed to do secret work. After Fuchs and Nunn May they've taken every precaution."

"I know that," she said. "But I don't think the screen is so fine that nothing can get through it. Try, Daniel. Try very hard."

After a pause, he said, "It isn't a thing I can do, and you know it."

"You have your friends."

"It would cost——"

"Just send me the bill," Amanda said. "But make sure that the man you use is reliable. You know exactly what we want, don't you? We want some hold on Travaritch so as to make sure that he can't back out at the last minute."

"I know," said Daniel Ronn.

"Who will you use?"

Ronn smiled more broadly, and very slowly shook his head.

"That's a thing you mustn't know," he told her. "I shall work through a friend of a friend, so that no one knows who is so interested in Travaritch. But if there's a skeleton in his cupboard we'll find it."

Amanda Tenby and Daniel Ronn did not know, but up and down the country candidates and agents and their chief workers were discussing the possible weaknesses of their opponents, in different ways and with different emphasis. A kind of metamorphosis came upon many of these people. The election seemed to work in them as a stimulant and an intoxicant. Even a candidate with next to no chance, or with no chance at all, began to dream dreams and to imagine reasons why he should be returned as the member of Parliament. No one who stood for election really believed that he had no chance at all. Many pretended to think so, even in the privacy of their own homes, but at heart there glowed a spark of hope.

Richard Benwell felt that spark very vividly.

He was the Labour candidate for a north London constituency against a Conservative candidate who had been the sitting member for nearly twenty years, always elected with a big majority. The Liberal candidate had won a seat on the local council a year before, and now had a very good and improving election organization. A lot of people argued that this was one of the constituencies where the right tactics was for the Labour man to stand aside so that the Liberal had a real chance to beat the Conservative. Not only was such a theory in complete conflict with official Labour party policy, it was against everything Benwell believed in. He was sure that everyone, no matter what his political opinion, should have a chance to vote whichever way he wanted.

Benwell was a comparatively young man. His wife, Marjorie, had a great love for him, and shared one great sorrow with him; they had lost their only child three years before. At that time Richard had been deeply interested in politics but had never seriously aspired to becoming a member of Parliament. His wife knew that politics now filled the gap which the death of their child had made in his life. It didn't help her, for she was not very politically minded. She voted Labour because of his enthusiasm, but wasn't particularly convinced about socialism; she was, however, absolutely convinced that whatever he felt compelled to do she must support.

She was a good shorthand-typist and was working in the main committee rooms in the High Street, with the throb of passing traffic and the clatter and chatter of passing pedestrians now booming and now fading, as the door was opened. Half a dozen voluntary workers were sitting at the long trestle tables at the back of the shop premises which they had rented for a month, the duration of the campaign. Huge hand-painted bills were plastered all over the window so that it was almost impossible to see out. In the centre was a huge disk, carrying the slogan:

VOTE LABOUR

VOTE BENWELL

One of the problems in the High Street was parking, but special arrangements had been made with the police for the candidate and his agent to leave their cars outside for periods of not more than twenty minutes; for longer periods they had to use a parking place at the back of the shop. Marjorie, typing letters appealing for the Fighting Fund to all known or suspected supporters, had a sixth sense about Richard, and she looked up before he reached the door, although the growl of a diesel engine had drowned the sound of his car's arrival. She saw that he was by himself, and her heart rose. He pushed the door open and came striding in. He was tall, had rather long, very brown—nutty brown—hair, and hazel-coloured eyes which could light up with enthusiasm and with passion. There was something very clean-cut and Byronic about him. He even limped slightly on his left leg. She seldom noticed that, but for some reason she noticed it now.

"Hallo, Mag!" That had been his name for her since their early days together. "Hi, everybody." He waved to the workers, all of whom looked up and smiled—two old-age pensioners who addressed their envelopes with slow, almost maddening care but with exemplary clarity, one middle-aged housewife, and one teen-ager. Benwell gripped Marjorie's shoulder for a moment, and then went up to the workers. "Hallo, Mrs. Potts, good of you to come again. Glad to see you're better, Mr. Heppenstall, but don't overdo it, will you? Here again, Mrs. Gray? . . ." He mentioned each of them by name. That was his especial gift: a reliable memory for names and the ability to be friendly with everybody and to neglect none. Everyone who knew him liked him.

He came back to Marjorie.

"Spare five minutes before Clark comes in?"

"Love to!"

"Let's go in the back and make a cuppa."

She pushed her chair back. The workers nodded and smiled knowingly among themselves. 'The back' was a small office used by Clark Henderson, their agent and Richard; it was very small, but in one corner was an electric kettle, a plug, a small cupboard with everything they needed to make tea. They had ten contented minutes, during which Richard talked of support he was likely to get from places where she didn't feel any hope at all. She hadn't the heart to disillusion him; her one anxiety was that he should not lose by too many votes.

A door banged, and a man clumped across the shop, calling in a deep voice:

"How's the Working Party today, eh?" He pushed open this door, and stood on the threshold, a thickset man with a barrel of a body, grey-haired, grey-bearded. He wore thick-lensed glasses in a flimsy steel frame. He clapped his hands together.

"Morning, lovebirds! Did you think of me or is that teapot empty?"

"We thought of you," said Marjorie.

"Bless you, my child. And what have you been talking about—cabbages and kings?"

"Crime and candidates," announced Richard.

"*What?*"

"That's right, isn't it, Mag? Crime and candidates. We were just saying that if there was only *one* thing that would come out to Libby's discredit it would make all the difference in the world." The real name of the Liberal candidate was Libby, and that was likely to be a great help to him in the campaign. Already there was a rash of diamond-shaped posters and advertisements all over the constituency:

VOTE LIB . . .

VOTE LIBBY,

VOTE LIBERAL

Marjorie was pouring out tea, and something about Henderson's manner made her look up, so that some of the tea spilled into the saucer. Richard obviously noticed the change in the agent too, for he asked:

"Now what's up?"

"As a matter of fact I think I have a piece of information which would kill Libby's chances," said Clark Henderson. "That's *if* you want to use it."

10

PAST

CECIL LIBBY, the Liberal candidate for the constituency in north London which bordered Quatrain's, bustled out of his scarlet Mini-Minor and along the path to his little house, and saw three of his children rushing along the hallway towards the open door, eager and excited, "daddy, daddy!" on all their lips. There were two girls, aged seven and five, and a boy aged three. They spilled out on to the garden, the older girl trampling on a flower bed which had more weeds in it than leggy antirrhinums which should have been pulled up weeks ago. They had no special reason for exuberance, just *joie de vivre*, and they hurtled at him. He thrust out his stubby arms, hoisted the first one shoulder high, then swung her over his head and dumped her down; she laughed helplessly all the time. He treated the second girl in the same way, dumped her down and turned to the boy. He would never have admitted it to a soul, but this child, his fourth, won a spark of deeper response from him than any of the girls. God knew he loved them, but young Monk, well, he had come when Libby had almost given up expecting a boy.

Libby's wife, Jane, appeared in the doorway.

Libby held out his right arm, straight as a poker. Young Monk stood immediately beneath it, with nearly a foot of clearance between the arm and his head, although his father was only five feet six. With gravity which almost made his mother burst out laughing, Monk stretched up his arms and gripped his father's, tiny fingers only just keeping their hold. Then the boy crooked his arms and hauled himself clear of the ground. His two sisters watched with bated breath, for this was the moment of danger, when Monk might slip off. They were honour bound not to pick him up, just as he was honour bound not to cry if he hurt himself. He drew his chubby legs higher and higher, then shifted his grip so that he edged closer to his father. Suddenly, Libby raised his arm and let the child dangle in the air, then caught him as he fell. The child's face was a beacon of delight.

"Monkey, monkey, monkey!" screeched the girls.

"I'm a monkey," piped young Monk.

"You're all monkeys," Libby declared. He bustled up to the front door, the children clinging to him, to his wife. "Hallo, pet. I just managed to snatch half an hour off. Any chance of a sandwich?"

"Of course," said Jane. "We've had lunch, so we needn't worry about the children. Daisy," she said to the seven-year-old, "go along to the shop and ask Mrs. Smith for the usual groceries, and bring them back. Don't forget to let Monk carry some, and don't step into the road. Will you promise me that?"

"Yes, mummy."

"Off with you!"

Libby and his wife, probably two of the happiest people taking part in the election, turned into the house and closed the door. The bungalow was untidy, but not messy or dirty. The wallpaper had a worn look, and so did the kitchen furniture. The linoleum was patched in several places. Dolls were perched tidily in two small armchairs, a regiment of toy soldiers from a bygone age, their scarlet uniforms and bearskins appealing to Monk, were lined up on a window sill. The boiler which provided the hot water and two small radiators in the bungalow was on, and the room was warm. Libby took off his coat. He was two stone too heavy, and looked very fat, but he also looked jolly. As Jane cut sandwiches, he leaned forward in his chair and undid the laces of his shoes.

"How is it going?" Jane wanted to know.

"Not bad, not bad at all," replied Libby. "I've been canvassing like a vacuum cleaner salesman. People are jolly decent, really. I could have had twenty-eight cups of tea, five sherries, four coffees and a whisky and soda, but I preferred to come home with you."

"Bless you."

"How have the kids been?"

"Monk's been a bit naughty, but he's over it now. Darling, how are the envelopes getting along?"

Libby grimaced. "We could do with a couple of dozen more workers, and a couple of hundred more quid. But we'll get through. Had time to do any?"

"About a hundred."

"Jolly good!" Libby closed his eyes. "Guess what the main subject people ask about is."

"Your syntax, I should think," Jane, looking at him, saw that he was really tired. The lines at the corners of his mouth showed now that he was relaxed, the tiny tell-tale crowsfeet. "I don't know."

"The bomb."

"*The* bomb?"

"Quatrain's bomb! Would you believe it? With all these issues at stake, the economic situation, Africa, the Far East, labour troubles on the home front, the cost of living, automation, every damned thing—and four people out of five say isn't it terrible about that bomb! It's won Quatrain more sympathy than anything else ever could. I feel sorry for Talmad. It's an uphill fight for him anyhow, and this——"

"It won't make any serious difference, surely?"

"In Quatrain's own constituency it might make a lot," said Libby. "It happened three days ago, and instead of the interest dying down, it seems to be livening up. Oh, well." He hitched himself forward in his chair, and took a sandwich off his plate. "This looks good. I wish the police would catch the devil."

"They're sure to," Jane said. "Look at the *Mail*."

The *Daily Mail* had a front-page picture of Quatrain, and one of a man with a big, strong-looking face; under this was the name 'Commander Gideon'. Quatrain was quoted as saying that the police had already lost their opportunity of catching the assassin; Gideon was quoted as saying: "We have never yet failed to catch a man guilty of such an outrage."

"The copper's sticking his neck out," Libby remarked, and devoured the next sandwich, turned over the pages and glanced down them for election and general news.

Suddenly his expression changed. His wife, coming in with a cup of coffee, saw his eyes close as if to shut out some unwanted vision. She had noticed him behave like this before and wondered if these were moments when he felt that he really had no chance to win, no matter what he said.

She did not know that he had just read a short news item, which ran:

OFFICE THIEF JAILED

Ernest Cartwright, 19, of Seabright Road, Delton, was sent to prison for three months by the local magistrate for theft from the cashier's office where he worked.

He, Libby, had not been jailed when he had committed just such an offence; he had been bound over. A generous employer had helped him. He had needed the money so desperately then, and temptation had been fierce and ugly. He had taken twenty-two pounds ten shillings. Twenty-two pounds ten shillings could have ruined his life—and if it ever became known locally could ruin his political hopes even today. It had happened in the Midlands and he had moved away from there soon afterwards, so very few people knew.

Jane knew.

"Very tired, dear?" Jane asked.

He opened his eyes. "Tired? I can't afford to be tired for the next two weeks!" He took the coffee, dropped in a saccharin tablet, and stirred vigorously.

Soon he was driving off again, the children waving goodbye, to the committee rooms in a one time newspaper shop, where a dozen people were sitting and writing out the envelopes in which the election addresses were to be sent out. They would be delivered free, each candidate was allowed one delivery gratis to every house in the constituency, but each had to be addressed, and that meant over sixty thousand envelopes typed or written—and no more than twenty people to do it, together with all the other office work, the canvassing records, the day-by-day organization of the election.

Candidates all over the country were facing the same kind of problem.

In constituencies where the party organization was good, such as in 'safe' Conservative and 'safe' Labour seats, it was not really a problem, however. Helpers were available by the hundred, and part-time paid help could be used. In the fringe constituencies like Libby's and for candidates with little chance of success, it was a hand-to-mouth business, always worrisome, always creating pressures.

Richard Benwell said to Clark Henderson:

"Are you sure this was the same Libby?"

Henderson pulled at his beard. "Yes." He fingered a yellowed press cutting which told the story. "There's no doubt at all."

"How can you be sure?"

"Someone who used to know him up in the Midlands recognized him at a meeting two nights ago. He told me about it."

"What will happen if it comes out?"

"He'll lose a large proportion of votes, and they would come to you."

"Sure they wouldn't go to the Tory?"

"A few would, but in this constituency most of the Liberal votes will come from Labour."

"What do you think we ought to do?" Benwell asked.

Behind steel-rimmed glasses Henderson's eyes seemed hard and bright; like glass marbles.

"Get you as many votes as we can."

"Do you think I've got a chance?"

"There's always a chance."

Benwell said slowly, reluctantly, "I'm not saying I'm going to use it, mind you, but if we *did* decide that the electors ought to know, how would you set about telling them?"

"*You* wouldn't have anything to do with it personally, nor would any of your voluntary helpers," Henderson answered. "I would see that it came out."

"Clark, you won't do anything without telling me first, will you?" Benwell felt very young and inexperienced. His agent, a veteran of a dozen elections, knew so much more and was so sure of himself.

"You're the candidate," Clark Henderson said. "It's up to you." He put the cutting away in his wallet. "Now, these canvassing reports. There are two most frequently asked questions—what do you think about the Q bomb and what's your opinion of the Big Bomb? We've got to watch the answers to both of them—condemn them both without committing you to anything. And these F.F.P. Battle Committee weirdies are out in strength. They've started canvassing for support and persuading electors to ask candidates to promise to support them. It's very tricky, Richard—you need every vote you can get."

"I know," said Benwell. "Well, I've got to get on with some canvassing."

It was sheer chance that he passed a street where Libby also was canvassing. The tubby little Liberal looked thoroughly happy as he stood on a doorstep with half a dozen women talking to him earnestly. He had a most persuasive manner. Benwell walked past the end of the road and started on another street of houses, but he could not get Libby's half-forgotten crime out of his mind.

What was the *right* thing to do?

What was the *best* thing to do in the interest of his party?

If a man had been light-fingered twenty-odd years ago, he might still be light-fingered. Even if it was the only time he had been convicted, it might not have been Libby's only offence.

Benwell called at a house with a Fight for Peace 'Ban the Bomb' poster in the window. A clear-eyed elderly woman, with a beautiful complexion, and an earnest man came to the door and started to argue. That was the trouble: a garrulous couple could waste a quarter of an hour or even more, and the really talkative ones were always on the other side.

"I certainly believe in banning the bomb," Benwell said, "but I'm not convinced that we should do it unilaterally."

"Now you listen to me, young man . . ." the woman began.

At the end of the street where Benwell was canvassing, Detective Sergeant Whittle was talking to a uniformed constable, who had reported that a middle-aged couple, ardent supporters of the F.F.P. Action Committee, had received a lot of callers lately, including many of the most extremist members of the committee.

"I wouldn't like to say they're up to anything more than a campaign of heckling at meetings," the constable said. "But you put out a request for information about any exceptional activity, sarge."

"Yes, we did. Thanks. Can you give me the names of the members who've called there?"

"I've got it written down."

Whittle studied the list, thanked him again, and got into his car. A detective constable was at the wheel, and the car moved off as Whittle flicked on the radio and called the Yard. Information answered him.

"Superintendent Parsons? . . . He's engaged, hold on."

Parsons seemed always to be engaged. In the three days since the outrage he had worked himself harder than ever in his life. Provided he got four hours' sleep at night, he kept going and felt well, but he knew that he was being driven by a compulsion which, once it collapsed, would leave him not only flat but dangerously near a stage of nervous prostration. He had watched the way work was going at some of the committee rooms, talked to many of the candidates, and seen the same kind of tension in them; it was a driving compulsion, absolute preoccupation with the job in hand.

His maps now had three colours of ink painted carefully on them, as well as the pins, showing the committee rooms in the London constituencies, and the homes of the candidates, and places where open-air meetings were held. Constantly in consultation with Gideon, he had arranged a system by which all the election agents informed the local police of places where they intended to hold out-door meetings, and he made sure that uniformed as well as plainclothes police were in attendance. But there were limits to the way in which divisional and head-quarters strength could be stretched.

He was talking to White, of KL. He always seemed to be on the telephone to that division.

". . . all I can say is, this girl says that it was a big man," said White. "She's sure he drove off and came back later. She was waiting for one of the tenants at Park Towers—he'd put her in the family way. That's why she wouldn't come forward before."

"I'll see her," said Parsons.

"If you ask her to come to the Yard she'll faint right off."

"I'll come over," said Parsons. "How about seven o'clock?"

"I'll fix it."

"Thanks." Parsons rang off, stretched his hand towards the internal telephone and the outside one rang again. "Bloody thing," he said mechanically, and plucked it up. "Parsons."

"Sergeant Whittle calling you, sir, from his car."

"Put him through."

Parsons was holding on when the door opened without a preliminary tap, and Gideon came in. Gideon waved his hand, as if to tell Parsons to go on with what he was doing, and stepped across to the maps. Two sergeants started to get up. Gideon waved them to their desks.

"Skipper," said Whittle to Parsons, "I've been in Highgate and had a word with the policeman on duty in Braine Street. Where the Wallises live."

"I know." Parsons could picture the clear-eyed little woman and the sad-looking man, Lady Wallis and her husband, who were active members of the F.F.P. Battle Committee.

"They've had a lot of meetings lately, and among the visitors they've had Amanda Tenby," Whittle went on.

"And Ronn?"

"No."

"Any idea what they're up to?"

"No. Division's made two attempts to get men at meetings by offering help, but the Wallises said that they had all the help they could use for the time being. That sounds phony in itself."

"I'll say it does."

"Anything else?"

"No."

"Right," said Parsons. "Try the St. John's Wood lot next." He put the receiver down and looked up at Gideon, who was studying the little painted areas and the legend explaining them. There were small black crosses against the homes of two of the candidates, and he could see no explanation of these. Parsons joined him.

"What've we got here?" inquired Gideon.

"Candidates whose homes have been burgled while they've been at meetings."

"Much stolen?"

"Not a lot, no. They happened last night, I've only just

seen the reports. As it was election material it was channelled through me instead of to you. In a hurry for the details?"

Gideon said slowly, "Not really. Anything new?"

"Yes. There's actually a ray of hope in the Q bomb case," answered Parsons. He spoke in a calm, deliberate voice as if determined not to sound excited about it. "White's discovered a girl who was outside Park Towers on the night of the bomb. He says he's interviewed several hundred people himself, and in all the divisional chaps have talked to over three thousand. This is the first promising line."

Gideon was looking at him very straightly. "Well?"

"It's a young girl who was waiting in one of the cars for a tenant whose wife suspected he'd kept a little bit of fluff on the side, and delayed him. And was wifey right! The girl's in the family way. She didn't know what to do, and just sat waiting miserably. I haven't got any details yet, but she's supposed to have said that a man came out of the main doors, drove off in an old Bentley, and came back half an hour later in a smaller car. She's sure it was the same man. He was a big fellow wearing a raincoat. She's sure he's the same man, because a car came along with its headlamps on, and he hid his face by turning towards her. She saw it clearly."

"Ah," said Gideon softly. "Jefferson Miles has an old Bentley."

"Don't I know it. He's up in Birmingham today, helping the local Q candidate. He's due back to report to Quatrain tonight."

"When are you seeing this girl?" asked Gideon.

"About seven o'clock."

"I've got a late conference with the Commissioner," Gideon said. "Call me at his office if she confirms this story. Show her a dozen photographs, including one of Miles."

"I'll get 'em looked out," said Parsons. "My God, if Miles did that to David Smith——"

"If he did, he did himself a bit of good as he's now Quatrain's right-hand man for the election," Gideon observed. "Anything else?"

"Amanda Tenby keeps going to Battle Committee meetings all over the place, but I can't trace anything dangerous or illegal as a result. There's the Lord and Lady Wallis group, over at Highgate, and it's pretty hush-hush. I wish we could find an excuse for raiding that house."

"If we need to raid it we'd better raid it," said Gideon flatly. "We can use the Special Branch for it. I'll have a word with Ripple." He nodded and went out, closing the door very quietly. The two sergeants stopped what they were doing for a moment and watched Parsons. Parsons said, "I'm going to Photographs. Put any calls through there." He pulled open the filing cabinet which contained his dossier on Jefferson Miles, took out Miles's photograph, a very good one, and tucked it under his arm.

"I want a dozen photographs of men roughly like this chap," he said to the inspector in charge of Photographs. "Not too like him, mind you."

"That's Miles, isn't it?" asked the inspector.

11

'KEYBOARD'

GIDEON went back to his office, deeply thoughtful, and opened the door on Lemaitre talking into the telephone; Lemaitre always seemed to be on the telephone. He was virtually *locum tenens* for normal Yard work while Gideon concentrated on the ramifications of the election. Except for the constant fear that there might be another bomb outrage, the election campaign was proceeding as quietly as Gideon could have wished from the police point of view. There was as yet no outward sign of a clash between Quatrain's supporters and the Battle Committee. The Fight for Peace members were distributing leaflets door-to-door and making thorough nuisances of themselves at meetings, but they were behaving strictly in accordance with the law. Sooner or later there might be a clash, but every day that passed strengthened the position of the police, for every day they learned more about the F.F.P. supporters, their plans and their members.

Lemaitre's tone changed. "Hold on, pal," he said and pressed one palm over the mouthpiece. "This one's too big for me, George, you'd better handle it."

"Who is it?"

"Dancy."

"*Jacob* Dancy?"

"Yes."

Jacob Dancy was probably the most efficient, most highly paid and the least publicized of all the private inquiry agents in the country. Most of his work was on divorce cases, inevitably, but he was consulted by a number of insurance companies and had been employed on arson investigations where the police were not justified in taking action. Gideon disliked Dancy as a person, respected him as a man and occasionally half wished that he was attached to the Yard. He had been here as a young C.I.D. officer and had known Gideon slightly.

Gideon picked up his telephone.

"Put the call on Mr. Lemaitre's line through to me, please . . . Hallo, Dancy. How are you?"

Dancy had a high-pitched voice, rather husky; a little like Roger Livesey's. It came over the telephone badly.

"Glad I'm not in your shoes," he said. "Have you found your bomb man yet?"

"Can you put a finger on him?"

"Wish I could, I'd get some of the glory," said Dancy. "I wanted a word with you about a different matter altogether. Much though I like friend Lemmy, I didn't think I should talk to anyone but you about this." Dancy's overfriendly manner, his tendency to ooze a kind of affable sarcasm, explained why a lot of people did not like him.

"I know you wouldn't call me if you didn't think it important," said Gideon. "Someone planning to steal the crown jewels?"

"That's not worthy of the great Gee-Gee," reproved Dancy. "No, George. It's just a little oddment of information which might interest you. I had an unusual commission the other day. I was asked to check back over the history of a certain Professor Ivan Travaritch."

"*Trav*-aritch."

"Not Tovarich," said Dancy waggishly. "Travaritch is a brilliant young worker in nuclear physicist circles. I'm told that he's one of the most brilliant we've ever bred in England. What's in a name, after all? He's two-generation English, yes

—and as I understand it, very, *very* patriotic. I'm sure the Special Branch screened him thoroughly before he went to work at Harwell."

Gideon had forgotten his irritation with Dancy, Lemaitre, the election problems, even Jefferson Miles. This was the way serious crises often threw their shadow: a whisper here, a whisper there, a hint, a vague possibility—and spy hunts were the most difficult and the least popular carried out by the Yard.

"What did you have to find out about him?"

"I was asked to look for any skeleton in his cupboard. It didn't matter what it was. Reading between the lines I assumed that some bad lads wanted to be able to exert pressure on poor Professor Travaritch, and hoped I could dig something murky out of his past."

"Who wants the information?"

"Now, Gee-Gee, you know that I can't betray the confidence of a client! It wouldn't be right, would it? In any case no crime has really been committed, yet—I'm just passing on a piece of interesting information. Up to you, old boy. Have Travaritch watched, won't you?"

"You could help a lot by naming the man who made inquiries about him."

"I can tell you but I don't think it would really help. You know how these jobs come, Gee-Gee. A friend of a friend of a friend wants a little information. I was offered two hundred and fifty pounds for this job, so it must be someone who seriously wants to know."

"Did you accept it?"

"I said I'd consider it."

"Ask for five hundred pounds, as it's about a man at Harwell, will you?" suggested Gideon. "Then we'll really know how badly the information is wanted."

"Will do."

"And you'll call me?"

"Will do."

"Thanks," said Gideon. "Do you know anything else?"

"I know that Travaritch is working on what is called Keyboard," Dancy told him. "That's about all, I'm afraid. You won't forget to remember this old friend of yours if he ever wants a favour, will you?"

"No," said Gideon. "I won't."

He sat for a few seconds, staring straight at Lemaitre, seeing but not noticing him, not even aware of the fact that Lemaitre was looking across, apparently greatly puzzled by his expression. Gideon moistened his lips. It was as if a gigantic shadow had passed over the office, and it made the election troubles almost non-existent.

"Seen a ghost, George?" inquired Lemaitre.

"Wouldn't be surprised," said Gideon. "I'm going to talk to Ripple, and by the time I've finished with him I'll have to go and see the old Man. Better telephone your wife to say you'll be home late."

Lemaitre made a great to-do about groaning.

Gideon went out, walked halfway along the passage, and stopped outside a door marked: *Commander Ripple, Special Branch*. He gave a perfunctory tap, although he knew that if Ripple wanted to make sure that no one could interrupt him his door would be locked. It wasn't. Ripple, a big, fat, brown-looking and brown-clad man, was sitting in his shirt-sleeves in a room that was stiflingly hot. As the administrative head of the Special Branch, he was in charge of all matters concerning enemy aliens as well as those matters which touched the police and also touched upon the security of the State. It was big brown Ripple who was at all the royal occasions, who organized the protection of the Royal Family, of the Prime Minister, and of somewhat lesser but nevertheless very important persons.

He was smoking a small black cigar.

"Come in, George." Gideon was already halfway in. "What can I do for you today?"

"What do you know about an operation called Keyboard?" asked Gideon bluntly.

"*Key*board!" Ripple almost dropped the cigar.

"You heard me."

"We were talking about it at the commanders' conference last week, remember?" Ripple said.

"It was mentioned in passing but no one elaborated on it," Gideon replied. "Can you tell me more?"

Ripple toyed with his cigar, as if gaining time for his reply. "What's on your mind, George?"

"What operation is it exactly?"

"You don't know?"

"No, I don't."

"It's the project for manufacturing the smallest reactor yet known to the physicists—a portable reactor not much bigger than a typewriter," Ripple answered. "You can carry it about with you. As far as we know we're pioneering it in this country. It's got enormous economic and industrial potential, could be the biggest boost our exports have had for fifty years."

"Very hush-hush, then."

"Absolutely top secret," Ripple said. "And well on the way to completing the prototype. The only stumbling block left is the carrying case. Lead's much too heavy, and it's got to be absolutely safe from radiation. They're working on it at Harwell. What's up, George?"

Gideon told him.

"My God," breathed Ripple. "I'll see that Travaritch is watched closer than a hawk. Thanks a million."

Gideon eased his collar.

"Thank Dancy," he said. It did not occur to him that this could be even remotely concerned with the election. And he forgot to arrange for a raid on the Wallises' place.

While Ripple was talking to his opposite number at the Home Office, while Parsons was talking to a frightened girl at the divisional headquarters, showing her the different photographs including one of Jefferson Miles, while Gideon was reporting to Scott-Marle, while candidates up and down the country, including Libby and Benwell, Quatrain and Talmad, were taking a breather (or a respite, according to their phraseology), most Londoners who worked in the City and the West End were on their way home. Millions of them were reading the *Evening News*. One of these was Fred Wilcox, who was going straight from work to a meeting where he was to be a steward; he went to meetings straight from work on most nights. He saw a short paragraph about the bogus doctor, put in for no apparent reason, gritted his teeth, and stared straight ahead.

He made himself look at the paper, made himself read the snippets of London news, and saw the little headline about the 'Office Thief Jailed' and another 'Candidate's Home

Burgled.' Nothing really sank in. He just wished he could get the hatred for an unknown man out of his mind.

When he reached the British Legion Hall, where the meeting was to be held, no one but the caretaker was there, putting out the chairs. Fred helped, for the sake of something to do.

"These elections," the caretaker complained. He was in his seventies, grey-haired, grey-faced; and he was crippled from rheumatism. "Always a lot of bother, they are and what for, that's what I want to know. How many do you expect to-night? A dozen?"

"Oh, there'll be more than that."

"Not many more if the other two parties is anything to go by," the caretaker declared gloomily. "What with television and meetings at street corners, no one attends indoor meetings these days. If I put out fifty chairs, that ought to be plenty."

A man came stamping in from the end of the hall.

"Couple of hundred, more like." He was the local agent, a youthful, bony, optimistic man, his arms overflowing with posters and leaflets. "Hallo, Fred, you're just the man I want. Here's some drawing pins—put up these posters, will you? You know how. Dolly Gray is coming in to put a leaflet on every chair, and she'll look after the literature stall. As more of our chaps arrive, get them to help with the chairs, will you? I've got four more meetings to go and check."

"All a waste of time," muttered the caretaker.

"That's the trouble with you young chaps, you've got no faith. You never do get big meetings early in a campaign, but mark my words, we'll be spilling out of the doors and windows before this one's over. It's going to be big, and I mean big." The agent heard footsteps, and turned to see a middle-aged policeman in the doorway. "You chaps will have your work cut out, I can tell you. Look after grandpa here."

He breezed out.

Fred, pinning the posters up round the walls and round the platform, felt almost cheerful.

12

OPPORTUNITY KNOCKS

In other parts of London, where the paragraphs were read avidly, London gossip being a staple diet of Londoners everywhere, three men were together in a public house. They were in a corner, on their own.

"Well, me lucky lad!" said Barney Spicer, the biggest of the trio. He thumped his cronies—both small men—on the backs, then spread his great hands over their heads and bumped them together. "Who are we going to vote for, eh? Let's have it."

"Pack it in," Shins Mason protested.

"Lemme go!" squealed Wilf Darlington.

Spicer gave their heads another bump, and released them.

"Trouble with you is you don't know your own strength," protested Shins. He earned his nickname from his habit of kicking in the shins anyone who threatened him; many a policeman in the NE Division had carried bruises left by Shins Mason. Shins was easy to identify because he was pigeon-toed, and his thin face was vaguely like a pigeon's too. "What's it matter who we vote for, anyway?"

"It matters plenty, don't it, Wilf?"

"I know who I'm *not* going to vote for," Darlington said. He was broad and stocky, with a very low forehead and thrusting eyebrows, which fooled many people into believing that he was half-witted.

"Who's that?"

"Mr. Flicking Barney Spicer!"

"That, Wilfy boy, is exactly where you're wrong." Spicer, a boxer who looked exactly like everyone's conception of a boxer, grinned from one man to the other. "You're going to vote for me *and* for yourself."

"What's the matter? You gone crazy?"

"Never been so sane in me natural. Listen—what do we want most on a dark night, eh?"

"A bit of skirt," said Darlington promptly.

"You've got a nasty, immoral mind, Wilfy. Your turn, Shins."

"An empty house," hazarded Mason.

"That's it, me lucky lad—an empty house! A nice, respectable house which will remain empty for a given time, so that we can have a good forage round and help ourselves to a drink or two. What kind of houses are going to be without the lord and master and the missus in the next two weeks or so, eh?"

"Same as usual," Shins Mason said, puzzled.

"No, you slob."

"Then what?"

"There's an election on, ain't there?"

"What's that got to do with empty houses?"

"Well, you can't address your election meeting with wifey by your side *and* be at home, can you? A lot of these places will be wide open. Couple have been done already." He slapped a copy of the *Evening News* on his arm. "We've just got to do a bit of research, and then we can get to work. All we need are the addresses of the candidates, see, and they're all posted up outside town halls *and* police stations, for all the world to see. We're in the world, aren't we?"

"You know, Wilfy, I think he's got something," Shins conceded softly.

"Not a bad idea at all—good enough to have thought up myself," boasted Darlington. "When do we start?"

"First of all we collect the names and addresses," said Spicer, who had obviously given this a great deal of thought. "Then we make out a visiting list, see. We do six a night, in different parts of the big smoke. Six a night for three nights running, all in different districts, and then we lay off. Okay?"

"Okay!"

"Will you handle the stuff?" asked Shins anxiously.

"You know me," said Barney Spicer. "I'll get the best terms any fence will give us. You know me."

That was the moment, the very moment, when the Q candidate in the Birmingham election was stepping into his car. It was a small, dilapidated old Ford Anglia which he had driven until it clanked and rattled but was still capable of a good turn of speed. He pulled the self-starter without giving it a second thought, and the front of the car blew up. He saw the windscreen crack and instantly become a mottled silvery colour, felt sharp pain as pieces flew into his forehead, and took in a deep breath of acrid, smoke-laden air.

Then flames began to leap out of the engine.

The Q man was so dazed that he did not know what was happening. He sat absolutely still, blood trickling down his forehead. Men came running from the door of the committee rooms, where the window was painted with a huge Q and with pictures of Quatrain and of the local candidate in the middle. They pulled open the car door as the flames roared, and dragged the injured man out. With every passing second the flames grew fiercer and the danger became greater.

Catherine Miller hated being at the police station. It seemed to add to the guilt that was already almost unbearable, and she was tormented because she did not think that her lover would carry out his promise to divorce his wife, and marry her. She was already heavy with his child. She lived alone in a small bed-sitting room and had not been to her parents for over three months because she was afraid of what they would notice and what she would have to tell them. She carried with her bitter memories of the night when she had waited for her lover, who had promised to come down and comfort her, after telling his wife what he was planning to do.

He had not come down.

She knew that in such circumstances some girls would have gone storming up to his apartment, but she had not; it was not in her. She had left Park Towers after one o'clock, scared, anguished, fearful of what would happen next. The following morning her lover had telephoned her.

"My wife's taking it so hard, Cathy, it's very difficult. Give me a little more time."

She had seen him only once since then, and she had realized that 'difficult' was more than a word.

She had seen the television and heard the radio requests for information from anyone who had been in the vicinity of Park Towers on that particular night, but she had been frightened of the publicity she might get if she went forward, and by the possible repercussions. When it had been repeated so often and the importance became so obvious, she had screwed up her courage to go to the police station. Its bleakness, the air of restrained activity, the passing to and fro of men in uniform and in plain clothes, the arrival at the station of two unhappy-looking men handcuffed together, all these had made her hate what she was doing.

Now she was with friendly, paternal-seeming Superintendent White, who had told her that a Superintendent Parsons was on his way from Scotland Yard. It was nearly seven o'clock. She had a nagging headache. She believed that the child stirred within her, but she could not be sure. It should be a matter of such joy, and instead of that it was one of misery and despair. She kept closing her eyes. She felt very tired.

The door of Superintendent White's office opened, and a man came in slowly.

"*No!*" cried Catherine Miller, as she saw him. "*No!*"

She half rose from her chair, and then slumped back in a dead faint. Parsons, at the door, looked dumbfounded. White jumped up, and said:

"I've seen fright at first sight plenty of times, but this beats the band." He seemed to talk for the sake of talking as he poured water from a carafe into a glass, eased the girl to a more comfortable position, and put the glass to her lips. Parsons, still baffled and more shaken by the little incident than it really warranted, stood in a corner of the room watching her. She stirred. Soon her eyes opened.

"Now you'll be all right," White assured her. "No one is going to hurt you. Superintendent, Miss Miller is nervous lest she get personal publicity out of this—she doesn't want her parents to know about her—ah—predicament. I've assured her that she needn't worry at all as far as we're concerned, but if you confirm that she'll be happier."

The girl was staring at Parsons, her eyes rounded and huge, her lips parted.

"You needn't be worried on that score," Parsons told her. He hardly knew how to phrase the assurance, because the effect he had on her was so startling.

She said weakly, "I—I thought you were my father."

"Your *father?*"

"Yes, you—you're so like him."

Parsons said, "Well, that's remarkable, isn't it?" He began

118

to understand. "And it's your father's attitude that troubles you over this baby, is it?"

"Yes. Yes, it is." She sat up straighter, still staring at him. "It—it was just as you came in. Just for a moment—I suppose I'd been thinking about him so much."

Parsons asked, "Fond of him, Miss Miller?"

"Oh, he's been wonderful to me! I hate the thought of hurting him. I think if he—if he knows what's happened he'll never recover from it. He'll be so disappointed in me." She was utterly woebegone, and yet so pretty with the promise of motherhood blooming in her cheeks. Her young breasts were full and thrusting against a dress which was too tight for her and which fitted glove-like round her spreading waist. Parsons, forgetful of the fact that Gideon was waiting for him and that so much was dependent on this identification, saw her as a pathetic young girl. For a few moments he just stared, wondering how to help.

White put in: "Fathers are often very understanding, aren't they, Superintendent?"

"Yes," said Parsons slowly. "Yes, very often." He drew a deep breath. "I certainly shouldn't worry, Miss Miller, and if we can help we will." He became brisk. "Now, we hope you can help us." He gave her a few moments to recover before going on: "You say you remember the man at Park Towers very clearly?"

"Yes, I do."

"Will you look through these photographs—there are twelve altogether—and tell us if he is among them?"

Cathy stretched out her hand for the photographs as the telephone bell rang. White muttered, "Why do they have to worry me just now?" and picked it up. The girl took the photographs. "Well?" barked White into the phone and glowered, but on the instant his tone changed. "Oh, *is* he. Thanks, Joe." He turned to Parsons. "Gee-Gee's on the way up."

The girl heard the absurd word 'Gee-Gee' and looked from the pictures to the men, because this so obviously mattered to them. Heavy footsteps sounded at the door, which opened. A very big man came in. He was so solid and massive that he gave the impression of being huge, compared with the others.

She looked into his face, a familiar one although she could not place it. The respect that these others had for him was apparent in their manner.

The man said in a deep voice, "So this is the young lady." He smiled at her. The smile wasn't broad or particularly attractive, but it gave her a kind of reassurance. He stepped to her and shook hands.

"I'm Commander Gideon of Scotland Yard," he said. "I want to thank you personally for coming forward."

"Have you had a chance to look at those photographs yet?"

"No," she said hastily, and dropped her gaze. The face of a man on top of the pile was unknown to her, and she put it aside on a corner of White's desk. She was aware of the tension in all three men, even in Gideon; not until this moment had she fully understood the importance of what she was doing. She stared at the next picture even more closely before putting it aside. The third, the fourth, the fifth, and the sixth were all of men she had never seen before. She looked at the seventh, and on the instant exclaimed:

"That's him!"

In a very clear voice, Superintendent Parsons, who was so like her father, said, "We've got him."

"Are you absolutely sure, Miss Miller?" Gideon was looking at her in a way which was almost alarming—as if he was drawing something out of her. But she did not hesitate, because there was no possibility of doubt.

"Yes, absolutely."

"It was dark when you saw him, wasn't it?"

"Yes, but the headlamps of the car shone on him. I'd seen him before, anyhow."

"You mean earlier that night?"

"Yes. *And* on other nights, when I'd gone to see—to see my friend." Her lips quivered.

"And would you swear to this in a court of law, no matter how serious the charge against the man?"

"Well, it really is the man," she said simply.

The telephone bell rang again. White muttered another imprecation and moved to pick it up. Gideon stepped closer to the girl and took the photograph of Jefferson Miles. White said, "I thought I told you to hold calls . . . Oh, I see. Yes. All right." He held the telephone out to Gideon. "It's for you, Commander." The formality was used because of the girl, and he added, "It's Lemaitre." Gideon took the instrument, smiled at Cathy and gave her greater reassurance than either of the others had done. He said into the telephone, "Yes, Lem?"

After a pause, he caught his breath. Catherine Miller did not know, but both men realized that only devastating news could make him show such a sign of surprise and could put such consternation on his face.

Then he said, "Yes. Yes, I understand. I'll go to Q's place." He put down the receiver. "Miss Miller, Mr. Parsons and I have to leave at once, on an urgent matter. Mr. White will look after you. You've been of very great service to us and also to your country. Very great service indeed. In fact, if you hadn't been there I don't know what would have happened. I hope to see you again, to express our thanks more effectively." He smiled at her warmly, and shook hands.

"What's up?" demanded Parsons as he hurried with Gideon to his car.

"Another Q bomb," said Gideon briefly.

"God. Where?"

"The Q candidate in the Midlands. There was a bomb under the bonnet of his car."

Parsons said in a thin voice, "Miles has been up there today!"

"I know," said Gideon. "He left half an hour before the explosion. He's supposed to be on his way to Quatrain now. I'd like to get there first. Come in my car, you can have yours sent on to the Yard." He climbed into the back and his driver started off as soon as Parsons had got in and slammed the door. "Could have been planning a series."

"Looks like it," said Parsons.

Gideon leaned over the seat in front of him, and took the radio transmitter off its hook. He clicked on, and called the Yard. Information answered. "I'm speaking for Superintendent Parsons," he said. "I want all Q candidates warned that they may be in danger from plastic bombs planted in their cars or in some other thing or place which they use frequently.

Have that sent to the nearest headquarters and transmitted to the candidates immediately."

"Right, sir."

Gideon rang off.

"Thanks, George," said Parsons. "I hope to God——"

"What?"

"He hasn't planted any others."

Gideon didn't speak. The car sped through the thinning traffic of the West End and along Park Lane and finally swung into the carriageway of Park Towers, opposite the dark mass of Hyde Park with its hidden lovers. No other police were there yet, but a group of men were standing near the entrance, talking to the doorman. As the police car drew up, several of these men swung round and hurried towards it. As Gideon and Parsons stepped out, a man called:

"Half a mo', Mr Gideon."

Gideon paused for a fraction of a second, and a flashlight dazzled him. Two other photographers took their chance, and reporters began to pour out questions, walking step by step with Gideon and Parsons.

"Have you heard about the bomb in the Midlands?"

"Did you expect another explosion?"

"Any arrest made yet?"

"Are you anywhere near making an arrest, Mr. Gideon?"

Gideon paused at the entrance to the lift.

"Very near," he said. "Thanks to Superintendent Parsons and the divisional police, we know who our man is." He stepped into the lift, and the doors closed, almost trapping Parsons. The doorman squeezed himself into a corner and did his best to stand to attention. One of Quatrain's men waited at the seventh floor. He was wearing the same uniform as when out of doors, but it had a white Q on each shoulder, in the form of an epaulette.

"Mr. Quatrain in?" inquired Gideon.

"Mr. Quatrain gave orders that he wasn't to be disturbed, sir."

"Who's with him?"

"Mr. Miles, sir."

Gideon nodded, and turned towards the apartment. Out-side the door were two more of Q's men, big and powerful.

Gideon went straight up to them. Parsons, a yard behind, wondered if they would obey their leader or whether the authority of Gideon would overawe them. They moved closer together, blocking the way.

Gideon saw the movement, noticed the way their hands bunched and knew that they did not intend to let him pass. Quite suddenly another crisis had come upon him, a swift conflict between police authority—for these men knew who he was—and a political group.

He stood very close to them.

"I want to see Mr. Quatrain, at once."

They didn't speak and didn't move aside or touch the door or do anything to suggest that they would inform Quatrain.

"I am Commander Gideon of the Criminal Investigation Department," Gideon announced clearly. "Step aside, please."

They did not move.

"I will give you thirty seconds to stop interfering with the proper process of the law," Gideon said. "Tell Mr. Quatrain I am here." When neither of the men moved or spoke, Gideon half turned his head and said over his shoulder, "Superintendent, go down and get all the available uniformed and plainclothes men in the vicinity, will you? Bring them up here at once."

Parsons began to object. "But you're alone——" He didn't finish, for it dawned on him that Gideon wanted him out of the way. The doorman was standing at the top of the stairs and close to the lift, looking scared. The Q man on duty at the lift seemed as if he would get in Parsons' way, and Parsons caught his breath, quite prepared for trouble. The man moved aside. Heart thumping, Parsons went into the lift. The doorman followed him and pressed the button; the doors closed.

Gideon was left in the passage with three of Quatrain's men.

He said, "If you know what you're doing, you'll let me in at once." He drew back, as if preparing to wait for reinforcements, and there was a slight relaxation in the manner of the two men in front of the door.

"And if you lay a finger on me," Gideon said, "I shall see that each one of you, Quatrain included, spends the night in jail and comes up before the magistrate for assault and conspiring to obstruct the police." As he finished speaking he moved forward and kicked the door twice, making dull, heavy thuds. Then the men struck out at him. Gideon thrust his right hand forward, spanned one man's face with his fingers and banged him back against the wall; the noise was louder than that caused by the kicks. The other man brought his knee up towards Gideon's groin. Gideon turned, took the knee on his thigh, saw the third man standing and hesitating as if he could not make up his mind what to do. The man whose head had been banged was sliding down the wall, the other victim was momentarily off balance. Gideon punched him in the stomach, and as his head jerked forward struck him under the chin, putting all his massive strength behind the blows.

He heard a shout from the stairs, and two newspapermen came rushing.

"Hold it!" one of them called.

Flashlights made lightning in the passage and footsteps made thunder. Gideon did not look round, but tried the handle, turned and pushed. The door opened. He stepped inside. Two more of Quatrain's men stood just inside the door, and Quatrain and Jefferson Miles were together in the doorway of the big room overlooking the park.

13

ARREST

QUATRAIN was moving forward, hands clenched, handsome face blazing with anger, Jefferson Miles stayed in the doorway. Gideon could not see him clearly. The door of the passage was open, and the newspapermen were trying to get into a position for a picture, but the two Q guards rushed forward to block their path.

Quatrain reached Gideon. His lips were working, his lean body seemed to be aquiver with passion.

"What is the meaning of this unwarranted interference? What do you mean by——"

"Just a minute, Mr. Quatrain," Gideon interrupted. "I want a word with Mr. Miles." He stepped forward, too big and strong for Quatrain to stop him. Miles was holding the door frame, and his expression told Gideon that he knew what to expect; yet there was a lingering mask of surprise too, as if it had only just dawned on him. Gideon was ready for him to dart back inside and slam the door in his face. He was within arm's length when Miles seemed to realize his danger and did exactly as Gideon had feared. He sprang back, snatching at the door to close it. Gideon thrust his foot forward. The door struck it, and swung away from him. Miles was rushing across the room towards the great window overlooking the park, the lights of Park Lane, and the highway through the park and the dark distance. He tripped over a stool.

"This won't help you, Mr. Miles," Gideon said equably. "I want to ask you a few questions." He was calm and matter-of-fact now, and still moving forward, crowding Miles back until he banged against the window with a booming sound. "Where were you at eleven forty-five on the night of October——"

Miles snatched his right hand from his pocket. In it was a cylinder, cigar-shaped, black in colour. He drew his arm back to throw this. Gideon, knowing the danger, realizing what was likely to happen from the moment Miles had heard the truth, closed with him and thrust out his right arm to clutch at Miles's wrist. Gideon saw the cylinder drop from the man's fingers. He let Miles go, stretched out his hand, and caught the thing.

For a terrifying moment he held it in his hand, expecting the explosion. He turned his face away and covered it with his free hand. He heard Quatrain exclaim, felt movement about him, lived in anguish for seconds which never seemed to end.

Then he realized that the impact had not been hard enough to explode the bomb.

"If it had gone off, it would have injured you as badly as it injured David Smith," Quatrain said stiffly.

"I daresay," said Gideon. He had a tumbler half full of whisky and soda in his hand and was sitting on the arm of a large chair. The danger had been over for fifteen minutes, but he still wasn't quite free from tension.

Jefferson Miles was on his way to Cannon Row, under arrest. Two more cylinders had been found in his pockets, and

Parsons was en route to the mews flat to see what else was there. The press had taken advantage of the confusion to take photographs and were still waiting outside for Gideon. Now there was a strong force of police on duty—in the passage, at the lift, and in the hall as well as outside. Crowds had gathered, Gideon knew; the sound of shouting came faintly through the big window.

Quatrain looked very pale.

"Yet you took an extreme personal risk," he said.

Gideon sipped his drink.

"That sounds a bit daft, coming from you," he remarked. "Would you send one of your chaps to risk getting his head blown off if you thought there was a chance to stop it yourself?" When Quatrain didn't answer, he went on: "Once I knew it was Miles—and I've told you about the girl who saw him that night—there was only one thing to do. Get him quick. He must be insane if he'll go to these lengths to drive you to extreme measures. Was he always one of your worst extremists?"

Quatrain said, "Yes. Yes, he was."

"It's the kind of thing that's bound to happen if you play at soldiers instead of work at politics," Gideon said flatly. "You understand that this means that we shall have to make a comprehensive search of your apartment, of your offices, of the committee rooms, and of the homes and offices of all your known supporters, don't you? Jefferson Miles might not have been alone in this. Has he the technical knowledge to make the bombs?"

"No, he hasn't," said Quatrain in a still voice. "I will, however, give you the names of others who may have such knowledge. And of course my files and records are at your disposal." He seemed to stare past Gideon, as if at some awful disaster; Gideon had never seen such pain in a man's eyes. "Thank you for your part in this, Commander. It was an act of very great courage, the ultimate in the acceptance of human responsibility. Thank you again."

Scott-Marle, in the study at his St. John's Wood home, held Gideon's hand for what seemed a long time, and said as if with difficulty:

"That is the greatest debt we shall ever owe you, George."

Kate was at the front door when Gideon reached the house, and Malcolm, Priscilla and Penelope were just behind her. It was nearly ten o'clock. Gideon looked up in surprise and, without thinking, asked:

"What's this royal reception about?"

"George," said Kate huskily, "are you all right?"

"You've been on television, dad," said Malcolm eagerly. "It wasn't a motion picture, but it was a jolly good still. It's a jolly good likeness too. Everyone at school will have seen it."

"Pity they didn't drop the camera," Gideon said. With Kate's arm in his, and her manner telling him how acutely the realization of danger had come upon her, they went indoors. He broke a rule, and talked freely to them, dramatizing the scene with the two Q men outside the door. He said nothing about the effect of it all on Quatrain, but added for the children's benefit:

"It was all due to the powers of observation of a girl—not much older than you two"—Priscilla and Penelope, the one so fair and the other so dark. Priscilla was nearly twenty-three, and engaged, and Penelope at nineteen was already dividing her spare-time-enthusiasm between the piano, which she was learning to play professionally, and a boy friend who seemed as serious over her as he was over his violin. Gideon watched their listening faces and went on: "This girl who put us on to the truth had plenty on her mind as it was. She had been waiting for a man who'd let her down pretty badly, but she remembered seeing Jefferson Miles so vividly that she was able to identify him. Teaches you the usefulness of keeping your eyes open and remembering what you've seen, doesn't it?"

"I take you, pop," said Malcolm half impudently.

Upstairs, when Kate was in bed and Gideon was pulling on his pyjamas, Kate said:

"Do you know much about the girl who identified Miles, George?"

"I only know she's been let down by one of the tenants at Park Towers. The usual promise of divorce and marriage. She isn't the type who would make a wealthy man want to leave wife and home. According to Parsons, she daren't tell her parents. I hope we haven't had that effect on any of our kids. If they do get into trouble——"

"Don't be absurd," Kate said. "Penny and Priscilla would never——"

She broke off, for her husband's grin reminded her of the time when Matthew, their second son, had caused a family crisis.

Catherine Miller slept better that night than she had for some time. First Gideon and then the man she had momentarily mistaken for her father had been so helpful and understanding. She knew now what she had helped the police to do, for the story had been on the radio as well as on television. Gideon's name had been displayed too prominently for her to doubt where he had gone after talking to her.

If only she could get rid of the baby.

Effie Wilcox did not sleep well that night; she had not slept really well since the time Fred had come tearing up to the flat about the bogus doctor. For a night or two he had slept badly too and had left for work looking red-eyed and exhausted, but he had soon got back to normal nights, and he was asleep now. She was looking at him. It seemed only a few days ago that she had loved lying awake and studying the outline of his face and prominent nose against the window and the stars, but it hurt whenever she thought of that now.

If she had been unfaithful he couldn't have taken it worse.

She didn't understand him, but did know that he was desperately unhappy and was avoiding her as much as he could. The election had been a godsend to him. He was out most nights, and seldom got home until eleven o'clock or later, and so she saw him only for a few minutes in the morning, to get his breakfast, and half an hour or so at night. What little he had to say was about politics. He didn't even mention the bogus doctor. Since the one time when she had stood up against him she had been baffled and defeated by his silence, and she did not know how to handle him.

At times she almost wished she could get rid of the baby; *that* might wipe out the memory.

Also at times she began to feel indignant that Fred could behave like this over something which hadn't been her fault. It was almost as if it had turned his mind. He had always been ludicrously jealous, but she had never dreamed that it could affect him like this.

He didn't seem to want to be at home; and when he was at home, he didn't want to touch her. He studiously avoided doing so. She had not felt his hands upon her in passion or in gentler love since that awful morning.

She did not know what to do.

If she did get rid of the baby——

There were moments when she told herself that it was ridiculous even to think about that, but at other times she felt that she hated the thought of the child. She did not realize that even had things been normal, even if she had never seen that fake doctor, she might have felt these moments of revulsion, that there would be times when the emotional stress of carrying her first-born would have given her absurd ideas and have made her feel as if life was a nightmare. But had things been normal there would also have been the times of a deep, ecstatic delight because of the child.

She had not known this golden mood for a long time.

Fred turned and muttered something in his sleep; he often did these days. She could never be sure what it was; the words ran into one another as if they were scrambled over the telephone, but now and again she thought she could make out two words:

"*Kill him, kill him, kill him.*"

Then she would tell herself that it couldn't be true, that such a thing would never be in his mind.

As he got up next morning, as he kissed Effie perfunctorily, as he went downstairs for his motor scooter and rode off, Fred Wilcox was thinking about the bogus doctor. Over and over again he told himself that if he ever found the man he would kill him, not only because of what had been done to Effie, but because he felt that the man had ruined their marriage. Now and again he argued with himself that it wasn't Effie's fault and it wasn't right to blame her, but he couldn't get rid of the weight of depression that was with him all the time. His works manager noticed this and watched him carefully, and the plain-faced girl with pimples and the beautiful legs watched too. She had always had a soft spot for Fred Wilcox, and had told herself that the time would come when he would want a bit more fun and games than the milk-and-watery girl he had married could give him. Sooner or later he was going to grow up and she would like to help him.

Two nights later a man named Scott Hannaford sat well back in a leather armchair and studied the copy of the *General Practitioner* which had come by the morning's post. Hannaford was a man of thirty-nine, slimly built, with a very pleasant manner. He had been on the fringe of the acting profession in his youth but had never made any success of it. One or two of the things he had learned at that time, however, came in very useful today. Make up, for instance. He knew how to dye his hair and how to restore its natural appearance without any difficulty; his natural shade was drab, and no one was ever likely to take special notice of it. There were changes one could make ,with the shape of the nose, by thrusting little cylinders up the nostrils; there were changes one could make to one's cheeks, and to the line of one's mouth, all of these without using make up.

He had another gift, too, which helped him a great deal: his ability to change the tone of his voice. He could alter it and could mimic other people without difficulty, and he enjoyed doing so. In fact he enjoyed most of life, including the spice of danger that was with him whenever he went to see a doctor and offered his services as a replacement. He selected doctors who worked alone and not in partnership, of course, and he talked to them by telephone first to get some idea of the working conditions, and whether many other people would be around—receptionists and nurses were a problem. In fact, the receptionist often controlled his decision whether to take a job or not; an alert and really competent receptionist was dangerous, but in these days when high salaries were so easy to get, a lot of doctors with a small practice employed girls who were fresh from school. They were no problem.

He had one precious certificate, stolen years ago from a doctor's surgery, and he used a liquid eraser to clean off a name once he had used the certificate. He kept it folded across the name, so the traces of roughness did not attract much attention.

He found himself getting bolder and bolder with each success.

He was never *quite* sure what had started him on this; it had been a bit of a practical joke really. And yet it had been more than a joke. He had always been strangely tongue-tied and diffident where women were concerned. Possibly a dragon of a foster-mother had been partly responsible for that. At first he had got satisfaction out of looking at pictures. There were a lot of books of nudes about, on sale almost anywhere in London, with girls whose statistics were utterly unbelievable; whose breasts were positively *balloon*-like. He had pored over the pictures and next had read a few mildly pornographic stories, then had felt a desire to see whether any girls *were* like the pictures or whether they were fake photography. In his days as an actor he had once played the part of a doctor, having to examine girl patients behind a screen, to the enormous delight of the audience if not of the actresses. He could remember to this day being slapped in the face by a redhead.

The idea had gradually developed from his remembrances of those days. Why should a doctor be able to see everything when *he* couldn't? Supposing he posed as a doctor? Now he had posed so often that he almost felt like one.

It was several days since he had been active, and although at one time he had allowed weeks to pass between getting one job and another, it was more difficult these days. He walked about, seeing women who passed by, seeing neighbours, even seeing little Gerda, the German maid at the house where he had two rooms, seeing all the women as they probably were when they had no clothes on. It was a compulsion, and he could no longer wait patiently. Graphic pictures and recollection of the different women who had passed through his hands were not enough. If he was out of a job he was restless.

A Dr. Osbert Jones was advertising for a locum for a period of three weeks. Dr. Jones asked for a married man but did not insist on it. His surgery was in a street which lay behind Putney High Street, the kind of middle-class area which Hannaford preferred. He did not enjoy the slum areas or the big working-class areas, and he did not think he would feel safe in the better-class residential areas. Dr. Jones's district should be just about right. He would telephone the good doctor first thing in the morning, for the advertisement said that the position was urgent as Jones had already been let down by another locum who had been taken ill. A doctor in a hurry was more easily satisfied than one with plenty of time.

Hannaford went to bed and filled his mind with fantasies, but there was one fantasy which did not even occur to him— the fantasy that a man was lying in bed and saying in his sleep:

"*Kill him, kill him, kill him.*"

There was another thing he did not know; that the police had searched all medical journals and had talked to all doctors who were advertising for locums.

On his way to work next morning, Fred Wilcox was slowed down behind a Jaguar, and saw the word 'doctor' on a windscreen sticker. He was alongside the car for several minutes, because of a roadblock, and kept glancing in. The doctor was middle-aged and grey-haired, and in no way resembled the bogus one. It was a shiny magazine Fred saw lying on the back seat which made him begin to think, a professional magazine, the *G.P. Weekly*.

The roadblock gradually cleared. Fred sped on, already late for work, but more preoccupied than worried. If you wanted to get a job as a *locum tenens*, or whatever it was, how would you go about it? You would advertise, of course—in the *G.P. Weekly*! Now that he thought about it, that was what one of the newspapers had said: that the bogus brute had answered advertisements from doctors. So why shouldn't he find out which doctors in the London area were advertising for a locum?

Where could he get hold of a *G.P. Weekly*? Were they on sale at news-stands? He was in Sydenham High Street, and knew where to find a big W. H. Smith news-stand and bookshop. He slowed down, turned into a side street, parked, and went to the counter.

A teen-age girl smiled at him.

"We don't keep it in stock, but we can get it for you."

"I—er—I just wanted to see something in one," muttered Fred. Now that he was running up against a difficulty, the idea seemed to lose much of its attraction. "I don't know that I'd want it every week."

"I'll see if we've got one you could have a *look* at," said the girl.

She ducked under the counter and reappeared with a copy of the paper he had seen in the doctor's car. He smiled his thanks, not realizing how attractive his nervous manner made him. He moved to the end of the counter and turned over the pages, finding the classified advertisements at the back. There was a column headed: *Locums Wanted.* He read it eagerly, his hands tightening on the shiny surface of the paper. Several of the advertising doctors were out of London, but one was in London—not really near Smith's, but not too far away: at Putney. A Dr. Osbert Jones wanted help urgently. The address was easy to remember: *66 May Street, Putney.* He repeated that to himself over and over again: *66 May Street, Putney.* He closed the book, thanked the girl, and did not realize that she watched him until he was out of sight. *66 May Street, Putney.* He went to his motor scooter and straddled it, the number and name of the street going through his mind. Why shouldn't he watch the place, and if the swine turned up in answer to the advertisement—well, why shouldn't he?

He started the engine, and suddenly thought: "What about the garage?" He tried to remember where there was a telephone kiosk, then saw a Post Office on the other side of the street; there would be a kiosk in it. He hurried, and was half-way across the street when he realized that the engine was still running, so he had to go back to switch it off. He kept licking his lips, he was so tense. *66 May Street, Putney.* He knew the number of the garage, and recognized the voice of the boss's secretary who answered.

"It's Fred Wilcox here," he said. "I've got some trouble with my hand, can't get in today. Tell the boss, will you?"

"Why, of course, Fred. I do hope it's not serious."

"Not too bad," he said. "I expect I'll be in tomorrow."

He rang off before the girl could speak again, and went out to the motor scooter. Now that his mind was made up, he felt as if everyone was staring at him. His heart palpitated as he drove off, and he had travelled a mile towards central London before remembering that to get to Putney it would be best to cut across towards Clapham and Wandsworth. He knew the

London district well and, once he was thinking clearly, made good speed.

Putney High Street, thronged even at half past nine in the morning, was familiar to him because he and Effie had often come there in their courting days; it had been a complete change of district, just like a day's holiday. Along there, not far from the old windmill, was the bower where he had first made love to Effie.

He turned into May Street, saw the numbers, and realized that Number 66 was on a corner. He propped the scooter up against the kerb, opened the repair kit, and took out a spanner, the largest tool in the kit. He slid the spanner down his trousers, the belt holding it firm, and began to walk towards the house where a doctor's red lamp showed and the sun glistened on a brass plate. Two men were working on a water hydrant near the corner, but he took no notice of them. He hardly knew what to do now that he was there. He walked past the house, and for some distance up the street, looking over his shoulder from time to time. Then he walked back. He could not possibly know whether the man he hated was there or not, even whether the doctor was in. He stood by the brass plate which said that surgery hours were from nine o'clock until ten daily, and in the evening from six until seven. The front of the house needed painting, but the lawn was beautifully kept and the flower beds were already planted with next year's wall-flowers. He walked across the road again, feeling awkward because of the spanner. The two men seemed to be having trouble with the hydrant. He recrossed the road. It was a quarter to ten, and several people came away from Number 66, while several others went in. Some were women. That was what Effie had done one day: gone to a doctor——

He clenched his fists.

If he ever got his hands on the phoney he would kill him.

A shiny Triumph Herald turned into the street, slowed down and stopped just beyond Number 66. A man got out, about Fred's own build, looked at the house and then went through the gateway. The men at the hydrant appeared to be intrigued by this, which was a change, for they spent most of their time looking about aimlessly. Fred Wilcox drew closer. He had never seen a picture of the man he sought, except the

one made up by the *Identikit*, but from what Effie had said
and from the description he had read in the Sex Special, this
could easily be the one. The suspect did not go to the surgery
entrance, but along a path which bisected the lawn and to the
door marked: *Private*. A young girl let him in and closed the
door.

Fred's heart was hammering now; it was as if he knew that
his compulsion had brought him there at the right moment.

He walked across the road, back again, then up and down,
up and down, fighting against the impulse to rush to the
house, to bang the door down, to attack the man inside. His
fingers itched to take out the spanner. *Supposing it wasn't the
bogus beast?* But it must be, he was the same build, he looked
like the description, and the newspapers had made it clear that
he always changed the colour of his hair, so that didn't matter.
Fred paced back and forth, but stayed close to the door
marked *Private*. More people went in at the surgery, but no
more came out.

The door opened when Fred was only twenty yards away
from it, and two men appeared, the young motorist and a
grey-haired man.

"On Friday, then," the older man said.

"Friday it is," agreed the young man briskly. "Good morning, Dr. Jones."

The speaker turned and walked towards the street, and
as he did so, Wilcox reached the gate. Something in Wilcox's
manner must have signalled a warning, for the young man
missed a step. The door closed behind him. A man called out
from somewhere nearby, but all Fred could hear was the drum-
ming in his ears. He pushed the gate open with his foot, and
said:

"I'm going to kill you."

He snatched the spanner from his waistband, and leapt.
His victim jumped back, thrusting out his hands to fend off his
assailant. He saw the glare in Fred's eyes, saw the spanner
smash down towards his head.

He screamed.

The spanner struck him on the forehead, the blow diverted
only by an inch or two by his right arm.

Fred drew back to strike again when the two men who had

been by the hydrant rushed at him from behind, carrying him down. He fought desperately and wildly, but they mastered him.

The young man, who was not Scott Hannaford, lay on the neat lawn, with blood oozing from the wound in his head.

14

REASON TO FEAR

ON that particular morning Gideon was feeling as satisfied with his job as he was ever likely to be. No crime of major importance had occurred to compel the Yard to swing most of its attention over to it, and the daily calendar of crime was being handled with that smooth efficiency which always showed to best advantage when nothing major had occurred to throw the Yard off balance. Only Parsons was really working all hours, and since the capture of Jefferson Miles, even he had been much less tense, though he still had his work cut out, for the F.F.P. campaign was hotting up. The real danger as far as the police could see, however, had threatened from the clash between Quatrain's party and the F.F.P. group, but now the teeth of the Q Men had been drawn by one of its own leaders. The irony of this greatly reassured Gideon and he knew it also reassured Parsons. It was as if a kind of benign fate watched over England, and whenever real trouble threatened to break up the continuity of political freedom, something happened to remove the threat. It was due simply to the fact that on the whole the British were not receptive to any cause presented by extremists or fanatics. The Fascists had never made great progress, despite those times in the middle thirties when it had looked as though they might one day become a power.

Gideon knew that he was being very smug whenever he allowed himself to think or talk like this, but the present mood of satisfaction was not one which he could easily lose. That was undoubtedly due to what had been so abruptly terminated at Park Towers.

His only present anxiety was shared by Ripple, of the Special Branch, about the interest which had been shown in the nuclear physicist Travaritch. So far Ripple had discovered nothing against the man, either past or present. He had checked the screening which had been routine when Travaritch had first gone to Harwell and could find nothing wrong with it. He had not heard again from Dancy, and was sure that if Dancy had discovered anything else about Travaritch, and who was taking an interest in him, he would have telephoned.

Lemaitre came bustling in.

"You going across to Great Marlborough Street, George?"

"No," said Gideon.

"Why not, you mug?" Lemaitre, on this cold day, had on a thick yellow sweater beneath his greeny-grey Harris tweed jacket, a suit for the Highlands which lent a touch of brightness to the office. He wore a tartan bow tie, and his face was as shiny as if it had been polished. "Just because you think they'll take more pictures of you? You ought to be there, George. The Great British Public and the Benighted British Press expect you."

"I know they do," said Gideon. "But Parsons can handle the Jefferson Miles job better than I can." He leaned back in his chair, smoothing the bowl of a large pipe which he kept in his pocket. "You look as if you're all dressed up for the Highland Games. What's the idea?"

"Want to cheer this morgue up a bit," said Lemaitre. "Listen, George. Miles is up for the second hearing, he's bound to be sent for trial today. You ought to be there."

"I'm not going," said Gideon flatly.

"Just because——"

"If you must know, it's because Parsons has worked his guts out on this case, and I want him to see it through. If I have to turn up at the Old Bailey later, all right. Just now it's his job, and I've got plenty to do here." As he looked down at reports on his desk his telephone bell rang. He answered. "Gideon."

"Yes, right away," he said, and rang off. "Piper's coming down." He thumbed through the reports, noticed that on the one marked *The Quack* there was a recent note that a Dr. Osbert Jones had advertised for a *locum tenens* and was due to interview applicants that morning. Piper had two men watching his house in case the Quack applied for the job. Gideon closed the file as there was a tap at the door and Piper came in. As always when he was edgy, Piper was cracking his knuckles. "Morning, Joe, I was just checking your case."

"Morning, George," Piper said. "There's been a hell of a do this morning."

"The Quack got away again?"

"I wish that was all," said Piper. "You remember that one of the women he examined was named Wilcox? Well . . ."

Piper told the story he had just been told by telephone. Lemaitre stopped working and watched him, while Gideon's thumb ran over and over the bowl of his pipe. Piper finished at last, leaning against the mantelpiece and scowling. "Don't see that we could have done anything else. Our chaps had no idea what Wilcox was after. In fact, except for his beak of a nose he fitted the description of the Quack, and they thought he was going to apply for the job. They hadn't any reason to expect him to go berserk."

Gideon said slowly, "Not a case for blame anywhere. How is the injured man?"

"On the danger list. The blow cracked his skull, and he's being operated on now."

"What does Wilcox say?"

"Apparently it sobered him up with a jerk," said Piper. "He'd been shouting and raving that the Quack had it coming to him, but when they convinced him that he'd got the wrong man——" Piper broke off.

"Sure it *is* the wrong man?"

"Positive. The one Wilcox attacked is a Dr. Fairweather. A couple of telephone calls were enough to prove that he was somewhere else when the Quack was active. In fact, Fairweather was in France during the time the Quack was busy at Sydenham and examined Mrs. Wilcox. We're no nearer the Quack than we ever were. Now this——"

"Wilcox's wife know about it?" interrupted Gideon.

"Dowsett's going to see her," said Piper. "I'm not too happy about that, he's a cold-blooded beggar, but it's not a job we can take away from the division. Fairweather's wife is at the hospital."

Gideon felt as if cold fingers were clutching him.

"So he was married too."

"Married, with two-year-old twins."

After a long pause Gideon said slowly, "Go and see Littleton, will you, and ask him to handle this with the press. It's a public relations job rather than a news item. We want as much sob stuff sympathy as we can get from the *Globe* and anyone else, and we want that *Identikit* picture displayed as often as we can get it. Also we want a special appeal made through the press to all the women whom this bogus swine saw, asking them to keep a very close lookout wherever they go."

Piper was looking brighter.

"I'll see that it's stepped up, George. I won't worry you unless something goes wrong."

"That suits me," said Gideon.

Piper went out, and the morning's usual routine briefing began. There was still no clue in the search for the murderer of the woman whose body had been found in a well in Cornwall. Three other provincial investigations, with Yard men on the spot, also were negative. A chief inspector had arrived in London from Stockholm the previous night, with a report on an investigation into the activities of an Englishman who was suspected of a big art theft in Sweden.

"He's their man all right," the inspector asserted. "They want me to dig as deeply as I can into his background and let them know the result."

"Do that, stay with it, and keep me in touch," said Gideon.

A grey-haired superintendent who had spent a week in Paris came in. He had been working with the Sûreté Nationale in a search for a Bristol solicitor who had disappeared, leaving his clients' funds in a sad way.

"He's there all right, I've seen him," the superintendent said. "The Sûreté are keeping a watch on him and will make sure he doesn't do a flit."

"Fix the extradition papers with our solicitors and the Home Office, and go and get him," Gideon ordered.

Detective Sergeant Whittle, standing in for Parsons, who was already at Great Marlborough Street, came into the office for the first time in his life. He was so stiff and formal with nerves that Gideon felt sorry for him. He sent Lemaitre out of the office to help the man feel a little more at ease. Whittle, in his early thirties, very fair haired, with darker eyebrows and exceptionally pale grey eyes, stood at attention.

"The superintendent particularly asked me to report to you, sir."

"What about?" asked Gideon. Parsons was doubtless blooding Whittle, who was believed to have great potential.

"The burglaries at the homes of election candidates, sir."

"We had more of them?"

"There were three more last night, yes, sir."

"We had two isolated ones, then three on each of three consecutive nights, and then a lull for a few days. Is that right?"

"Yes, sir. And—I'm afraid I slipped up."

"How?"

"It's a very busy time, sir. We need men at the meetings where the F.F.P. people are likely to be in strength, as well as at the usual places, committee rooms and suchlike. After the arrest of Jefferson Miles I thought it safe to take the surveillance off certain candidates, including Robert Talmad. He was one of those whose home was burgled last night."

"What about the others?"

"They wouldn't have been watched in any case."

"Can't see why you should blame yourself for that," said Gideon. "How've you been trying to handle this?"

"Through the divisions, sir. I have been acting as liaison on behalf of the Yard. I've talked to the three divisions affected last night, and there is one possible line of inquiry."

"What is it?"

"A member of Mr. Talmad's committee went to his house for some papers, and met the thief coming out. It was just one man, sir. He kicked the committee-man on the shins, and escaped. Among the men I've been checking on is one called Mason, Shins Mason, who——"

"I know Mason."

"I expect you do, sir." Whittle became beetroot-red. "Well, I thought it would be a good idea to ask Mr. Christie of NE to find out what Mason's been doing lately, and where he was last night."

"Do just that," approved Gideon.

"Thank you, sir." Whittle, only slightly relaxed, turned and went out, and closed the door too hard.

Lemaitre came in, with a grin.

"They do breed 'em these days, don't they? What's old Parsons up to? Think this is a kindergarten?"

"Whittle will do," said Gideon. His internal telephone bell rang as he spoke and he glanced at his watch. It was a quarter past eleven, and the Jefferson Miles hearing was due at eleven-thirty. For some reason he was very jumpy about it, and wondered if he had made a mistake in staying away.

"The Commissioner would like a word with you," a woman's voice told him. Gideon wrenched himself from the doubts about staying away from the police court hearing. "A moment, please." It was a long moment, and Gideon straightened his collar and then suddenly remembered how Whittle had been affected, and wondered how he, George Gideon, had behaved when he had first seen the Commissioner himself.

Scott-Marle was back to formality.

"Commander."

"Yes, sir?"

"I assumed you would be at Great Marlborough Street this morning."

"Nothing there that can't be handled without me, sir."

"I see. Well, I didn't ring up about that, but I would like a report on the hearing tonight," said Scott-Marle. "What can you tell me about a man named Travaritch, Professor Travaritch?"

Gideon's pulse began to beat fast.

"He's a physicist at Harwell, sir, working on a project called Keyboard. I heard from one of our informants—the private agent Dancy, in fact—that interest was being shown in him by some unknown person. As you will know, I discussed it with Commander Ripple. Nothing has developed from that, as far as I'm aware."

"I certainly didn't know about it," said Scott-Marle, Gideon was disturbed, for that could only mean that Ripple had not sent through a report about Travaritch. Now Scott-Marle would realize that Gideon had thought one had gone through. "Have you any idea who is making the inquiries about Travaritch?"

"No, sir, not yet. He is being very closely watched."

"Not very well, I fear."

Gideon's heart thumped.

"Apparently Travaritch has disappeared from the Harwell Establishment," said Scott-Marle. "He appears to have realized that he was under observation. The establishment security officials say that our men were not discreet enough."

Gideon did not speak right away. He knew the sensitivity of the various service ministries and everyone associated with nuclear research. Security had been tightened up, and a number of C.I.D. men had been seconded to the various ministries; that had resulted in some feeling between the existing security chiefs and the seconded men. It was all a little silly but probably inevitable, as he had realized when he had worked out the new system with Ripple and others. He had been one of an advisory committee of five.

Somewhere along the line he had slipped up.

He knew just how it was; he had left the reports and the handling of the situation to Ripple, and Ripple had left it to him. Each should have checked with the other and made absolutely sure. It was no excuse for him that Ripple hadn't reported; he himself should have, and risked duplicating the report. As he admitted that to himself he felt a flush creeping up from his neck to his cheeks.

"I would like you to confer with Commander Ripple and prepare a joint report for me," Scott-Marle said. "Can it be ready by five o'clock this afternoon?"

"An interim report can."

"That will do. Thank you, Commander."

Scott-Marle rang off. Gideon sat absolutely still, the blood still darkening his cheeks. Lemaitre began, "Did he tear a strip off——" and stopped, as if he realized that something had happened which affected Gideon profoundly. He went on with the report he was writing, but kept glancing up at Gideon covertly.

Gideon stood up slowly, and went to the window, to the view he loved, the smiling water, London. He could just see the lamps on the terrace of the House of Commons. For the first time for weeks he looked at it without thinking of the election.

Amanda Tenby walked with her long strides and her feline stealth towards Braine Street, Highgate, where she was to meet Lady Wallis and would get a message from Daniel Ronn about Travaritch. She was aware that a uniformed policeman was always on duty within sight of the Wallis house, but that was common to the houses of many of the Action Committee, and she did not worry about it. Demure-faced Lady Wallis opened the door for her, and drew her inside.

"Is there any message?" Amanda wanted to know.

"There is and there isn't," said Lady Wallis. Her voice was so gentle.

"Has he got it?" Amanda demanded.

"I don't know, I really don't know," said Lady Wallis. "I do understand that the security officers have been showing some interest in him, dear. Isn't it a good job that Daniel made sure that no one was likely to connect him with us?"

Amanda didn't speak.

"Amanda, my dear——"

"If we don't get it, we've wasted our time and our money and we won't have a chance to show how serious we are," Amanda said in a taut voice. "Has Travaritch betrayed us? Is that what you're trying to say?"

"I don't think so, dear. But Daniel says that he is asking for more money, in view of the extra risk involved. And he says that he thinks it may be necessary for him to get out of the country at very short notice, so he needs a passport, I'm afraid, and tickets and things."

"If that man's fooling us, I'll murder him!"

"Don't talk like that, Amanda, please. There's no reason to think he *is* fooling us, you know. If the security men are watching him, then the risk is indeed much greater, and he would naturally expect to be paid. After all, if a man was found guilty of taking one of these things *away* from Harwell and offering it to a third party who might represent a foreign power, it would be a very serious situation, wouldn't it? I mean, he could be sent to prison for forty years—isn't that the term that the naval dockyard people were sent to prison for?

think we have to be realistic, Amanda. After all, this *was* our idea, dear, and we always knew that it would cost a lot of money."

Amanda asked, through her teeth, "How much more does he want?"

"Daniel said something about ten thousand pounds."

"How much will *you* find?"

"Well, you know that we're not as well off as we used to be, but we will certainly make a contribution—ten per cent, say. Or perhaps fifteen—I really don't think we could go above fifteen. Daniel is going to telephone early this afternoon, for an answer one way or the other. The trouble is, Amanda, that if we refuse what Travaritch now asks, then he might turn spiteful, and report what we have been suggesting to him. It was a thousand pities that you and Daniel ever showed yourselves to Travaritch, so that he knew whom he was dealing with. I'm afraid that was a grave mistake."

Amanda said, "Lucy, do you trust Daniel?"

"Trust him, dear?" The old lady's voice rose. "Why, of course I do. I think I am shocked to hear you ask. What on earth made you?"

"Daniel isn't very well off, is he? If I thought he was putting up the price without telling Travaritch——"

"Oh, I'm sure that it's nothing of the kind!"

"I hope you're right," said Amanda. She went to the window, where Venetian blinds were drawn. A policeman walked past slowly, and she could just hear the plodding of his footsteps; it was as if she was suspected, as well as Travaritch—if Travaritch really was. After a long pause, she said, "All right. But that must be the last increase. Make them understand that, Lucy."

"I will, I will indeed," said Lady Wallis.

Gideon did not go to see Ripple immediately; he wanted to be sure that he handled the interview in the right way and did not imply criticism. Ripple could be touchy, and on his job that wasn't surprising. Gideon felt no easier than he had when the flush had crept over his face and when Lemaitre had stared at him so anxiously. To try to make sure that Lemaitre had no chance to ask questions, Gideon opened some files, but he did not study them closely until he reached the slim one about Travaritch, which he always kept locked in his desk. There was so little information. A record of Dancy's telephone call, of what he himself had arranged with Ripple—there were only a few notes about that—and his own notes about the importance of the investigation. There were three reports from Harwell and three from Special Branch men whom Ripple had detailed to watch Travaritch.

Gideon sat back in his chair, forgetting that he didn't want to show his feelings to Lemaitre. It was over half an hour since Scott-Marle had talked to him, and he felt no easing of the fear. And it was fear. He could look back over his years at the Yard and see in retrospect the long line of security failures —some even disasters—which had occurred in England. Sometimes it had been the fault of the Yard, more often the fault of one of the service ministries or the Foreign Office. He had never studied the cause of the failures closely, as it was Ripple's job, and the job of other men who had led the Special Branch, but he had studied it. He was fully aware of the repercussions and the ramifications of the big spy trials. He knew how the rest of the world would feel and what they would say and how they would think if there was another leakage of secrets from Great Britain. Fuchs, Burgess and MacLean, the trio of spies at the Portland Dockyard—these were the more disastrous failures, but there had been others. British security had suffered too many setbacks. It could not really be trusted. Then had come his part in it, the great reorganization of security arrangements after the Portland scandal. Six top Yard men had gone to the research establishments to organize security, and as far as he knew had made a good job. He, George Gideon, had certainly been satisfied.

The reputation of Scotland Yard remained high throughout the world. In spite of a few minor failures, it was still regarded as incorruptible and super-efficient. It was a part of him. His pride was never in himself but in the Yard, and now he—he himself—had slipped up in such a way that another great scandal might blow up and smear not only the country but the Yard itself.

"George," Lemaitre said.

Gideon looked up.

"You all right, George?"

"Yes."

"What's up?"

"Nothing," Gideon lied. "Nothing that can't be put right." He hoped to God that was true. "The Old Man doesn't want me to discuss it with anyone."

After a pause Lemaitre said, with that prescience which sometimes gave him a promise of brilliance:

"That Travaritch thing or the Tenby bitch?"

Gideon said, "When I can tell you, I'll tell you." He got up, and it was on the tip of his tongue to say that he was going to see Ripple but he realized in time that if he did he would confirm Lemaitre's guess. "I'll be back in half an hour or so. You carry on, will you?"

He went out.

Lemaitre leaned back in his chair, stared at the door, and said very slowly:

"My God, what's on? I've never seen him like that before. Never."

Gideon was thinking: We've got to find Travaritch. If we have to call on every house in the country, we've got to find him. In any other mood he would have told himself that he was talking like Lemaitre; there was no way of making house-to-house calls, for it would take the whole of the police force weeks, and there was so little time.

15

OUTBURST

PARSONS, at Great Marlborough Street, was feeling on top of himself and the situation, but also feeling puzzled. Jefferson Miles seemed to have no one to defend him. He had expected to find that Quatrain had briefed counsel, even for the police court hearing, but there was not even a solicitor, except the man watching for the Home Office and the Yard. Quatrain and two of his supporters were in the packed public gallery. The Press benches were just as crowded, and seething with the kind of excitement that any *cause célèbre* generated. The only completely dispassionate people present seemed to be the magistrate, Mr. Thompson; the magistrate's clerk, a young man who appeared set on following the tradition of irascibility-cum-confidence; and Quatrain.

The magistrate's clerk read the charge.

Thompson, who looked rather like an American Indian, partly because he had just come back from a cruise to the Bahamas and his skin tanned easily, sat with his hands clasped in front of him. His hooked nose, with the rather wide, distended nostrils, added to the illusion.

"Has the accused anything to say?" he asked.

Everyone looked at Jefferson Miles, who was looking at Quatrain. He did not speak, but gripped the rail of the dock tightly.

"I will repeat my question," said Thompson. "Has the prisoner anything to say?"

Miles drew in a deep breath, which puffed up his chest like a balloon.

"I'll say what I've got to say at the trial."

"It may have escaped your notice that you have not yet been committed for trial," the magistrate said. "It has not passed my notice that you appear to be unaware of the gravity of the situation in which you find yourself. Who represents the police?"

A grey-haired solicitor stood up.

"I do, your honour. And I would like first to call evidence of arrest. Ah—Superintendent Parsons, sir."

"And the accused?"

"I understand he wishes to conduct his own case," said the clerk.

Miles nodded.

"Very well," said Thompson.

Parsons had done it all so often, had held the Bible and sworn the oath and stepped forward to depose, but he had never felt anything like this. All the tension that had been injected into the election campaign because of what had happened at Quatrain's house seemed to have been compressed into this small, oak-panelled courtroom. The situation was as explosive as one of Miles's bombs.

Parsons gave simple evidence of charging and arresting Miles, and went on:

"I would like the prisoner to be committed for trial, your

honour. I believe that it would be in the public interest not to submit any but formal evidence at this hearing."

"And who is the best judge of the public interest in this matter?" Thompson had obviously been annoyed by Miles, and was not going to make things easy.

"With respect, sir, I am the officer in charge of the measures necessary to ensure that the general election takes place in an atmosphere free from all prejudice, and for that reason I submit that it is in the public interest to present as little evidence as possible. I can if necessary produce witnesses, including Mr. Roland Quatrain, to testify that the accused was in fact arrested after being prevented from starting another explosion which would have caused considerable damage. I can produce a witness to identify the accused. I can also call witnesses to testify that among the accused's close friends is an employee of a firm of pyrotechnic manufacturers who has had access to and facilities for making the kind of explosive unit which has been used in this case. Between now and the time of the trial by jury, if your honour so directs the trial to be held, the police expect to be able to submit evidence which will prove that the accused's objectives were two-fold: one, to stir up sufficient public unrest and agitation to make the holding of the general election difficult in the proper atmosphere and, second, to remove from proximity to his then friend and leader certain individuals whom he believed to be exercising a moderating influence on his leader. I think I may venture to say that there is no doubt whatsoever that these witnesses will be forthcoming, and some of them are in fact available today. Nevertheless, I ask for a committal, your honour."

Thompson said, "Ugh." He looked at Quatrain and at Miles. Miles seemed to be clenching his teeth, and his grip on the dock rail was so tight that even across the courtroom one could see his knuckles gleaming white.

"And have you still nothing to say?" Thompson asked him. Miles opened his mouth.

Quatrain sat with a hand raised in front of him, as if to command the accused to say nothing in his own defence. There was almost unbearable tension in the court, generated partly by the conflict between Quatrain and Miles, and partly by awareness of the influence they had tried to exert on the political scene. Miles licked his lips. Quatrain kept his hand up. Parsons glanced at Thompson.

"Very well," the magistrate said at last. "In the circumstances I shall accede to the request from the police, particularly as the accused obviously has nothing to say."

"*Nothing!*" Miles cried. He raised his clenched hands towards the raftered ceiling. "*Nothing?* What I have to say is the most important thing in the whole world. *That* man has betrayed his country and betrayed everything he stands for. *That* man, Roland Quatrain, should be here, not I." Thompson opened his mouth as if to protest, but Miles's torrent of words swept over him. "*He* should be standing in the dock arraigned before the people of all England. That man had the vision and the opportunity given to no one in history before, of leading the nation from the brink of disaster, the brink of famine, the brink of economic collapse. There is the man who could have led this nation to the bright uplands of prosperity, who could have won the devotion of a people who have lost greatness, and given them vision and greatness and power. He could have led the British people so that once again they would lead the world. And he has betrayed them."

"Please stop at once," Thompson said clearly.

Miles did not seem to notice the interruption.

"That man has preferred the vain trappings of a so-called democracy. He has submitted to the sell-out of our history to Europe and to the United States. He has helped to tread this great nation into the dust. He could have wiped opposition from the face of the land, he could have created the perfect state, a shining example to the whole world, to the universe beyond the world. He should be dragged out of this place and strung up on the nearest tree. *You!*" screamed Miles, and he leaned forward and shook his fists at Quatrain, his face suffused with red, as if he would burst, his great body thrusting against the oak of the dock. "You, you devil, you ought to be hanged and drawn and quartered, like traitors of our greatest age. I worshipped you. The country could have worshipped you."

Thompson seemed stunned to silence.

Parsons, three policemen, two warders, and an usher drew

close to Miles. Saliva was showering from his lips, the only part of his face without colour were those lips. He began to shake the dock, and soon the inevitable happened. He swung over the front of the dock to try to get at Quatrain, but the group of men made a solid barrier and they bore him down, struggling, screaming, shouting.

Among those who watched was Catherine Miller, who had been told that she might be called upon as a witness, and had been terrified in case she was, for fear her name should get into the newspapers, and her parents find out. Since Parsons and Gideon had talked to her she had known moments of comfort, but the gloom of unhappiness shrouded her most of the time. She had not seen her lover again, but he had telephoned her twice, at the shipping office in the City where she worked. She knew that it would not be long before everything was over between them. He had talked of money, and she had shrunk from the very idea of being paid off, but as she watched the proceedings and realized that her immediate dread was over—for she would not now be called as a witness—she thought of her predicament. She could not work much longer; already some of the other girls were pretty sure of the truth. Without money she could not live on her own. She dreaded having to confess to her father, and her mother would be horrified too.

Parsons came across to her when it was over.

"Glad we didn't need you," he said. "Will you come with me, below the dock? There are one or two little formalities to go through." As he took her arm it crossed her mind that it was remarkable that after having so much on his mind he could spare time and thought for her, but she had come to take that for granted. He led the way through a doorway and down a short flight of stairs, and then said:

"Did I tell you I've a good friend in the Brighton Police Force?"

"No," she said. Brighton was near her home.

"Well, I have. And I had a word with him yesterday and he went to have a word with your father. Everything will be all right."

Alarm flared up in her.

"Oh, you shouldn't! You'd no right to. Oh——"

That was the moment when she saw her father. It was no illusion this time, no passing likeness. It was—*Dad*. He was coming towards her across a wide passage which was crowded with people, including policemen and warders. He was very close to Quatrain. He was smiling. He nodded to Parsons, and said:

"Thank you very much, Superintendent. Thank you indeed. Cath, I've got a taxi waiting outside. We're going straight home in it. Somehow we have to work this problem out between us."

Parsons watched the girl as she went off, her father's arm about her. Tears were spilling down her cheeks. No one took any notice, because Jefferson Miles was still making abortive attempts to free himself.

The editorial, London *Evening Times*:

In a London police court this morning we saw an exhibition of megalomania, unbridled and uncontrolled, and caught a glimpse of how hideous the face of this nation could become under the control of such men. It may seem absurd to contemplate even the possibility, but it is a sobering thought that other nations, once believed to be thoroughly democratic, have in fact fallen under the spell of ranting dictators. If we go near to contempt of court in speaking thus frankly, we do so humbly but with a deep conviction that it is necessary to tell the British electors exactly what happened. It is to some degree reassuring that the man now committed for trial by jury in the best English tradition was not the leader of the men among whom he worked. The leader has shown a quality of statesmanship which, considering the circumstances, can only be admired.

One of the gravest features in this case, the full truth of which will not come out until the trial, is the fact that Jefferson Miles—what a tragic irony that the name Jefferson should have been given to a man who rejected freedom—believed every word he said. Fool, bigot, fanatic he might be; but in his way he followed his star, and believed it the right star to follow.

From the London *Evening Times*, page 1:

Attacked by Man with Spanner

Dr. Eustace Fairweather, who was about to act as *locum tenens* for Dr. Osbert C. Jones, of 66 May Street, Putney, was attacked by a man with a spanner as he left Dr. Jones's surgery this morning. Dr. Fairweather is in hospital in a serious condition.

Frederick Allen Wilcox of Stepp Street, Sydenham, the attacker, has been charged with attempted murder and will appear at West London Police Court tomorrow.

From the London *Evening Times*, page 4:

MORE CANDIDATES ROBBED

The police are baffled by the series of daring burglaries at the homes of general election candidates. Money and valuables have been stolen, but there is a possibility that the burglaries have some political motivation. Three candidates' homes were entered last night.

At the home of Mr. Robert Talmad, Independent candidate for Williton, a friend of Mr. Talmad's was attacked by the thief, who hacked him on the shins.

Scotland Yard are redoubling their efforts to apprehend the thief, who . . .

From the London *Evening Times*, page 5:

WHAT IS THE BATTLE COMMITTEE
PLANNING?

Behind the Scenes Threat

The Fight for Peace campaign, or that part of it controlled by the Battle Committee—which is quite distinct from the Committee of 100 and also from the Group led by Canon Collins—is planning a great demonstration.

No one yet knows what it will be.

So far their members, like those of other groups with the same objectives, have heckled at out-door and indoor meetings, making things uncomfortable for candidates who refuse to answer their questions. The members of the committee have drawn up a questionnaire about attitudes towards Nuclear

Disarmament and have sent it to all candidates, all election agents, all newspapers, and leading citizens in most constituencies. A door-to-door distribution of Fight for Peace leaflets has been made in many constituencies, showing that the organization is nation-wide. There can be no one in the country who is unaware of what they require—to force this country to give up the nuclear deterrent, to send the bombs back to the United States or to Europe. The rights and wrongs of this belief are irrelevant at this time. What is important is the rumours of some sensational demonstration planned between now and the date of the election, and intended to sway electors to cast their votes for those candidates approved by the Battle Committee.

If the methods of persuasion are within the law, no one will complain.

If they are against the law, they constitute a threat to our free system of government, and we hope that the Home Secretary will instruct the police throughout the nation to act swiftly and with whatever severity is called for. This is a democracy. Any attempt to influence political decisions or the electors of the country by illegal or unconstitutional methods must be stamped out.

From the London *Opinion*, page 3:

Everyone in this country has a right to his vote, to freedom of expression, and to his opinion—and unless he or she is uttering treason—that is, the overthrow of the Government by force, or the overthrow of the monarchy, or endangering the safety of the realm—he or she should be allowed to say what he likes where he likes within the bounds of decent language.

This journal feels strongly that there are a great number of genuine idealists in the various groups who wish us to withdraw from participation in nuclear armament races. They believe what they preach. They make considerable sacrifices for their beliefs. Yet there is something suspiciously—dangerously—like a witch hunt going on among these people. They cannot meet in one another's houses without the police watching. They cannot ask a question at a public meeting without the eye of the police upon them. This is wrong. This is not democracy. This is not what we fought two great wars for.

The police have plenty to do in the perpetual battle against crime. They have too much to do with the warm-hearted idealists who—even if mistakenly—believe that they are serving humanity in the only way humanity can be served.

Gideon read all of this.

Barney Spicer, Shins Mason and Wilfy Darlington read the stories and editorials too.

Amanda Tenby, Daniel Ronn and most of the other members of the Battle Committee read them.

Fred Wilcox did also.

So did Cecil Libby, relaxing for a few minutes between meetings. He felt on top of the world, for his canvass was showing more support than he had expected, and the two meetings he had already addressed tonight had been enthusiastic and well-attended. He had two more before going home. His wife would be at the next one, provided their sitter-in turned up, and he always liked Jane to be on the platform whenever possible. There was even a sneaking hope that she would be at the next hall, the Catholic school hall near the café where he was sitting. That paragraph about the clerk who had been sent to prison no longer worried him.

He walked along to the meeting, saw two dozen cars parked outside, and was elated. As he entered the door a little group started cheering. The speaker, one of Libby's ward workers, stopped and began to clap. The hall, which would hold two hundred people, was three-quarters full. Two or three men stood up, and others followed. Libby felt very excited; nothing like this had ever happened to him before. He kept his wits about him, and noticed that one man in four or five was still sitting down; they would be the unconverted. But a welcome such as this was wonderful.

He began his speech. He knew that he had never reeled off policy so easily and had never felt more confident when answering questions. Let 'em all come! To put the finishing touch to his triumph, he saw Jane at the back of the hall, sitting down unobtrusively. He waved to her, and she smiled and waved back.

Then a tall, very dark man rose to ask a question, and Libby's heart missed a beat. Somehow he thought he recognized the questioner from distant days—from those days when he had been such a reckless fool. If he was right, this man had been in the general office of the firm where he had worked.

The man asked: "What does the candidate think about the condition of prisons in this country? Does he believe that convicted criminals are punished with sufficient severity?"

Libby never remembered how he answered.

At his next meeting he was flat and dull, and the meeting was unresponsive.

On the way home he told Jane what had happened.

"Oh, they'd never use that," she protested. "You're worrying yourself about nothing." Soon she went on with forced brightness: "Darling, I must tell you what Monk did today——"

Monk had climbed his first tree, but the story did nothing to dispel Libby's gloom.

"You've got to make up your mind soon," said Richard Benwell's agent. "I got that chap to ask Libby a question at his third meeting tonight, and Libby recognized him at once. He folded right up. He knows what will happen if the story gets around. And believe me, Ricky, you need every vote you can get."

Effie Wilcox had read the *Evening Times* too.

She was in the little room which she had once loved so much because it was hers and Fred's. Her mother was there, a big, bustling, hearty woman, very different from Effie, but overflowing with affection and with deep understanding. She did not keep on talking to Effie but watched her from time to time. Effie kept looking through the evening papers, making herself read most of the things, including the snippets of news about the election, especially the constituency Fred was so interested in.

Suddenly she looked up.

"Mum."

"Isn't it time you thought of bed, dear?"

"Mum—that doctor won't die, will he?"

"Don't talk nonsense. Of course he won't die."

"It says here he's in a serious condition."

"That doesn't mean that he's going to die."

"If he does——"

"How about a nice cup of tea, and an early bed?"

"If he does," persisted Effie evenly, "it would be murder, wouldn't it?"

"Now, my girl, don't let me hear you say anything like that again!"

"But it would be."

"Now, Effie——"

"Mum, do you think Mrs. Mullery will let me use her telephone?"

"What on earth do you want to use a telephone for to-night?" The big woman stood in front of her daughter, arms akimbo, and went on with pretended suspicion, "You haven't got a boy friend in the background, have you?"

"Oh, don't be ridiculous," Effie said. "You ought to know better than to say that. No, I want to find out how that doctor is. If I telephone the hospital, they'll tell me, won't they?"

After a long pause, her mother said, "You won't get any rest until you know, will you? Shall I go downstairs and ask?"

"No," Effie said. "No, I'd rather do it myself."

The telephone was in the hallway of the neighbour's flat. The light was on, the living-room door closed, the muted tones of a television sounded against the background of buzzing and squeaking on the line. At last a man answered:

"Putney Hospital."

"I want—I want to make an inquiry about a patient," Effie said, in a voice that was so low-pitched she hardly heard it herself.

"Can you speak up, please?"

"I want—I want to inquire about a patient."

"What ward, please?"

"I—I don't know. It's—it's the man who was—it's the man who——"

The operator said in gentler tones, "No hurry, miss, just tell me the name of the patient."

"Fair-Fairweather." It almost choked her.

"Dr. Fairweather? I can tell you that myself, miss. He has been operated on and the operation appears to have been successful. He is as well as can be expected. No further bulletin will be issued until tomorrow. Is that all you require?"

"Yes," Effie said weakly. She was thinking, Oh, thank God, thank God. "Yes, thank you ever so."

"Quite all right," the operator said.

"I don't know who that was," the operator confided in a nurse who was passing his office. "It wasn't Mrs. Fairweather, she's only just left the hospital. Sounds cut up, though. I wonder if Doc F has a little bit of fluff tucked away somewhere."

"Telephonists," sniffed the nurse, and went past.

Scott Hannaford read the *Evening Times* too, and he re-read the story about the attack on Dr. Fairweather at Osbert Jones's house. Nothing had yet been said in the newspapers, but several reports had made it almost certain that the attack had been on a locum. The name Wilcox made Hannaford very thoughtful.

"That's the last thing I ever expected," Hannaford said to himself. "I'll have to be careful. I wonder if the poor devil will die."

In Brixton Jail, where he was spending the night before appearing in court the next morning, Fred Wilcox kept tossing and turning on a bed which was quite comfortable. He had seen the newspapers but taken little notice of anything, except the piece which told everyone what he had done. From the moment he had realized that the man he had attacked had not been the bogus doctor his whole world had smashed —his real world, as well as the nightmare one of the past week or so. The horror of what he had done, the fact that his victim was on the danger list, the fact that he would *gladly* have killed, seemed like a new kind of nightmare. He kept shivering. He felt dreadful, and he felt so lonely. He couldn't talk to anybody; not *talk*. There had been a solicitor, and some of the policemen had been kind although some of them obviously thought he ought to be horse-whipped.

He wanted to talk, desperately, and there was only one person in the world to whom he could.

Effie.

He wanted to tell her that it had been like a cancer in his mind, that nothing he had said or done or tried to do had helped, that he had hated himself as well as the bogus doctor, *and that he had hated her* in those awful days when his mind seemed to have been twisted by the shock and by his own jealousy. He wanted to tell her that he loved her, that he couldn't live without her, that he wanted their child now, now, *now*; and he longed to talk to her about his dread of what would happen if the victim died.

He was so afraid.

Gideon wished he could talk to Kate, but it was impossible to discuss a security case with her, just as it was impossible to conceal his anxiety from her. She did not ask questions, for she knew that as soon as he could tell her he would.

There had been no word of Travaritch.

There had, as yet, been no word about anything stolen from the research unit where Travaritch worked, but he might well have photographed the documents and the *data*. That was the great danger now; that he had walked out with those vital statistics in his pockets, and might turn up in Moscow, or in Peking, or in any part of the world where Operation Keyboard had a cash value.

As he left his house next morning Gideon saw a group of a dozen people at one end of the street, each carrying sheets of paper, each holding a pencil, each sporting the yellow rosettes of the Liberal party in this constituency. As he strolled along, a plump young man came towards him; he had sheets of the electoral roll in his hand.

"Good morning, Commander. I'm John Seal."

Gideon shook hands.

"My son's been standing in for you at school, Mr. Seal. How are things going?"

"Very well, I think. We're starting the day's canvass, and hope to cover every house before we're through. It's a bit tricky with a comparatively new—well, revived—organization, but we're doing all right. Daren't ask you who you're going to vote for, dare I?"

Gideon smiled.

"You can ask," he said. He nodded to all of the others, who

were receiving instructions from an elderly man. He was at the corner, heading for his garage, when he stopped short.

"My God!" he breathed. "There *is* a way!"

Scott-Marle said thoughtfully, "I think it might be possible, Gideon. I'm not sure what the Home Secretary would feel about it, but in circumstances like these I think he would agree. Tell me again exactly how you would like to handle the situation."

"I'd like to go to the headquarters of each main party, sir. The Conservative Central Office, Transport House and Liberal party HQ in Victoria Street. I'd ask them if they would request all their constituency organizations to co-operate with the local police in requesting information about Travaritch. It wouldn't take long to get enough copies of a photograph made, we could get cracking on that at once. Within three days we could show that photograph to practically every household in the country. Any streets already canvassed by the parties we could cover ourselves."

"I see the advantages of such opportunism," agreed Scott-Marle. "I will talk to the Home Secretary at once."

"He will realize that this isn't a time for being long-winded, won't he?"

"No time for protocol," said Scott-Marle dryly. "Yes, he will realize that."

"Gideon."

"Yes, sir?"

"Go ahead with your plans for the canvass inquiry. It must be arranged separately with each local constituency, through the local police, and one simple question may be asked: 'Do you recognize this man?' Is that understood?"

"Perfectly," said Gideon. "I'll get moving."

In the turmoil of the most open general election for twenty years, the organizational leaders found time for Gideon. He pushed his way through seething crowds sorting out posters, bills, slogans, envelopes. He sensed the tension and the excitement and that mood of dedication which seemed to be as deep in one party as in another.

159

Each of the leaders listened attentively.

Each said, in effect, "Yes, of course. We'll send the request to the constituencies. Then the local police will take it from there."

Gideon, back at the Yard, felt suddenly on top of the world; here was something he could do to fight back and also make amends. Teleprinter messages went out to all provincial forces and divisions; then he, Lemaitre, Parsons and Ripple talked to chief constables. Copies of photographs of Travaritch were already coming off the presses in their tens of thousands, and being sent by special messenger or by passenger train or even by air, picked up at their destination, taken round by the local police to the local committee rooms. There the strength or the weakness of the party's organization at constituency level showed up. As the reports came in to Gideon he was impressed by the efficiency of most of them, by the number of divisions which would in fact be covered in a door-to-door canvass by at least two of the parties. Everyone would be visited, and most of the canvassing had still to be done, so the simple question could be fitted in.

A photograph of Travaritch was shown, and the simple question asked:

"Do you recognize this man?"

When it was all in hand, Gideon sat back and smiled almost cheerfully at Lemaitre and Parsons, then said:

"Now all we can do is wait. Who's coming across for a drink?"

Cecil Libby was alone in the front room of his bungalow, which was littered with envelopes, election addresses still not mailed, bills, streamers, posters, poll cards, bits of string, bottles of ink—a room which was hardly recognizable. In a small corner cupboard he kept the bottle of whisky against emergencies—he seldom touched spirits—but tonight he went across and opened the cupboard, took out the bottle and a glass, poured himself out a finger, then realized that there was no soda water. He went to the kitchen for some tap water. As he reached the door of the cloakroom he heard Monk call:

"Daddy!"

He looked up. The child, in pyjamas, was standing at the

end of his cot. A Teddy bear, almost unrecognizable as such, was on the floor.

"Daddy, Teddy was naughty," Monk fibbed. "He climbed out."

Libby gulped. "We'll have to make him pay for it, won't we?" Glass in hand, he went towards the bedroom, and as he did so his wife opened the kitchen door wider.

"Is that you, Cecil?"

"Yes," Libby said. "Monk—I mean Teddy climbed out of his cot."

He was very conscious of the glass in his hand, and did not drink the whisky then. They spent a few minutes with Monk, before shutting the door on him. Outside the room Jane said quietly:

"If you drive after drinking and anyone smells your breath, you might offend a lot of voters."

He said, "I suppose I would."

"What is it? That questioner?"

"Yes," he said miserably. "The same man. He comes to meeting after meeting and asks the same question. It's affecting me so that I hardly know what I'm doing. The first thing I do when I get to a meeting is to look round to see if he's there. Jane, I don't think I can go on."

Only half a mile away from Libby's home, Richard Benwell said to his agent, "Clark, I don't think I can use that skeleton out of Libby's cupboard. I've been thinking a lot about it. If I'm going to beat him, wonderful, but I'm not going to rake up old dirt. Keep that Midland chap away from the meetings, will you?"

The wily old campaigner pulled at his beard.

"It would help you a lot, Ricky."

"I've got to live with myself afterwards."

"Yes, so you have," agreed the agent. "All right, I'll fix it." He smiled into his beard. "From what I can gather, the harm's done. Libby's gone all to pieces at his meetings."

"Oh."

"And no one's actually *said* a word about his wicked past!"

At home with his wife, at half past twelve that night, Benwell talked over the happenings of the day, the canvass results, the meeting attendances and the progress report, and finally told her what he had decided and what the agent had said.

"I feel a swine about it as it is," he went on. "I know what it's like when a questioner starts needling you. Remember, I said last year that I thought Ban the Bombers ought to be shot? How I've paid for that! Every time I get asked whether I still think they ought to be shot, or wouldn't I rather kill them by radiation?"

His wife said, "I know, darling. I shouldn't worry about Libby, though."

Jane Libby seldom got away from the bungalow during the day, and her husband looked up in surprise when he saw her. He had just popped in after visiting a nurses' training college and talking to the off-duty nurses. He was tired and dejected and almost hopeless, and hadn't much heart even to have a cheery word with his committee room helpers. The sight of Jane did him good, for she looked so happy. He wondered what Monk had been up to now.

"Darling," his wife said, as soon as they were alone. "I had a telephone call from Mrs. Benwell half an hour ago. I just had to come and tell you. She said that she thought it might be helpful if you knew that Ricky Benwell does not believe in raking up the past."

Libby didn't speak, just held her hands tightly, and closed his eyes; they were like that when a helper called out that the candidate was wanted on the telephone by the local newspaper. His voice was husky when he answered.

16

'TYPEWRITER'

DANIEL RONN knew that he was being watched by the police, but he also knew that the police were stretched tightly and that many policemen felt that the surveillance over members of the Battle Committee need be only nominal. He had always known that the time would come when he would want to evade them, and he had deliberately moved about openly so that he was easy to follow and report on; he expected that as a result of this some of the police who watched his flat would take it for granted that he was just a nuclear disarmament weirdie. Twice he slipped his watchers without going anywhere of importance, and turned up again quickly, to the obvious satisfaction of the men who had been watching him.

He was acutely conscious of the fact that he had made a serious mistake when he met Travaritch at Cleo's Restaurant, with Amanda, but it did not look as if that was going to catch up with him. He had not seen too much of Amanda since the night she had come to see him, bursting with the great idea. He had been to some meetings with her, but most of their business had been transacted by telephone, or through Lady Wallis, who was always ready—in fact eager—to help. Lady Wallis, Amanda Tenby and he had one thing in common—a passionate belief in the wickedness of nuclear weapons and a determination to risk everything to compel Great Britain first and if possible the rest of the world later, to give such weapons up. On this issue, Ronn was absolutely ruthless.

Two mornings after Amanda had agreed to find the extra money and one morning after he had received it—in cash— from the little house in Highgate, he got into his battered MG car, waved to a constable who was watching the street, and grinned. The man smothered a grin in return. Ronn drove along steadily until he came to a garage, fully aware that he had passed two policemen and one plainclothes man en route, who had noticed him and would report his normal movements. He went into the garage, talked to the foreman about some imaginary distributor trouble, left the garage and walked along until a taxi picked him up. He asked to be dropped at Swiss Cottage Underground Station. That was one of the easiest places in London to lose oneself and to shake off pursuers. In a side street he walked boldly up to parked cars until he found one unlocked—a Ford Consul. He did not think he was seen when he got into it. One of his own keys fitted the ignition.

He dumped the case containing the money into the back of the car, as if it were full of old clothes, drove past the pond, and headed northwest. He was not followed. He put on speed once he was on the A41 but he was cautious. South of St. Albans he turned off the A41 road, and half a mile along a narrow by-road he pulled in outside a solitary cottage. There was nothing attractive about it: it was ugly in the worst Victorian way, with fading red brick and a slate roof. The garden was neglected, and the surrounding privet hedge badly needed trimming. He took the case with him and walked up to the front door.

It opened as he stepped on to the porch, and Travaritch stood there. Travaritch, with his huge glasses and pale face and shiny forehead, looked almost like a troglodyte. He was wearing a polo-neck sweater, a pair of slacks and brown leather sandals which showed most of his feet. He needed a shave and a haircut—and also a bath.

"You're late," he said.

"I know I'm late," retorted Ronn. "I had to shake off the police."

"Have you got the money?"

"Yes. Have *you* got the keyboard?"

Travaritch said, "I've got it. I want to see the money first. And don't make any mistake, Ronn. The machine can be safe or it can be deadly, and if you don't know how to handle it, it will be deadly. I can show you how to handle it, but you can't find out by yourself."

Ronn, so spruce and well-groomed, gave the kind of laugh which made people feel that he was a thoroughly nice chap.

"You don't trust me, do you? It's a funny thing, but nobody does, really. Not even Amanda. And I'm so trustworthy." He pushed past Travaritch into a tiny kitchen. The table was littered with cups and saucers, dirty plates, knives and forks, half-empty marmalade and jam jars. The old stoneware sink was filled with more dirty crockery, and one of the draining boards was piled high with empty meat, soup and fruit tins which also spilled out of a bin on the floor. Flies hummed and buzzed against the window and over the empty tins.

Ronn wrinkled his nose in disgust, but made no comment. Travaritch cleared a corner of the table and Ronn put the suitcase down, then unlocked it and threw the lid back. Travaritch stared at the closely packed wads of five-pound notes. He moistened his lips. He gulped. Then he said thickly:

"Wait a minute."

He went out, but almost at once he came back and stood in the doorway.

"I forgot the passport."

"It's here." Ronn handed one to him from his breast pocket. Travaritch took it. His own photograph stared up at him, but the details of his name, address and birthplace were all very different from the real ones: he was shown here as Ian Thomas. Folded inside the passport was a BOAC envelope, and inside this was a ticket to Vienna on an aircraft leaving London Airport that afternoon. There was also a train ticket from London to Vienna, including a sleeper for one night. "You have alternative means of travel," Ronn said dryly.

"That's what I asked for, isn't it?"

Travaritch went out. Ronn did not follow him, but stood looking out a window which had not been cleaned for weeks, perhaps for months. There was a buzzing blanket of flies in this window, too. The cottage was in a shallow valley, in the fold of gently sloping hills, brown with stubble. At one end of it was a copse of beech and oak, the leaves already changing colour. The sky was a clear, pale blue. Rooks wheeled and circled about the tops of the trees.

Travaritch said, "Here it is."

Ronn turned round, slowly. The physicist was carrying what looked like a portable typewriter, but it was larger than most —nearly as large as a table-size record-player. It was in a black leather case, which he opened. Inside was a shiny metal box. When Travaritch put the box on the table it looked as if it were almost hermetically sealed, there was no outward sign of a join. In the centre was a slightly mottled piece of metal, about the size of a shilling. Travaritch's right forefinger, the nail broken and dirty, hovered over this.

"Closed like this, it's absolutely safe," he declared. "It's unbreakable and it's fireproof. Nothing can go wrong—absolutely nothing. You close it, and it's self-locking. This is the only way to unlock it."

He pressed the mottled round mark. Very slowly, the top of the box began to open. As he watched it, Ronn found himself clenching his teeth. There was no sound, and it was uncanny to see that lid rising and to know what was inside. When it was at right angles to the main case, the lid stopped moving. Another layer of shiny metal, with four mottled marks, showed now.

"At this stage the unit can be injured by impact and by fire, and would be dangerous if it was damaged." Travaritch said. "When it's at this stage you have to be very careful with it. Do you understand?"

Ronn moistened his lips.

"Believe me I understand."

"Don't make any mistakes; they could be fatal," said Travaritch. "Each of the controls has to be operated at this stage —and it is operated by a built-in electronics system. At this stage you press each control—a disk, as you see, not a switch because of the amount of space switches would take up. The essence of it is simplicity and compactness. Watch."

A fly buzzed on to his glasses and settled; he brushed it off impatiently, then poised that broken nail over the disks.

"They are marked—1, 2, 3 and 4. You press them in that order."

Ronn began, "Are you sure——" and broke off.

"If there were any danger now I wouldn't be doing this, would I?" asked Travaritch. "But if your foreign friends have any sense they will wear protective clothing when they are taking this to pieces—but of course they will. Who are they? —Russian?"

"How does it work?" asked Ronn.

Travaritch shrugged. "Suit yourself what you tell me," he said. "Press in the order, 1, 2, 3 and 4. Now the inner protective lid will rise."

It did, and inside the inner shell of the container was a small instrument which looked rather like an electric motor, with a cylindrical body and flywheels at one end.

"Now we are down to the pile itself," said Travaritch, moistening his lips. "I invented this, you know. But for me it would be years before any such thing was available. It can be used to generate power in factories and workshops, for the heating of blocks of flats, for almost any purpose. It will create enough electricity to light a small town, and a dozen of these could provide all the power required for a city of a hundred thousand people. Its potential value is enormous. When it is perfected it will solve the power problems of the world."

Ronn echoed in a hard voice, "Perfected?"

"There are refinements to be made yet," explained Travaritch. "It is not yet absolutely foolproof, but I told you that. If this were to be used without effective precautions, such as being in its insulating case or under other insulated conditions, the radiation from it would cause all the ill-effects which we fear from fall-out, plus the immediate danger from exposure to a concentrated radiation." He pointed to another disk on one side of the outer cover of the little motor. "When the unit is connected—and the installation is quite costly—this outlet controls the power. It is really worked on principles very similar to those of the atomic-powered submarines, but is so much smaller. Aircraft will soon be powered by even smaller units, and——"

"Tell me about that outlet," said Ronn.

The forefinger hovered.

"That outlet must be sealed off, but the seal has to be broken in order to connect it to the installation. It is sealed now. It can be unsealed by electronic waves or by electric shock—much the same way as in electrical shock therapy—or by a severe blow. That is what makes it dangerous, and why you must handle it carefully. Once both containers are secured nothing can damage this or unseal it—nothing at all. It is dangerous only when it is opened for use. Is that clear?"

"Yes."

"I will close it, and open it again," said Travaritch.

Ronn kept clenching his teeth as he watched, and his jaws hurt. Travaritch went through all the processes again, and at last turned to Ronn.

"Try it."

For a few seconds Ronn hesitated, fully aware that Travaritch was grinning at him derisively. He placed his forefinger upon the outer disk and forced himself not to jump when the lid began to lift. He touched the inner disks, 1, 2, 3 and 4, and that lid rose also. He moistened his lips when he saw the unit inside, so neat and compact, metallic grey in colour. Then he closed the inner container and the outer one. When he had finished he wiped sweat off his forehead.

"Now tell me it isn't worth fifty thousand pounds," said Travaritch. "You ought to get a million for it."

"You forget something," said Ronn.

"Do I?"

"I'm not going to sell it."

"Don't give me that."

"I've told you from the beginning why I want it," Ronn said. "It isn't to sell to Russia or to anyone else. If that's ever going to be manufactured in big quantities and sold, it's going to be in England. I'm no traitor."

Travaritch said in a husky voice, "You mean you're serious about using this for your Battle Committee?"

"Dead serious."

"I can't believe——"

"You don't have to believe me," Ronn said. "All the same, I'm going to use this to show its power. I'm going to give them a demonstration of the danger of nuclear weapons—I'm going to make the police, the politicians and the public realize what it feels like to know that I can press a button and spread disaster. They won't dare to touch me. They will be too terrified. The newspapers will have the biggest story of their lives, and the whole world will read about it. That is the only way they will ever come to their senses. But I'm going to make absolutely sure that the police can't find out before I'm ready to use it. Do you think they're looking for you yet?"

"Of course they are. I've been here over a week."

"Nothing has appeared in the newspapers," remarked Ronn. "The authorities won't want to admit that another nuclear scientist has sold out. You wouldn't have worried if I'd been Khrushchev or Mao himself, would you?"

"It makes no difference," Travaritch said. "The Atomic Research Commission pays me a miserly three thousand pounds a year, for work like *that*. They're so mean they can't think in terms of real money. If they paid——"

He broke off.

"That's real money," Ronn said, lifting several wads of the five-pound notes. "As much as you would get in eight years —if you were going to live eight years." As he finished he drew a knife out of the case—out of that fortune—and the blade glistened.

Alarm sounded shrill in Travaritch's voice. "What do you mean? What——"

Ronn said, "You've just told me what I've been afraid of,

168

that you can't be trusted not to sell your knowledge to some other country. I'm going to make sure you can't."

Travaritch made a wild swing at the knife, missed, struck at the reactor, touched it but did not make it fall.

"I'll never sell it to anyone, this is all I want! I swear it!"

Ronn lunged forward with the knife.

Ronn wiped the handle of the knife clean. He had touched nothing else except the 'typewriter' and the suitcase, and he carried them both out towards the car. In a field a long way off a combine harvester was working. Along the narrow lane a labrador retriever with a glossy black coat sniffed the hedge. Ronn put the two cases in the back of the car and then started off for London. He left the car in an Islington side street, went by bus to Baker Street, and took a taxi to Paddington. He felt quite sure that he had not been seen or followed. He left the reactor unit in the left-luggage office, in its black leather case, and carried away the suitcase containing the money. He went in another taxi to Amanda Tenby's bank, and took the money in.

The bank manager, already puzzled by the large amount of cash which his client was drawing, was even more puzzled when Ronn said:

"Miss Tenby intended to use this for the campaign, but she finds that it won't be necessary now—we have enough funds. Will you have it counted, and credit it to her account, please?"

"By all means," the bank manager said.

Ronn left the bank twenty minutes later, took another taxi to Highgate and the garage where he had left his car.

"It wasn't the distributor head, it was the pump," the foreman told him. "I fitted a new one. Was that all right?"

"Yes, thanks," said Ronn. He paid the bill in cash, had the car filled up with petrol, and drove round to Braine Street, where a uniformed constable nodded and smiled. Lady Wallis opened the door. She looked as mild and gentle as ever.

"Is everything all right?" she demanded.

"Yes," said Ronn. "I've got it. Tell Amanda I'm going to see her right away, will you?"

"Yes, yes, I will, Daniel. Oh, how wonderful!" She flung

her arms round him and hugged him. Drawing back, she went on excitedly: "And it's going to be the biggest, the very biggest demonstration we have ever had. There'll be a hundred thousand people there at least, I'm sure."

"You were a thousand times right," breathed Amanda.

Her soft, supple body was wonderously a woman's. Passion and ecstasy, born in their certainty of the coming triumph, seemed to create a whole new world.

Afterwards, as she lay and looked at him, and he sat over her, leaning on one elbow, playing with the unexpected firmness of her breast, he said:

"I won't see you again until tonight, my darling. You be at the demonstration. I'll be there at nine o'clock exactly. I'll have it with me. It will be interesting to see how the police will behave when they know that if I press a button I can destroy half London."

17

LOSS AND DISCOVERY

GIDEON saw the way Kate looked at him, and guessed how much she wished that he would talk, and wondered whether he was making a mistake, whether he ought to confide in her a little. The thought was hardly in his mind before he drove it out. They were in the kitchen, having breakfast. The meal was later than usual because he had been up half the night, part of the time at the Yard and part at Harwell. Now he pushed his chair back, went to her, slid his big hands to her breast, and said:

"It'll work out, darling. Don't worry."

"You're worried," she said simply.

"It'll pass."

"I've never seen you so—so down."

"I must put on a better show in future."

"George."

"Yes?"

"Is it do with the election?"

"No," said Gideon, quite positively. "It will all come out

in the wash, Kate. Don't worry about it too much." He gave her a squeeze, and straightened up. "I must get along. There's another conference with Scott-Marle at eleven."

It was now half past nine.

"Is there any hope at all of you getting back early tonight?"

"I'll try. Any special reason?"

"Yes, in a way," said Kate. "It's election day at the school, and Malcolm will be dying to tell you all about it. It was Eve of Poll yesterday, and he was so disappointed that you weren't back. He knows you can't help it, of course, but——"

"Doesn't alter the fact," Gideon said. "If I can possibly be here, I will. Don't see any reason why I shouldn't." He moved to the door as the telephone bell rang. It should not have made him start, but it did. Kate was frowning with anxiety when he stepped into the hall to answer. "Gideon." He listened, and then drew in his breath sharply. "Yes, all right. I'm on my way."

He rang off, and walked towards the front door, and his wife knew that in those few seconds he had actually forgotten her, the telephone call had affected him so much. She felt that if he walked out without turning round, she would scream.

He turned round. She went to him. He kissed her cheek lightly, but suddenly she put her arms round him in an embrace which drew their bodies close, and which told him how deep her tension was.

He went off . . .

He was at the Yard twenty-five minutes later, went straight to his office and found Ripple there with Lemaitre. Lemaitre now knew the essentials of the Travaritch situation; it would have been impossible to keep it from him. Ripple was looking flabby and miserable. Gideon could almost hear Lemaitre on the telephone, saying:

"Ripple says there's a new development which makes things even worse."

Ripple said glumly, "Hallo, George."

"Half a minute," Gideon said. He hung his hat on a peg and rounded the desk. "What's in, apart from this, Lem?"

"Nothing I can't handle, except——"

"George!" protested Ripple. "There's nothing half as important as this. Everything else can wait."

"In a minute. Except what, Lem?"

"Parsons says he needs ten minutes with you."

"Tell him to come along at a quarter to eleven. I can give him the ten minutes then, no more." Gideon sat down. "Take a pew," he said to Ripple, and his right hand slid into his pocket for the comfort of the smooth, shiny bowl of his pipe. "Even worse, you say?"

"Much worse," said Ripple. "Not—not from our angle, perhaps—this isn't something they'll say is our fault. But it's bad. They've just reported that one of those portable units is missing along with Travaritch."

"*Just* reported? Why, it's a week since he disappeared!"

"Just reported to us might be better," said Ripple. "From what I can gather, the loss wasn't discovered right away. Travaritch was assembling one of these things with some other chaps. One has been on sick leave, another on holiday. It's just like these bigheads not to be sure how far the experiments had gone or how many models they'd finished. There were five, anyhow. Now there are four. Travaritch must have smuggled the fifth out." Ripple sat with his chin on his chest—three chins, framing his face, making him look like a despondent Buddha. "Once they knew it was gone, they told the director and, once he was sure, he wanted to tell the Prime Minister, but the Prime Minister was in Berlin. They pussied around with it from minister to minister, waiting for the Prime Minister to approve that we should be told. The theory is that when we find Travaritch we'll find the pile itself, and we couldn't be looking harder for Travaritch."

Gideon said, "Fair enough, I suppose." He felt very, very old. "A whole atomic unit missing."

"Yes."

"Not just microfilm or documents."

"No."

"My God." It was a cry of despair.

"I know how you feel," said Ripple. "Well, that's it. I've told the Old Man. You won't be even a split second late, will you?" Ripple really meant: *Need* you see Parsons?

"I won't be late," Gideon promised.

Ripple went out, the seat of his brown trousers baggy and shiny. Lemaitre, who could never be in deep gloom for long, looked at Gideon with an eyebrow raised and a half grin on his face.

"Looks like an elephant who's lost his memory, doesn't he?"

Gideon actually laughed.

He glanced through the reports on his desk perfunctorily, yet sufficiently to convince himself that Lemaitre was right and that nothing else of real importance had come in. Three more candidates had been robbed the night before, and that racket was assuming the proportions of a major scandal which could do the Yard a lot of harm. There was a long report from Parsons about the situation he was so anxious to talk about, and Gideon did not have time to read it carefully. There was a note in Lemaitre's very fine handwriting, pinned to the outside of the file on the Quack case. It read: *Dr. Fairweather now out of danger.* So the young fool Wilcox wouldn't be charged with murder, and he could think himself lucky. The harshness of Gideon's reaction was partly due to the overriding anxiety. He kept thinking: *A whole unit smuggled out.* There would be some kind of excuse for its being possible— there always was. On top of the file from the Cornish skeleton case was a note: *Skeleton now believed to be that of a Mrs. Myrtle Brown, of Penzance, who disappeared at the same time as her husband seven years ago.*

Gideon made a note: *Is Curson looking for husband?*

There was a tap at the door, and Parsons came in.

"Morning, George. Glad you could spare a minute."

"Wish I could spare an hour," said Gideon. "Things are going all right, aren't they?"

"As far as I can see, yes," said Parsons, almost reluctantly. "I've only got one real worry. Shall I run through the odds and ends first?"

"We've nine minutes left."

"Quatrain's four candidates outside London are all withdrawing, but Quatrain himself is going through with his campaign. There's guts for you. There isn't any reason now to think that the burglaries at the candidates' homes are political. There have been twenty-one altogether, and nine Conservatives, six Liberal, five Labour, and one Independent have been the victims. All fairly well-off, too. The biggest loss was Talmad's, Quatrain's opponent, but he can afford it."

"How much?"

"Several hundred in cash—election fighting fund contributions. He hadn't checked it and says he just hasn't had time to take it to the bank—and about a thousand pounds' worth of jewellery, a camera and some binoculars. We're putting a call out for stolen cameras and binoculars—we know the most likely places to find them. There have been no major disturbances at meetings. Now and again the Battle Committee boys get really vicious with a candidate they don't like, but there's no violence, no breaches of the peace. Just questions—and the door-to-door canvassing."

"By the F.F.P. people?"

"Yes."

"What angle?"

"The horror of what it would be like if a bomb did go off. They reduce it to personal terms—what it would do to *you*. On the face of that it's no more than the Civil Defence people keep saying, when they're trying to strengthen local units, but the F.F.P. people are really hammering it home. I've talked to most of the divisional chaps and twenty provincial chief constables, and there's a fairly general agreement."

"What is it?" Gideon glanced at his watch: there were four minutes to go.

"The F.F.P. people think that this will be a stalemate election, with the Liberals holding the balance of power, or at least with a government in with such a small over-all majority that it won't last long. The consensus is that the Battle Committee and all the others concerned with Nuclear Disarmament are working up to the point when they can put a large number of candidates up at the election that will follow. They're using the canvass to test their strength."

"Could be," said Gideon thoughtfully. "Needn't worry us, if that's all it is. Two minutes."

Parsons stood up.

"I'm not satisfied it is all. I think that there is going to be a big Eve of Poll rally in London, probably at Trafalgar Square, and probably in all big cities. I think they're going to use it as a great demonstration of the strength of the Fight for Peace movement and the danger of having nuclear weapons. And I wish to God it wasn't Guy Fawkes Night.

There will be fireworks in more ways than one, and there could be a lot of damage.

Gideon was standing up too.

"You mean, we need our chaps at the demonstration centres and also at the party Eve of Poll rallies, and we can't stretch 'em."

"I don't really know what I mean. I'd say we ought to cancel all leave and have every man we've got on duty that night, in spite of the fact that they'll all have to be at the polling stations next day."

Gideon said, "I'll think about it. Thanks." He nodded and went out without another word.

Lemaitre exploded. "What's up? You out of your mind? Fancy worrying him with trivia at *this* stage."

Parsons rubbed his fleshy chin.

"Known him for over twenty years and you still don't know him, do you, Lem? If he didn't think he was right up to date with the general situation he wouldn't be able to concentrate upon this big problem, whatever it is. There's a rumour that it's another spy case—and someone's slipped up."

Lemaitre, who knew what it was, just glared.

Gideon tapped at the door of Scott-Marle's room, and opened it when the secretary called. Her door was open. Ripple was already there, with three Security chiefs from the service ministries and Atomic Control. Rogerson looked very old. Chairs were in a half circle in front of Scott-Marle's big, leather-topped desk, but Scott-Marle wasn't there. It was one minute to eleven. Gideon took the only vacant seat, nodding round to the others; he had seen them all last night and there was only a murmur of "good morning." It was obvious from their faces that all of them knew the latest development.

Scott-Marle opened the door as the stroke of eleven from Big Ben sounded faintly in this high, bright room. He took his seat, said "Good morning, gentlemen," and placed his hands on the desk.

"Commander Gideon, is there any trace of Travaritch?"

"None has been reported to me, sir."

"Commander Ripple?"

"No, sir."

"At this time yesterday I would have said that it was impossible for the situation to get any worse," Scott-Marle told them in his clear, dry voice, "but of course it is now immeasurably worse. I have just come from the Prime Minister, from the Home Secretary and the Minister for Atomic Research. We can be left in no doubt of the gravity of the loss. In the wrong hands, this one unit could spread radio-activity at danger level over a very wide area, and the immediate effect would be considerable, with much damage to human tissues." Scott-Marle spoke as if the words were being forced out of him and that he could not really believe they were true. "The example given to me—and I believe to everyone from the service ministries—is that if it were to be damaged or misused in Trafalgar Square, for instance, the effect of its radiation would be felt over a radius of more than a mile, affecting or possibly affecting over a million people. I have no reason to believe that is an exaggeration. Such a demonstration is quite conceivable. It would demonstrate once and for all the effect of radiation on people in the West, and extremists might believe that this would frighten a vast majority of the people into demanding an end to the bomb here. There may be reason to think that the portable atomic unit has already been taken out of the country, but until we know for certain——"

A telephone bell rang.

Scott-Marle broke off, and stared at the phone. Gideon fancied that the Commissioner would have gladly shouted at it. Instead, he stretched out his hand and picked up the receiver; and in that second Gideon sensed that he had been wrong, that Scott-Marle half expected this call. Feared it, perhaps.

"This is the Commissioner speaking." He kept his voice low, and stared out the window. Everyone waited tensely.

Then Scott-Marle exclaimed, *"Are you sure?"*

Gideon had never heard him raise his voice like that before, never seen his eyes flash so, never known him to show such signs of excitement.

Then Scott-Marle said, "Yes, at once." He put the receiver down, and looked at the men in front of him. He moistened his lips. It was impossible to tell whether he had had good news or bad.

"The Watford police report that they have discovered the

body of the man Travaritch in a cottage between Watford and St. Albans. They are sure that it is the man. Gideon, Ripple, I want you to go there at once. Final identification will be from an associate of the dead man—I will arrange for him to join you at the cottage. A Hertfordshire police car will meet you at the junction of the A41 and A4088 on the south side of Watford. Presumably you will wish to go . . ."

He was already talking to the service chiefs.

Gideon and Ripple were halfway across the room.

"George," called Lemaitre, as Gideon strode along the passage past his own office door.

"Not now," Gideon said.

"Dancy says he must talk to you."

"I'll call him later."

"He's been on three times already."

"I'll call him the moment I can."

Lemaitre said, "Okay." He withdrew reluctantly, but re-appeared a moment later and called in a different voice: "George!"

"What the bloody hell do you want now?" Gideon demanded, swinging round and banging into Ripple.

Lemaitre was rushing forward with Gideon's hat thrust out towards him.

There was not room for all of them in the kitchen of the cottage. The place stank. The flies buzzed, some of them round the wounds in the dead man's belly and in his chest. He had not bled very much, and the two knife thrusts had been made at close quarters. The knife, cleaned of prints, was on the table. Also on the table were the marks of two cases which had rested there—marks which showed clearly against the dust and in patches of grease, in spots of jam and marmalade. The Watford police had already made preliminary investigations and carried out the essential routine. A police surgeon stated with assurance that the body must have been there for days. It had been discovered early that morning by a tramp who had called to beg for breakfast, found the back door open, and stepped in.

The Geiger counter test showed that the radioactivity in the cottage was normal.

18

EVE OF POLL

GIDEON never ceased to marvel at the way the subconscious mind worked. As he sat alone in the back of his car that afternoon, being driven by someone else's chauffeur, he thought of what Parsons had said about his fear of a big demonstration, a rally to outdo all rallies. Gideon had not given that a moment's conscious thought, but his subconscious mind must have been working for now he felt as if he had assessed the situation and could issue reasonable instructions. The burden of the murder of Travaritch and the possibility that the 'keyboard' unit was still in the country in the hands of a man who did not know how to operate it, was still heavy on him, but that did not make Parsons' problem any less intractable.

Gideon leaned over the back of the seat in front of him.

"Hand me that telephone, will you?"

The chauffeur leaned sideways, unhooked the phone, switched it on. When Information answered, Gideon said:

"This is Commander Gideon. Give me Superintendent Parsons."

"At once, sir." There was a pause, and then the same man said, "We're getting Mr. Parsons, sir. Mr. Lemaitre would like a word with you."

"All right, I'll talk to him."

"George," said Lemaitre obviously bursting with suppressed feeling, "Dancy says that if you don't talk to him soon, you'll regret it for the rest of your born days. I think he means what he says."

"Where is he?"

"He's going to call every half hour, on the dot."

"Tell him I'll be back at the office by five o'clock" said Gideon. "Anything else in?" That was almost a mechanical question.

"Parsons is bursting himself to talk to you, too," Lemaitre said, "but I told him——"

"Put me through."

"Listen, George——"

"Put me through."

Lemaitre didn't argue again, and after a moment Parsons came on the line. He was almost as tense as Lemaitre had been. It was as if the election nerves were affecting him, as they were all the candidates, whose fight was nearly over.

"George," Parsons said, "ten minutes ago I had a call from the Conservative Central Office. One of their canvassers got a 'yes' on the T question. He was canvassing Soho this morning, and saw a restaurant proprietor, Cleo. Cleo says he's seen the man once. I went over the minute I heard, and brought Cleo back with me. He saw T with Amanda Tenby and Daniel Ronn, about four weeks ago."

"I am quite sure of it," asserted Cleo, when Gideon was back in his office. Cleo was in a black suit with a bow tie, his hair shone, his face shone, his shoes shone. "It is the kind of face I would not forget. That photograph is a very good one, very good indeed. He had luncheon with Mr. Ronn and Miss Tenby. The date was October 15th, I have the reservation in Mr. Ronn's name, and neither he nor Miss Tenby has been to my restaurant since, so that must have been the day. I hope that I have been helpful, Mr. Gideon."

"You'll never know how helpful," Gideon said.

Parsons showed Cleo, still shimmering, out of the office.

Gideon had talked to Parsons and checked what Parsons had already laid on: calls at Amanda Tenby's Chelsea flat and at Ronn's rooms in Mayfair, calls at every Battle Committee meeting place where either the man or the woman was known to have visited. All the members of the Battle Committee were on the list for questioning, all their helpers too. Parsons, anticipating the steps which Gideon would take, had withdrawn all the plainclothes men he could from Eve of Poll duty, and had sent a teletype message to every division in London as well as to all the Home Counties police. The railway stations, air terminals and seaports were being watched.

"Think roadblocks would do any good?" Parsons asked.

"Shouldn't think so," Gideon said. "We'll leave that until the morning anyhow." He did not ask if there had been any news at all; even a whisper would have reached him by now. He pushed his fingers through his hair, and then his telephone bell rang. He leaned across and picked it up as Lemaitre said:

"That'll be Dancy. It's six o'clock."

"Gideon," said Gideon.

"Dancy," said Dancy. "You're the most evasive copper in England, a damned sight slipperier than a crook. I have some real dope for you. I would have given it to Ripple but he's unavailable too."

"Sorry," said Gideon. "I've been tied up."

"Well, you ought to untie yourself, Gee-Gee, you really ought. I've been casting my bread upon the waters and I've reaped two harvests of considerable interest, about our friend whom we had better call T. In the first place——"

"He had lunch with Amanda Tenby and Daniel Ronn at Cleo's Restaurant, Dean Street, on October 15th," said Gideon.

Dancy's garrulity was stilled.

"Or have you got some other news for me?" demanded Gideon heavily. It was in a way a relief to feel that the Yard had got the information in time for him to be able to say that it was the result of police work; it was an added burden to know how soon this man had discovered it.

"Gee-Gee, you're a sly old fox, that's the truth of it," said Dancy. "I didn't think you knew. But that's right. Has it helped at all? I've heard rumours that T hasn't been home for a few nights, and I wondered if you'd lost him."

"We've found him," Gideon said heavily.

"Oh. Oh, I see. Quite a success story for you, then. I'd better stick to my unfaithful wives and roving hubbies."

"You do all right," Gideon said, "and I won't forget this. That's a promise. There's one other thing you can do for me. Keep all this under your hat. As soon as I can, I'll buy you a dinner and tell you the whole story."

"Good old Gee-Gee! I'll hold you to that." Dancy, delighted, rang off. Gideon, disconsolate, put the receiver down. He sat for a few seconds, frowning, then called Scott-Marle and reported. He told Rogerson, whose reaction was very slow, and began to work on the Yard men and the divisions to step up their efforts in the search for Ronn and Amanda Tenby.

It was half past seven when he realized that he had promised to try to get home, and could not. He closed his eyes momentarily against the image of Malcolm in his disappointment, then put in a call to Kate.

Malcolm answered.

"Hallo, old chap," said Gideon with forced brightness. "I can't get home for a bit, but I'm anxious to know whether I've got a member of Parliament for a son or not."

"Well, no, not exactly," said Malcolm. "Jolly nearly, though. The Labour man beat me, but it was a jolly close thing, and I just pipped the Tory. I'll tell you what the big surprise was, though."

"What was it?"

"That fourth candidate, the one I nearly forgot," answered Malcolm. "We thought he would lose his deposit, nobody took him seriously. He got nearly as many votes as the Tory and me, though. And he looks such a weirdie!"

"I'm glad he didn't beat you," Gideon said heavily. "Nice work, old chap, second is a good place to be in. Tell your mother I won't be home until late, and not to wait up for me, won't you?"

"Okay, dad," said Malcolm. "Ooh, just a minute! There's a big Eve of Poll rally in London, some people have just told me about it. Is it all right if I go?"

"I don't think I should," said Gideon slowly, "I think there'll be too much of a crush. Give it a miss this time, will you?" He rang off before the boy could argue, understanding how much he would like to go, then looked up as the door opened. Parsons came in, carrying two photographs.

"What is it?" Gideon demanded.

"Two fingerprint fragments were found near Travaritch's body," Parsons said. "I've identified them as George, Ronn's. I've put out a general call. Right?" Parsons' eyes glittered.

Gideon dialled Information and said harshly: "Give that call for Ronn absolute priority." He rang off. "That might save us. Thanks. Anything else?"

"There's to be a monster rally in Parliament Square tonight," said Parsons. "Not Trafalgar Square, after all. It's been organized by word of mouth—nothing printed, nothing officially announced, but they're marching in from all over London. Uniform keeps getting reports of new lines merging on the main roads. It's the big demonstration, George—there will be a hundred thousand people in Parliament Square, at least, and God knows how many in the overflow. And it's happened too suddenly for us to stop them. They're on the march."

From the outskirts of London they had left in ones and twos and little groups; by car, by bus, by train and taxi. From the inner suburbs they had started out in single lines of marchers, picking up more and more supporters on the way. They walked in silence. The banners and the placards they carried did their talking for them. They kept at the same steady pace all the time. At every crossroad a few more joined, from houses and apartment buildings, from shops and pubs and restaurants, from bus garages and stations they came on their silent march, all heading for Parliament Square.

As the single lines of marchers reached the main arteries leading to the heart of London, they formed in double and at times in treble file, as if they had been trained for it on some parade ground. There was no stopping them. They simply marched on and on, ignoring traffic, which had to crawl behind them, and scores of frustrated motorists passed them with a snarl and a blast of stinking exhaust.

None complained.

The very young, the early teen-agers, the young married with babies in their arms, the middle-aged, the elderly and the old all marched, until the streets of London were filled with the ghostly battalions, the soft padding sound of footsteps taking the place of martial music. In the light from street lamps banners and placards showed white and ghostly with the pictures of the mushroom which they believed would kill the world, and pictures of the sick and the maimed and the idiot who could be left, they said, when the nuclear war was 'won.' At the windows, at the doors, at gateways, people who did not know what it was all about watched the marchers. Some talked, a few joined, a few cursed, but nothing made any difference. Those who passed along any particular street or road or highway were soon lost to sight but behind them they left a restlessness all over London and a tension which spread from the meeting places and big halls where the politicians gathered in their last frenzied or impassioned or reasoned appeals.

Police helicopters and military helicopters went to get a complete picture. The Press of London and of the world soon heard what was happening. Reporters joined the throng, radio and television units were rushed to the most advantageous positions. The roofs and windows of buildings were taken over for television and for newsreels, and radio carried word of the silence around the world.

The wealthier newspapers hired helicopters too, until the night sky seemed to reverberate.

Gideon went up in a police helicopter, just after nine o'clock.

In the dim light of the streets and the brighter lights of the main roads, he saw the files of marching men and women and children, who did not stop but only slowed down the nearer they got to the true heart of London. He saw the way they filed into Parliament Square. He saw the police, trying to keep them on one side, but the battle was lost almost before it had begun. The police could arrest a thousand or five thousand, but here the demonstrators were in their tens of thousands, the mass thickening until they blocked all roads leading to Parliament Square.

With Gideon was Ray Cox, recently promoted from deputy to commander of the Uniform branch. He was a young, eager, aggressive man, whom the sight below subdued. He kept giving radio orders to the ground. Now and again on the perimeter of the crowd fireworks exploded, and Cox ordered the arrest of everyone who let one off. Movement below showed where he was obeyed. He gave orders where to re-route buses and where to halt private cars outside the centre of the metropolis; that was now the only thing to do.

Once Cox said, "Look at the river, George."

Gideon had already seen the river, teeming with a fleet of small boats, like a Dunkirk by night in the heart of London. Hundreds of them, thousands of them, moved quietly and steadily up- and downstream towards Westminster.

"Look at those *bridges*!"

Westminster Bridge and Lambeth, Hungerford Bridge and even Waterloo, were thick with masses of people. The flashes of fireworks became more frequent, the flashes of cameras up here and down below were brighter, but there was no sign of panic or of fear and resentment. In the distance a few rockets soared, but that was all.

"I've seen everything now," Cox said in a pause.

"I hope you have," said Gideon. "Can you go nearer Parliament Square?"

"I'm going."

"And a bit lower?"

"Yes."

As they went, he saw that the marchers were sitting in Parliament Square, along Whitehall, in front of the Abbey, along the Embankment, even on Westminster Bridge and Lambeth too. The pace of the marchers in the rear was slowing down, because those in front could go no farther. There were only stragglers now; the march was nearly done, the demonstration was soon to come.

"Let's put the searchlight on the middle of the crowd," said Gideon.

He believed that he knew what he was going to see, but the sight of it would stay with him to his dying day. In the middle of the square was a small clearing, and in the middle of the clearing a group of people were standing on a platform, made, if he could see aright, of a trestle table. The searchlight, switched on so suddenly, shone straight on to the group in the centre. There was Moncrieff and the chairmen of the other committees. There was Lady Wallis. There were the executives of the Battle Committee. And there was Amanda Tenby, in black, standing still as a statue made of ebony, with the pallor of her upturned face and of her hands like carved alabaster. In that moment, with the roar of the helicopter in his ears and the stillness of the silence below, she seemed like a modern Joan of Arc burning in the white-hot fire of flashlights and searchlights.

The beam passed over, and touched thousands of the squatting marchers, who did not look up. They sat in awed expectancy, as if they knew Amanda would speak to them in the clear small voice of truth.

Gideon, terribly afraid but convinced of what would follow, turned round to look again at Amanda and to make sure that Ronn was with her.

He could not see Ronn.

"Go over once again, will you?"

"Yes," said Cox.

The helicopter described its wide circle and went back; the beam of blinding white shone on Amanda once again, and the others on the platform, but Ronn was not there. For the first time Gideon began to hope. How could Ronn, how could any man, force his way through the denseness of that crowd? He saw the rows of police lining the empty roads. Then he saw the cars coming along the roads, saw men spring out of them and knew that some of Quatrain's men had arrived. All this—his greatest anxiety so short a time ago—was now the least of his worries. There would be some scuffles, but not with the F.F.P. demonstrators in the middle of those hundreds of thousands.

Then the helicopter's radio crackled.

"Hallo," said Uniform. "Helicopter Metro 1 speaking." There was a pause. "Yes . . . Yes, he's here." He handed Gideon the microphone.

Daniel Ronn knew that he must have sufficient time to get from Paddington to Parliament Square, but not too much, for every unnecessary minute added to the danger that he might be caught. He did not think it likely, for he was wearing a sandy-coloured beard and a moustache, he had thickened his waist with sheets so that he looked tubby, and he walked with a slight limp. At eight o'clock, an hour before he was due at the demonstration, he stepped off a bus and walked into Paddington Station, heading for the left-luggage office. He saw the uniformed police in strength, and knew that there were a lot of plainclothes men, but they were concentrated at the barriers and the ticket offices. He walked boldly across to the big counter, took out his ticket, and presented it.

"It's a black record-player," he said. "I brought it in in the afternoon."

He stood very still as the attendant turned away, for he knew he was very, very close to everything he had ever wanted to do. The man went towards the spot where the precious box was resting. He took it down. Ronn moistened his lips. The man brought the case, and dumped it heavily in front of Ronn, who thought: The fool, what does he think it is? A sack of potatoes?

"That the one, sir?"

"Yes."

"Two shillings, please."

Ronn said, "That's plenty." He took two shillings out of his pocket with one hand, and picked up the case with the other. His heart was thumping. He walked towards the main exit, face flushed with triumph; nothing could stop him now. He could make all England, he could make the whole world, realize what it would feel like to be under the immediate threat of nuclear explosion in the heart of a great city. As he passed beneath the arch leading to the taxi stand, a man appeared on either side of him.

"Good evening, sir."

"Excuse me, sir, I wonder if we can have a look in that case?"

Ronn froze. "No, you can't." His throat went so dry that he felt as if he were choking. "What right have you to ask?"

"We're police officers, sir, making a routine check. We won't keep you a minute." One man touched Ronn's fingers where they were round the handle of the case. "If you will please——"

Ronn kicked him, swung his left arm round to strike the other man, and tried to leap forward, but he did not make even a yard. He tripped over an outstretched foot and crashed down, and the unit crashed with him. As he fell, he twisted round, his face distorted, and he shouted:

"That will kill you! Don't touch it, it will kill you!"

"Well," one man said, "it didn't kill you, did it? May I have your keys, please?"

"Get me Commander Gideon, on Helicopter Metro 1," Parsons said in a clear, ringing voice.

That was the moment when Amanda Tenby began to talk over a loud-speaker, her voice inaudible to Gideon and doubtless to countless others, but as she raised her hands the people rose. Rising, they took the banners and posters and lifted the placards from their bodies, holding them high so that everyone above could read; perhaps they were hoping that the heavens had eyes too.

On one, on a dozen, on a hundred, Gideon read:

VOTE TO BAN THE BOMB

The leaders of the parties, all of whom had travelled the country by air and road and rail, who had become hoarse while addressing meetings morning, noon and night, who had known moments of exhaustion, of fear, of hope, of despair, were at last at home on this eve of their campaigning. Each was in his own constituency, speaking to electors whose votes he felt sure would come to him; the time of persuasion had passed. Each man, worn out though he was, felt the stimulus of a great crowd, of the deafening cheers, of clapping, even of the occasional boo from the ready voices of opponents not cheering their own candidate on.

Each leader spoke of nuclear disarmament. The leader of the party which had laid down the burden of government after so many years, and was eager to take it up again, spoke to a mass meeting where thousands roared their loyalty and thousands more thronged outside at overflow meetings, able to hear the voice if not see the familiar face and figure.

"Mr. Chairman, my lords, my ladies, ladies and gentlemen," he said in a firm, clear voice. "I want there to be no doubt about where this great party stands, nor where I stand, in the matter of nuclear warfare. We abhor the thought of it. I abhor the thought of it. Nothing we can do and nothing I can do will be left undone to banish the horror from the realm of mankind.

"But—and I speak from my heart and, I believe, I speak from the heart of this nation . . .

"When this hideous bomb is banned, it must be by all who possess it now, and in such a way that none who might possess it in the future can ever make use of it. To me, that is the only way to the peace mankind desires."

In Parliament Square there was the hush of a multitude waiting for the moment of revelation, which did not come.

In nineteen hundred halls up and down the land there was a tumult of acclamation.

19

POLLING DAY

"It isn't likely to get into the newspapers," Gideon said to Kate next morning. "The national dailies and the national news agencies have been asked to keep the news quiet, in the public interest, and I think they will—until the sensation's died down anyhow. If Ronn had threatened a demonstration with the unit, God knows what would have happened. And if Travaritch had got away, we couldn't have kept it quiet. I think we can now. Or let's say I hope we can." He looked tired but relaxed as he sat in his shirt-sleeves at the kitchen table. "I'll never know whether the Security men would have done a better job if we'd done ours better, but I know the ghost of this mistake will stay with me, Kate. At least it's only a ghost."

Kate didn't speak.

"The remarkable thing was the way Amanda Tenby behaved when she realized what had happened," Gideon said. "We had the news of Ronn's arrest broadcast to the crowd. Only one or two of them knew the significance of it, of course, and for all I know Amanda Tenby was the only one who really knew the lot. She took the loud-speaker, and asked them to sit down again, without moving or speaking, for half an hour. The Chairmen let her handle the situation, and—well, look at that."

The headline in the *Daily Globe*, on the table, ran:

THE SILENT VOTE

In the heart of London last night, on the eve of what might well prove to be the most momentous election in the nation's history, one of the most remarkable demonstrations of the power of silent protest was manifest. A crowd of at least two hundred thousand people (see the magnificent photographs on page 4) walked to the home of the Mother of Parliaments, and sat in silence, while their banners proclaimed their message: VOTE TO BAN THE BOMB.

This newspaper does not agree with the policy of the Battle

Committee, the Fight of Peace group, or any other such group. But it believes that, when any great weight of public opinion is demonstrated with the dignity and power that was shown last night, the foundations of a world at peace are slowly but surely being laid.

"What does that mean, dad?" asked Malcolm, coming in and knotting his tie.

Gideon read it again, aloud.

"I think it means that with a bit of luck the world will one day be a better place," he said. He was acutely aware of the inadequacy of the answer, but it seemed to satisfy Malcolm. "Why aren't you at school today?"

"Don't be a drip," Malcolm retorted. "They've taken over the school as a polling station. All the masters and mistresses are supervising, or whatever they call it."

"They're poll clerks, are they?"

"That's right. Mum, can I have some sandwiches and go up to Wimbledon Common for the day?"

"Yes," said Kate.

"Kate," said Gideon, "I'll be off. Coming along to vote? The booth's on your way."

"I'll slip in when I'm out shopping," Kate replied.

Gideon took his own car out, was recognized by the uniformed policeman outside the booth, went in, cast his vote, and came out again, all with an odd feeling of anticlimax. He drove along to the Yard, wondering what kind of poll it would be; on this fine day it might well be a big one. Outwardly it was an ordinary day, with no more and no fewer people in the streets and traffic was certainly as thick as ever. As he threaded his way through it he thought of Ronn, who had been charged with being in possession of stolen goods, and who would doubtless soon be charged with murder. Ronn had refused to implicate Amanda Tenby or anybody else, and the questioning of them all would soon begin; it might well be a long and wearisome business. There was never any end to police work, and there was not likely to be an end to the campaign for nuclear disarmament now. He wondered how many of the marchers had been true believers, how many had gone along for the ride, how many had gone simply because it was an Eve of Poll rally. He could not fail to be impressed himself, although it had not shaken his own conviction that the nuclear bomb was in fact a deterrent, that without it there would one day be war, with it the era of peace might well begin.

But he could understand others believing like Amanda Tenby and Ronn and Lady Wallis. Lady Wallis—she might be worth special attention, the blood of one of the old suffragette families ran in her veins.

He mustn't forget to tell Parsons that . . .

Scott Hannaford went to cast his vote, came back and read his newspapers. The report that Dr. Fairweather was recovering put new life into him. He had made no attempt to get a locum's job since the attack on Fairweather, but there couldn't be more than one idiot like Wilcox, could there? It would be safe to have another go in a few days. He got up and went to his bathroom, where there were two cabinets. In one were bottles of hair dye, rinses, eye black, some little cylinders of cotton wool, some cheek pads, both suction and solid. He took down the dye marked *Rich Auburn*.

Effie Wilcox had never voted before, and she would not have taken the trouble this time but for the fact that Fred wanted her to. She went out into the bright morning. A big policeman outside the Baptist Church hall, two streets away, was talking to a little man wearing a red and white rosette— the very man she was going to vote for! She looked at him shyly, and he called out:

"I hope you pick the winner!"

"I'm sure I will," she said. "I'm going to vote for you."

The hall, usually so bleak and bare, looked different from her recollection of her Sunday-school days and Bible class meetings. Wooden frames and black fabric made little booths where the shiny black ballot boxes stood. There were four tables with two people at each, and two men were standing about. It was all so strange: like going to a funeral.

She shivered.

"What's your number, miss, please?" A clerk smiled up at her.

She looked down at the Labour candidate's election address, which gave her all she required, including a facsimile of the ballot paper.

"Nine-one-seven-three," she said.

The clerk checked over the electoral register, found her name, ruled it off in ink, and gave her a ballot paper. She took this behind a black drape, put a clear X opposite Fred's candidate, popped it into the box, and went off. No one took any notice of her. The candidate had gone. She only wished Fred could cast his vote too. She bought a lamb chop for her supper, went home, and read all about the big demonstration. She did not think much about it, but the paragraph about Dr. Fairweather made her heart leap. Thank God, thank God!

Her solicitor, one her mother had recommended, said that the circumstances would be taken into account, and it shouldn't go too badly with Fred. The baby would be born while Effie was on her own, of course, but loneliness wouldn't last long. A year perhaps? Or two or three. It didn't make all that difference, because she had seen Fred and knew that he loved her. He also knew that if he was in prison for twenty years, she would be waiting for him when he came out. She would have to move from the apartment soon and go back to her mother and afterwards she would need a job. But her mother would help with the baby.

Lemaitre was at work, brisk as usual, this morning in a pale-brown suit and a dark-brown tie.

"You voted yet, George?"

"Yes. Haven't you?"

"I will on my way home. I've seen everybody on the list, by the way. The Old Man says he'll be calling you later. Rogerson's not coming in—had a nasty heart spasm last night, his wife says—he can't work much longer, can he? Parsons's been at Ronn again, but Ronn won't say a word. Stubborn devil. Oh, Curson rang up—he's found Brown, the husband of that skeleton, and he—Curson, I mean—thinks that's sewn up all right. Oh, Ripple's having a go at Ronn now. There were another three burglaries last night, and one of the candidates' wives caught a thief and got kicked on her shins. Pity we couldn't pull Mason in, but his alibi seemed all right. Paterson rang up from the House of Commons, and says he'll be looking in. Got a bit of a poser from the Bank of England—they've some five-pound notes they're not very happy about.

Body of a twenty-year-old man was found in the river at Wapping, head bashed in. Wasn't a very full night last night, though." He looked out the window. "Wonder how the voting's going. Not that it makes much difference to us, we'll still have to pay too much income tax. Politicians! They're all the same, if you ask me."

Watching him, listening to him, Gideon felt uneasily that Rogerson might be right, Lem might not be a good man for deputy commander. At least there was no urgency about it, but sooner or later he would have to decide whether or not to recommend him.

It was going to be a case of divided loyalties.

At eleven o'clock that night, the first result came through. *Williton:* Quatrain 2,509, Talmand 12,991, Talmad elected, Independent gain.

Gideon didn't wait up for any more. He would read all about it tomorrow, and by the next day it would be old stuff.